The # NECEN *Voyage*

A Fantastic Journey into the Heart of a Computer

The NECEN *Voyage*

A Fantastic Journey into the Heart of a Computer

WILLIAM S. DAVIS

Addison-Wesley Publishing Company, Inc.
Reading, Massachusetts • Menlo Park, California
Don Mills, Ontario • Wokingham, England • Amsterdam • Sydney
Singapore • Tokyo • Mexico City • Bogotá • Santiago • San Juan

Library of Congress Cataloging in Publication Data
Davis, William S., 1943–
    The NECEN voyage.

    Summary: A professor and members of the Special
Missions Forces shrink themselves to bit size and
enter a computer network to stop a sinister hijacker,
who has seized control of all computerized operations
from Washington to Boston.
    [1. Computers—Fiction.   2. Science fiction]   I. Title.
II. Title: N.E.C.E.N. voyage.
PZ7.D3213De   1985   [Fic]   84-24392
ISBN 0-201-11979-X (pbk.)

ABCDEFGHIJ-DO-898765
First printing, March 1985

Cover design by Marshall Henrichs
Set in 10 pt. Palatino by Techna Type, Inc., York, PA

Contents

1 *Premonition*

The Porsche rolled to a stop. As Professor Corbin cut the engine, he felt the afternoon sun blazing through the side window. For a moment, he regretted leaving the cool quiet of his Pennsylvania mountainside retreat, but he needed cash, and Mount Pocono was where the bank was. Could be worse, though, he thought, wiping his forehead with the back of his hand. I could be in Washington. He smiled, a contented smile; retirement agreed with him.

Reluctantly, he pushed open the door and stepped out. The parking lot's asphalt surface felt soft and tacky, and he flinched as he sensed the heat through the soles of his deck shoes. Bending to clear the fog from his glasses, he noticed how the thin vertical stripes of his tennis shirt clashed with his muted plaid walking shorts. Stripes and plaids. He chuckled. Marty would never have approved. A look of sorrow accentuated the deep lines that marked his face. Dear Marty. He thought of his late wife often these days. Had it really been ten years? They'd planned so much together.

He sighed and tucked the edge of his shirt back into his shorts, carefully smoothing it over an increasingly noticeable paunch. "Tomorrow," he said to himself, patting his midriff, "I am going to start exercising." With a shrug, and just the slightest hint of a limp, he set off toward the automatic teller machine. Quickly locating his bank card, he inserted it into a slot; with a whir and a click, it disappeared.

"GOOD AFTERNOON, AND WELCOME TO POCONO STATE," said the machine in its electronic monotone. "PLEASE ENTER YOUR PERSONAL IDENTIFICATION NUMBER." A metal cover slid aside, revealing a row of push buttons. The professor keyed in a four-digit number. The machine paused briefly, as though thinking, and then continued. "GOOD AFTERNOON, PROFESSOR CORBIN. I HAVE EATEN YOUR CARD. [BURP.] DELICIOUS. HA, HA. YOU ARE THE CHILD OF UNMARRIED PARENTS, ONE OF WHOM—YOUR MOTHER, I BELIEVE—EXHIBITED DEFINITE CANINE TENDENCIES. GOOD DAY, SIR." With an audible click the metal cover slid back into place, terminating the transaction.

Corbin's sense of shock passed quickly. Laughing quietly to himself, he turned and walked into the bank, stopping near the door to let his eyes adjust to the subdued light. He knew this bank well. Directly in front of him lay the teller stations. To his right, slowly coming into focus, sat the branch manager's desk. To his left he saw the door to the meeting room where he and Marty had signed the papers for their Pocono estate.

"Professor!" John Kline, the branch manager, was the loudest banker Corbin had ever known. "What can we do for you today, sir?"

"Your machine ate my card, John," he said.

"*Damn*! You too? You're the third one this afternoon. What's going on with that stupid machine?" He stepped toward the teller stations. "Linda! The machine just ate Professor Corbin's card. Get it back for him, will you please."

"Sure, Mr. Kline," replied a young woman standing behind the counter. She grabbed a key and started toward the automatic teller machine, when the sound of Corbin's voice stopped her.

"Linda. Could you get me a hundred dollars cash—tens and twenties? Take it from my checking account."

"Certainly, Professor," she replied. "Glad to."

John strolled back toward Corbin. "We apologize for the inconvenience," he said. "I have no idea what happened. It's never acted like this before."

"My guess is that a hacker penetrated your computer, John. Can't say I'm surprised, though. Your security isn't very good."

"A hacker? You mean some kid playing a joke?"

"Could be. A particularly bright kid, though, if that's any consolation."

"It isn't, Professor," sighed John, his tone revealing both frustration and anger. "You have no idea how much trouble this has caused. The tellers just can't keep up with both their work and the automatic teller machine's."

Perhaps, thought Corbin, if you stepped behind the counter and did a little work for a change . . . But, keeping his opinion to himself, he shook his head in apparent sympathy.

"On top of that," continued John, "we have to clean up after that stupid machine. I've spent most of the last hour apologizing to customers."

"Especially Mrs. Moran," interrupted Linda as she returned. "It told her to go mate with a bull elephant."

Corbin pictured the pompous 300-pound-plus Mrs. Moran reacting to the machine's obscene suggestion. He burst out laughing. Unable to control herself, Linda joined him.

"I don't think it's very funny," sputtered John. "Mrs. Moran is a very good customer."

"I'm sure she is," agreed Corbin, quickly regaining his composure. "That's pretty good, though." He chuckled again. "I'd say our hacker is very good, indeed."

"He'd have to be, to knock out every bank from Boston to Washington," said John.

"What did you say?" asked Corbin, suddenly serious.

"As far as we can tell," replied Linda, handing him his card and his money, "every automatic teller machine on the eastern seaboard is acting like this one—eating cards, badmouthing customers." A smile still played around the corners of her mouth. John glared at her and she, too, turned serious.

Corbin whistled softly. "Every teller machine."

"That's right. And it's not just the banks either," continued John. "Traffic is messed up in New York, the subways aren't running in Washington . . ."

"I've really been out of touch," interrupted Corbin. "I haven't heard any of this."

"There's a TV set in the employee's lounge. The networks have been running special news shows all afternoon. You're welcome to watch if you'd like."

"Well, thank you, John. As long as you don't mind."

"Of course not. Follow me."

The small, sparsely furnished lounge lay through an unmarked wooden door next to the bank's meeting room. An inexpensive couch and two folding chairs occupied one wall. A cheap coffee table heaped with empty cups, soft drink cans, and overflowing ash trays sat nearby. "Sorry about the mess, Professor," John apologized as they entered. A color television set glowed in the corner. "There's the tube. I'll turn up the volume."

"This is Connie Lopez at the corner of 50th Street and Fifth Avenue," intoned the announcer. The camera panned slowly over an intersection littered with disabled cars, twisted metal, and broken glass. Angry people milled about, picking through the debris. A bright red

Fiero lay partly hidden, its front end under the side of a bakery truck. A taxi, its hood raised, spewed steam. "Throughout Manhattan, traffic is at a standstill. Roughly twenty minutes ago, all the traffic lights in the city turned red. Every last one of them." As she spoke, the camera lingered over the scene. It focused briefly on a taxi driver beating on the side of a bus with a tire iron. On the northeast corner, a group of people chanted slogans; in the background, crude references to the mayor's ancestry and sexual preferences could be heard.

"Our New York offices are just a few hundred yards from this spot," continued Ms. Lopez. "I heard the horns and looked out the window just as the lights turned green on 50th Street. Apparently, at exactly the same time, they turned green on Fifth Avenue too, because both eastbound and southbound traffic surged into the intersection. You can see the results." The camera continued to pan. The back end of a pickup truck rested on the hood of yet another taxi. Near the southeast corner, a police officer struggled to break up a fistfight.

Corbin grinned. "Looks like a demolition derby," he joked. John frowned. Clearly he saw no humor in the day's happenings.

The announcer went on. "While we can't confirm it directly, we believe that literally every intersection in Manhattan looks like this one. I've never seen anything like it. Nobody's going anywhere this afternoon. Back to you, Bob."

The scene shifted to an anchor desk and a tall, well-dressed middle-aged gentleman with a deep, trustworthy voice. "Connie, are you still there?"

"Yes, Bob." The accident scene appeared again.

"Any idea what caused the lights to malfunction?"

"There's been no official statement yet, Bob, but rumor suggests a computer . . ."

"Look out!" cried an unidentified voice from off camera. A look of terror crossed Connie's face and she dove for an open doorway, dropping her microphone to the pavement. The camera turned quickly and focused on a taxi speeding down the sidewalk. Pedestrians scrambled out of the way, their screams and curses echoing through the still live, untended microphone. A trash can flew into the air, spun end over end, and landed atop a Toyota. Still the cab came on, right at the camera, filling more and more of the screen. Then, at the last possible second, brakes squealing, the cab skidded into a nearby fire hydrant, spraying water high into the air. Rivulets covered the screen, then it went blank.

"I think I know that taxi driver," quipped Corbin.

John shook his head, disgustedly. "New York has to be the craziest city in the world," he said. "Oh, there's the picture."

"We'll get back to Connie Lopez in New York as soon as possible."

Bob, the anchor, clearly shaken, struggled to maintain the calm de-meanor that had earned him his job. "Meanwhile, let's switch to Tim O'Brien in Washington, D.C. Tim, are you there?"

"I certainly am, Bob." The screen flashed to the crowded interior of a metro station. A train entered and, without even slowing, surged right through. In the background, people booed. "Since roughly 3:45 this afternoon, the trains have been rolling through the stations without stopping," the reporter said. The camera scanned the faces of hundreds of angry, sweating people packed tightly onto the subway platforms and stairways. "As you can see, the station is mobbed, and the mood is turning ugly. Metro officials shut down the escalators some time ago, but passengers keep pushing their way into the station. It's getting nasty out here, Bob."

"Any word from the people on the trains?" the anchor prodded.

"No. We can only imagine their frustration as their stations flash by, time and time again."

"Time and time again?"

"Yes. Apparently, when a train reaches the end of its line, it turns around and retraces its route. We've seen one train come through here three times since we arrived."

"Any idea what caused this mess?" asked the anchor.

"Everyone assumes it's a computer foul-up, Bob," answered Tim. "That's unofficial, of course."

"Thanks, Tim." Once again Bob appeared on screen, talking to the monitor on his right. "Stay on the line and let us know if anything develops." He shifted his gaze to the audience. "If you've just tuned in, here's an update. A rash of apparent computer failures has tangled traffic throughout much of the Northeast on this, the hottest day of the year. From Boston to Washington, computer-controlled traffic lights, toll booths, drawbridges, and public transportation systems have broken down, . . ."

Banking. Transportation. In Corbin's highly trained mind, a pattern began to emerge. NECEN. The NorthEast CENtral computer. Of course! NECEN controlled the computers that controlled both banking and transportation. Someone, some brilliant hacker, had managed to pen-etrate NECEN's security!

He tried to ignore his growing sense of anticipation, forcing his attention back to the TV screen and Bob, the network anchor. ". . . a particularly poignant piece of film taken by an amateur photographer near Egg Harbor, New Jersey. At precisely 3:45 this afternoon, the com-puter controlling the new, fully automated North Pass drawbridge failed, and the roadbed came crashing down. Here's what happened next."

The scene shifted. A hand-held camera panned quickly over an open drawbridge, moving up one side, back down to the water, across, and then up and down the other side. Returning to the water, it focused on a beautiful, high-masted sailboat moving slowly, majestically through the opening. Suddenly, the roadbed began to drop. As though in slow motion, the sailboat drifted into the steadily closing jaws. The teeth meshed, sheering off the top of the mast. Still the bridge dropped. Tons of concrete and steel settled on the sailboat, pushing it down, like a child sinking a toy boat in a bathtub. As the sea rushed over the sailboat's sides, it settled into the muck at the bottom of the channel.

"They say that all these incidents were caused by computer foul-ups," said John. "Is that possible?"

"Yes. Yes it is." Corbin seemed momentarily lost in thought.

"Something wrong, Professor?"

"What?" He snapped back to reality. "Oh—no, John. Don't mind me, I'm fine. My mind drifted. It happens more and more as you get older. I really do have to go, though. Thanks for your hospitality."

"Any time, Professor." They walked from the lounge and crossed the teller area.

"Take care, John. You too, Linda." Corbin hurried through the front door, waving as he left, but his mind was elsewhere.

2 *The Summons*

It had to be NECEN, the NorthEast CENtral computer. Nothing else could explain the traffic lights, *and* the subways, *and* the drawbridge, *and* the teller terminals. Corbin's worst nightmare had come true. Someone had penetrated NECEN's security and taken control of the most powerful computer in the world!

NECEN. Bitter memories flooded Corbin's mind. Once again he heard the technocrats arguing for a national data bank. He remembered their rallying cry: efficient government. He'd opposed them, of course, but the words of an outsider, even one with his reputation, had little impact. Then the President called. "I need you, Corbin. Come to Washington."

His mind returned to those unhappy days. He hadn't wanted to go. His writing and his robots kept him busy. His textbooks and his patents still generated income, so he didn't need the money. Prestige? He'd already won every award and honor the computing profession could bestow on him, and he'd advised presidents before. Power? He'd never wanted power. He was content; he had nothing to prove.

But he went to Washington. He fought, and fought well. "Large systems are inherently complex, extremely expensive, and error-prone," he'd argued. "We need efficient government," countered the technocrats. "Right," he'd agreed, sarcastically. "With a national computer center, the government can screw up ten times faster."

"What about security?" he'd asked. To protect a computer you start with the value of the information stored on the system, and add security features until the cost of breaking in (or the risk of getting caught) exceeds that value. But the value of a national data bank couldn't be measured. "Information is the key to knowledge, and knowledge is power," he'd argued. "He who controls the national data bank controls the nation. The proposed system will be a tempting target—too tempting. Eventually, someone will break through security and gain control. That's an unacceptable risk."

Against his precise, pointed, telling arguments, the technocrats offered little more than slogans. Effortlessly, he'd exposed their absurdly low cost estimates, their much too optimistic schedules, and their laughable security claims. Publicly he'd discredited them, made fools of them. He'd won. The national data bank was dead.

Or so he'd thought. Then the whispers started. "Old man Corbin is out of date, locked in the past. He doesn't understand the new technology. He's afraid computers will take over; he sees the national data bank as Frankenstein's monster." They never confronted him, of course; they never do. Instead they laughed at him behind his back. They couldn't beat him in an open, fair debate, so they turned to political dirty tricks. In their polite, diplomatic way, they undercut him, attacking his professional credibility.

And it worked! That hurt. The President, reluctantly, sided with the technocrats. The national data bank would be developed, step by step, region by region, starting with a prototype system: NECEN. Publicly, the technocrats praised Corbin, trying to claim him as one of their own. "We were moving too fast," they admitted. "Corbin brought us back to earth; thanks to him, we'll succeed in the long run. He's a genius." But everyone knew he'd lost. Angry and frustrated, he'd resigned. Now NECEN's security had been penetrated. It serves them right, he decided.

Suddenly, the sound of a cascading mountain stream pulled Corbin back to the present. He was almost home. He'd often joked that his years of practice had made the trip from Mount Pocono so automatic he could drive it in his sleep. Well, today, he'd done it. He had almost no memory of the twisting, turning mountain road that had brought him here.

Just across the bridge, the turn off to the right appeared as little more than an opening in the trees. The Porsche slowed, swung onto a narrow gravel road, and disappeared into the forest. Gradually, his eyes adjusted to the deep shade. Ferns and undergrowth brushed softly against the sides of the car, and low-hanging branches slapped occasionally against the windshield. Beyond a rise a chain link fence blocked the way. The car rolled to a stop at the gate. He leaned out and called in the direction of the nearby guardhouse: "Open up, Duke! It's me."

A squat, dwarflike robot emerged and rolled toward the gate. "Good afternoon, Professor." Duke's voice had just a hint of a metallic monotone; Corbin had programmed him well. "Welcome back." Grasping the lock in his clawlike hand, Duke began to slide the gate open. "How was your day, sir?"

"Fine, Duke."No point in explaining NECEN to a robot. "Any news?"

"We have an intruder, sir."

"Oh?"

"Yes, sir. His car is right over there." The robot pointed at a light green compact partially hidden in the bushes just outside the gate.

"See you later, Duke!" As the Porsche lurched through the almost open gate and accelerated toward the house, Corbin's mind raced almost as fast as the engine. An intruder. My god! He pictured his granddaughter, her soft, brown hair framing her pixie face. "Why did I leave her alone? If anything happens to her . . ."

He jerked to a stop, jumped out of the car, and rushed toward the cabin, trying desperately to remember the new code words. Locating the intercom just inside the door frame, he pushed a button and, almost out of breath, spoke into the receiver: "Strawberry. Mississippi. Inconsistent." A tiny display over the speaker flashed, again and again: REPEAT. He took a deep breath and, more slowly, more carefully, repeated the code words: "Strawberry. Mississippi. Inconsistent." This time the computer liked his voice print. The door buzzed; he pushed it open. And there she stood! Susie! He could barely contain his emotions as he dropped to one knee and hugged her.

"Are you okay, honey?" he asked, looking directly into her eyes. He could see his wife Marty in those eyes.

"I'm fine, Gramps," she replied, quietly, a slight quiver betraying her fear. "I was in the observation room when the alarm went off, and I came right up here, just like you told me."

"Good girl." Again he hugged her, tightly. "There's nothing to be frightened about." He stood and took her hand. "Let's see what's going on."

Together they crossed the hardwood floor, entered the control room, and stopped in front of a large computer monitor. Corbin flipped a switch, activating an audio input unit, and snapped a one-word command: "Status!"

Almost immediately, the machine responded, its words coming from a speaker just above Corbin's head. "We have an intruder in sector 14. The robogs have him cornered."

"Visual link!" ordered Corbin, ignoring the additional details displayed on the monitor. The scene changed. Through the eyes of a robot dog, he looked up into a large maple tree. From this perspective, so close to the ground, he could see a pair of shoes dangling from a lower branch, but little more.

"Dispatch Cedric!" Cedric, another robot, was designed specifically for emergencies such as this. His three legs gave him surprising agility on the uneven terrain of the forest; few human beings could escape his determined pursuit. Using his handcufflike claws, Cedric could patiently disarm and hold an intruder until the authorities arrived. Sophisticated video and audio units gave the robot sight, hearing, and speech, and allowed Corbin to identify and communicate with any unwelcome guest through him. A few words from this massive, ungainly, mechanical being scared off all but the most determined intruder.

"Cedric! Video!" The monitor image shifted to Cedric's perspective. He lumbered through a hardwood forest of white birch, maple, ash, and hickory, the ground hidden by dark green ferns. As he broke into a stand of evergreens the undergrowth thinned noticeably, and he moved more quickly. The pines gave way to a thick patch of rhododendron. Cedric slowed down again, carefully picking his way through the tangled roots.

Now Corbin heard the metallic yelping of the robogs, his robot dogs. As Cedric burst into a small clearing, the camera saw six of them surrounding a tree. The robot's gaze moved up the tree. There were the shoes. Next, a pair of massive legs with thick, muscular thighs covered by expensive, pin-striped slacks appeared. A matching vest hid a flat, hard midriff. The suit jacket draped a broad chest and powerful shoulders. Finally, a scowling face materialized.

Corbin stared in disbelief. He knew that man! Relieved, he smiled and grabbed a microphone. "Pete Smith! You old son of a gun. What are you doing here?" In the clearing, Cedric echoed his words.

Obviously startled, the man in the tree almost lost his grasp. "Bill Corbin? Is that you?" A puzzled expression replaced his scowl.

"Indirectly. Meet Cedric." The robot pointed to itself. "Hop down; he'll lead you to the house."

"Not until you get rid of these tin dogs of yours," said Pete. "They're vicious." In spite of his words, he smiled.

"Break!" snapped Corbin. The robogs loped off toward the house. "You can come down now; it's safe. Take your time, though," he teased. "You might want to dream up a good story. Hard to believe a couple of toy dogs chased you up a tree. You're slipping, Peter."

Pete dropped from the tree, grinning. "You really know how to hurt a guy, Corbin." He swung his arm in the general direction of the cabin. "Lead on, Cedric."

"Cedric! Return!" ordered Corbin. Cedric spun on his three legs and retraced his path through the rhododendron; Pete followed close behind. "It's been a long time, Pete," said Corbin through the robot.

"Hard to believe it's been eight years since we broke that insurance fraud case," said Pete.

"Yes it has, my friend. That's why I'm so surprised to see you today. Just what were you doing climbing my fence?"

"I tried to get in through the gate . . ."

"Ah—you've met Duke. The robots run the place when I'm not here."

"They do a good job, Bill. My compliments." As Cedric reached the stand of pine he picked up speed, forcing Pete into a jog. "Hey, tell this guy to slow down!"

"He'll be through the pines in a minute." Almost as Corbin spoke, the robot entered the thick undergrowth and slowed perceptibly.

"I'm surprised I haven't seen these robots on the market," said Pete. "They really are quite good. Where did you get them?"

"I build them," replied Corbin. "Fascinating hobby."

"Why don't you patent them? They'd be worth a fortune."

"If I applied for a patent, I'd have to publish the technical specifications. If I did that, somebody might be able to figure out how to disable one of my robots and break in. Right now, my privacy is more important than the money, so I prefer to keep them a secret."

"I understand. They're really something, though."

Through the trees, Pete could see the outline of the house. In the background, a waterfall added its relaxing rhythm to the quiet of the deep woods. "It's so beautiful up here, Bill," he said, "I almost hate to tell you why I came."

"Why *did* you come, amigo?" asked Corbin. Somehow, he already knew.

"We're in trouble. We need your help."

"I'm retired, Pete."

"I know that. But this is serious, Bill."

Pete reached the house. "Just push on the door—it's open," said Corbin. Cedric continued on, returning to his post; Pete stepped inside, closing the door behind him.

From the outside, the house seemed little more than a hunter's log cabin. Inside, however, it was magnificent. The cabin formed the foyer. Its back wall opened to a sunken living room, tastefully decorated in early American. A large stone fireplace, flanked by trophy cases holding the professor's many academic honors, mementos of his long career, and the first copy of each of his books, dominated the left wall. Directly in front of him, Pete noted a large picture window overlooking the falls. To his right sat a control room housing an impressive array of electronic equipment, and there, in the doorway, stood a twelve-year-old girl and a short, silver-haired, elderly gentlemen: Professor Bill Corbin.

"Good to see you, Pete," said Corbin advancing across the hardwood floor. They met, shook hands, and then hugged each other.

Pete reached out to pat the professor's stomach. "You've put on some weight."

"I'm getting old. Your chest drops when you get old."

"Right!" Pete grinned. "By the way, when are you going to introduce me to the young lady?" He gestured toward Susie.

"Oh, I'm sorry." Corbin turned to face his granddaughter. "Pete, meet Susie. Her parents are on vacation for a few weeks, and she's staying with me." He nodded toward Pete. "Susie. This is Pete Smith. He's a government agent—sort of a spy."

"A spy!" Susie's eyes grew wide. Then a look of puzzlement crossed her face. "If you're really a spy, how come the robogs caught you?"

Pete laughed and reached out to shake her hand. "Nice to meet you, Susie." She seemed momentarily taken aback by the man's sheer size, but then, shyly, stretched out her own small hand.

"Nice to meet you, too, sir," she said. She turned to her grandfather. "Were you a spy, too, Gramps? " she asked.

Corbin shook his head. "Not really, Susie," he replied.

"He's being modest, Susie," said Pete. "Your grandfather is the best electronic espionage agent in the world. Any time we get in trouble, we call him."

"Really, Gramps?"

"I'm afraid Pete exaggerates, Susie. Besides, that was years ago." He reached out and brushed a lock of hair from in front of her eyes. "Honey," he continued, "Pete and I have some business to discuss. Can you find something to keep you busy for a while?"

"Sure, Gramps. Is it okay if I go outside and look for deer?"

"Of course. Take Cedric with you, though."

"Okay. Nice meeting you, Mr. Smith." She kissed her grandfather on the cheek and walked gracefully through the door.

"She's a doll, Bill," said Pete.

"Yes, she is." Corbin had a pensive look. "She's bright, friendly, and very well behaved. My son and his wife are doing a fine job of raising her. I'm afraid I spoil her, though. Every year I send her mom and dad on a two-week vacation, and I get to look after her. They think I'm doing them a favor, but they're really doing me one. She keeps me young."

Briefly, they stood in silence; then Pete broke the spell. "As I said outside, Bill, we need your help again."

"Not here, Pete. Let's go downstairs."

The two old friends crossed the living room to a spiral staircase and descended, entering a library. Thousands of books lined the walls. Pete paused for a moment, pulled a well-worn copy of Frank Herbert's *Dune* from the shelf nearest him, inspected it, and smiled as though greeting an old friend. "I could get lost down here, Bill," he said, wistfully. "Based on what I saw from outside, I never would have imagined a library like this."

"Most of the living space it underground," said Corbin. "That way, there's less for thieves or the IRS to see." He paused, and grinned. "Really no difference between those two, is there?"

Pete smiled and shook his head as he replaced the book. "Still the cynic, Corbin. I'd hoped retirement would have mellowed you."

"Not a chance." Corbin pointed toward a doorway in the far wall. "Let's go out there. I think you'll like what you see."

Pete stepped through the door and into the observation room. To his right, a waterfall thundered into a pool fifty feet directly below. To his left, the pool became rapids, and then yet another waterfall. Around him, covered by mist and dark green moss, loomed the rocky walls of the glen. Above his head the overhanging trees framed a sliver of deep blue sky. "This is fantastic, Bill," he said, quietly.

"Thanks. Have a seat." Corbin motioned toward a hanging basket chair with an unrestricted view of the falls. Pete sat down, crossed his legs Indian style, and began swinging gently, looking out of place in his pin-striped suit.

"Can I get you something to drink?" asked Corbin.

"A glass of sherry would be nice," Pete replied.

"Coming up." Corbin crossed the room to a small bar nestled just inside the door. He opened the cabinet, removed two wine glasses and a bottle of amontillado, slowly poured the pale, amber fluid, and, retracing his steps, handed a glass to Pete.

"Thanks, Bill." Pete took a sip, closed his eyes, and licked his lips. "Delicious."

Just to the right of the hanging basket stood an ancient leather armchair. As Corbin settled into it, it seemed to mold itself to his body. "My favorite chair," he said smiling. Then his mood changed abruptly. "Let me have it, Pete. Why are you here?"

"We've lost control of NECEN."

The professor removed his glasses, rubbed his eyes, and frowned.

"The big one, Bill," continued Pete. "The NorthEast CENtral computer. The one that controls damn near everything from Boston to Washington."

"Can't say I'm surprised, Pete." He replaced his glasses. "I predicted this four years ago. They dug their own hole; let them get themselves out."

"The President asked for you. Personally."

"Tell him to go pound sand, Pete. I'm *not* coming." His tone grew suddenly angry.

"Bill, I know why you resigned the Cabinet. I wouldn't blame you if you didn't come. But . . ."

"I left because the President chose to ignore my advice and follow a bunch of bozos into this mess. Let the technocrats get him out."

"They can't. Have you heard the news this afternoon?"

"Yes, I have. Frankly, I rather enjoyed it."

"A lot of people have been terribly inconvenienced, Bill. We've had injuries, too. It's no joke."

"I know that, Pete. But look beyond the individuals. Focus on the situation." Corbin's index finger jabbed the air, as if to emphasize his words. "Some guy takes over a computer, *one* computer, and manages to bring the entire East Coast to its knees. He's doing us a favor. He's showing us what can happen when we put all our eggs in one basket." As Corbin spoke, his rising anger became more and more obvious. "These are pranks, Pete. We're lucky this guy's got a sense of humor."

"There's more, Bill."

"I know about the banks. An automatic teller machine questioned my ancestry about an hour ago."

"These 'pranks' are just the tip of the iceberg. Here, read this." Pete handed Corbin a letter clearly marked top secret. Carefully, the professer unfolded it, and began reading aloud:

My Dear Mr. President:

   I have NECEN. If you want it back, please transmit the sum of one billion dollars through NETEN. Address it to me; I'll do the rest.

   Perhaps you don't take me seriously. Fine. I'll give you a demonstration of what I can do later this afternoon. Don't try to go anywhere; you may get caught in traffic. Stay away from banks, too.

Don't worry, I'll fix things. At 4:45. Then you'll have twenty-four hours to pay me.

Did anyone ever tell you how much the country's financial health depends on NECEN? They should. Talk it over; you'll pay. If you don't, I'll just take the billion dollars anyway.

Respectfully
The Harlequin

The Harlequin, thought Corbin. Where have I heard that name before? A sense of foreboding crept into his mind. Suddenly serious, he refolded the letter and handed it back. "Any idea who this Harlequin is, Pete?" he asked.

"No. Not a clue," replied Pete slipping it into his pocket.

"Where did the message come from?"

"It showed up on the President's NETEN line around noon. No return address."

"NETEN?"

"The NorthEast TElecommunications Network. It went on-line about a month ago. Links everything from Boston to Washington."

"And NECEN controls it?"

"That's right." Pete glanced at his watch. "It's almost 4:45, Bill. If this guy is going to carry through on his threats, we should hear something soon. Do you have a TV set?"

"Sure do," replied Corbin. He flipped open the arm of his chair revealing an array of buttons and pushed one. The back wall slid aside, uncovering an oversize TV screen. Selecting a station, he settled back to watch.

Again, Bob, the network anchor, appeared. "This just in," he read, in his baritone voice. "We have reestablished contact with New York. The traffic lights appear to be working normally again. Let's go to Connie Lopez . . ." Suddenly he paused. "Wait a minute," he said, obviously listening to his earphone; finally he swung back to the camera. "We've just received some important news from our Washington correspondent. Tim."

"Thank you, Bob." The screen showed a crowded subway station. In the background, people cheered, loudly. Correspondent Tim O'Brien stood in the foreground. "Just a few minutes ago, a train stopped here in the L'Enfant Plaza station," he shouted over the din. "At precisely 4:45, the train pulled into the station, slowed, and stopped, as though nothing unusual had happened this afternoon. When the doors opened, the passengers scrambled out."

Suddenly the background noise grew even louder. Another train had entered the station; quickly, the camera focused on it. The train slowed, then stopped. Its doors opened. Once again the people cheered. "Well, you saw it Bob," said Tim, trying desperately to be heard above the noise. "It's beginning to appear that things are returning to normal. We . . ."

Abruptly Bob reappeared. "Sorry to interrupt, Tim," he said, "but we've just received a bulletin. At 4:45 this afternoon, the following message appeared, simultaneously, on all the news service wires." As the text of the message flashed on the screen, Bob read it, slowly, somberly:

THE HARLEQUIN HAS STRUCK.
TODAY, TRANSPORTATION.
TODAY, THE BANKS.
TOMORROW, WHO KNOWS?

Corbin switched off the TV. The Harlequin. Of course. How could he have missed it before? The situation was serious; they had *no idea* how serious. He stood and looked directly at Pete. "I'm convinced," he said. "I'll go."

"There's a plane waiting at the airport."

"Give me a few minutes. I have to instruct the robots, put the Porsche in the garage, and get Susie."

"Is there someone you can leave her with, Bill?"

"What do you mean? I'm responsible for her, Pete. She's coming, with me."

"We can't take her. This is top secret."

"No Susie, no Bill Corbin. Your choice, my friend."

"Bill. I can't." Pete's tone was almost pleading.

"I understand. Convey my regrets to the President." He started toward the door. "Can I interest you in dinner before you leave? I grill a great steak."

"Dammit, Bill, you are stubborn." Frustrated, Pete glared at his old friend. Finally he sighed, a resigned look on his face. "Okay, you win. Bring her along. I'm supposed to deliver you to Washington. I'll let the general worry about Susie."

"Fine. Why don't you wait here and enjoy the falls? I'll be ready in a few minutes." Corbin turned toward the door, but suddenly, half-way through, he stopped. "Pete," he said, over his shoulder.

"Yes, Bill."

"I think I know who the Harlequin is."

"Great! I knew you were the right man for the job. Who is it?"

"Wait a while; I want to be sure." He stood in the doorway motionless. "I'll tell you later."

"Okay. I hope you're right."

"I hope I'm wrong, Pete. If I'm right, we're in trouble."

3 The Briefing

The small jet locked onto the Potomac, far below. Quickly it descended, following the river's every twist and turn. Then suddenly, just beyond the wingtip, almost close enough to touch, lay Washington, D.C. Susie sat glued to the window, announcing every detail of their journey. "Look, Gramps! There's the Washington Monument! And the Capitol! Isn't that the White House? There's the Lincoln Memorial right down there!"

Professor Corbin smiled and leaned forward to share the view with his granddaughter. "It's beautiful, isn't it, Susie?"

"It sure is." Her eyes stared directly into his. "Do you think we can . . ."

"Sure, Susie." No sense fighting the inevitable; when she looked at him that way, he always gave in. "As long as we're here, whatever you want to see, we'll see."

"Great!" She kissed him on the cheek. "Thanks, Gramps!" In an instant, she had returned to picking out landmarks.

The plane banked to the right, dropped toward the runway, and touched down at the National Airport. Avoiding the main terminal, it followed a little-used taxiway toward an isolated hangar. As it approached, the massive doors slid open, and the plane rolled to a stop inside. Slowly, the doors closed behind them.

This was no ordinary hangar. In the distance, Corbin could see at least three aircraft shrouded in canvas, hidden from even accidental public view. Along the east wall a dozen military jets were undergoing repair or modification. Sophisticated helicopters lined the west wall. Just outside his window, four men pretended to work on a small jet. They might have fooled a casual observer, but his years of contact with the secret services had taught him to recognize a trained agent; these men were alert and heavily armed. As he glanced up, he noted a small observation booth mounted on the wall some twenty feet above the hangar floor. It was, he knew, occupied, and he sensed, with a shiver, the high-powered weaponry aimed his way. Without doubt, the opposite wall supported a similar booth. They were well covered.

"Nice flight, Pete," said Corbin, trying hard not to let his nervousness show. "You haven't lost your touch."

"Perfect landing," chimed in Susie.

"Thanks." Pete smiled. "Welcome to SMF." He unfastened his seat belt, stood, and stretched.

"SMF? I thought you worked for the Combined Miniature Deterrent Force," said Corbin as he swung from his seat. "CMDF was bad enough, but SMF is even worse. How do you pronounce that? Smuff?"

Pete laughed as he pushed open the door and hopped out. Susie followed, confidently rejecting Pete's assistance. Finally, the professor exited, a bit gingerly, showing his age.

"Need some help, Bill?"

"No thanks. I'm just a little stiff; it'll pass." He stepped down onto the hangar floor.

"Smuff." Pete chuckled once again. "I'll have to remember that one." They started across the hangar toward the helicopters, Pete in the lead.

"What exactly does SMF stand for?" asked Corbin.

"We are now the Special Miniature Force," replied Pete. "Insiders call us the Small Mission Force, but don't tell the general." He grinned.

"Why the name change?"

"Blame it on Isaac Asimov."

"Asimov! What does he have to do with SMF?"

"Several years ago we gave him a tour and he wrote a novel about us—*Fantastic Voyage*, or something like that."

"Oh, yes. I've read it."

"I read it, too," said Susie.

"Do you read a lot, Susie?" asked Pete.

"Sure. Especially science fiction."

"She's amazing, Pete," bragged Corbin. "I swear she reads five books at a time. I find them lying open all over the house."

"Terrific, Susie!" smiled Pete. Then, gesturing toward the professor, he continued. "Getting back to your question about the name change: Dr. Asimov's story was a bit too accurate, so we dropped CMDF. Changed our entrance, too; it's right here." They stopped near an inobtrusive gray door. "Excuse me."

He pulled an identification card from his pocket, inserted it into a scanner, and watched it disappear. Almost immediately a section of wall slid aside revealing a screen. He placed his palm flat against the glass. The gray door swung open and they stepped into a small elevator; the door closed behind them. Beside the door was a keyboard. As Pete typed the day's code, his identification card reappeared, and the elevator began to descend.

"That's it?" asked Corbin, incredulously.

"What do you mean, Bill?" responded Pete.

"An ID card, a palm print, and a digital code is all you need to get in these days?"

"You missed a few checks, Bill. The plane has a coded transmitter; that's how we opened the hangar doors. The hangar itself is a secure area; we were covered from the minute we rolled in."

"I know," said Corbin. "I saw the maintenance people and the observation booth."

"They had a complete description of me," continued Pete. "If someone else had jumped from that plane first, there would have been trouble. As soon as I hit the ground, I flashed them an all clear hand signal; a different signal, and they would have destroyed the plane. And we're not home free yet." He pointed to a side wall. "There's a camera behind that panel. A computer is busy analyzing my body shape right now. If I don't check out, we don't get off this elevator."

Suddenly Susie spoke up. "Can you really miniaturize people, Mr. Smith?"

"What?" Pete seemed puzzled, but then the sense of her question dawned on him. "Oh—Asimov's story. I really can't tell you what SMF does, Susie. It's a secret."

"Well, in *Fantastic Voyage*, they shrunk a bunch of people and put them inside a human body. Then . . ."

"Susie," interrupted the professor, "Pete really can't tell you any more."

"Okay, I understand. I'm sorry, Mr. Smith." She seemed just a bit disappointed.

"No problem, Susie," said Pete. "Someday I'll tell you all about it. Promise." He held out his palm. With a grin, she slapped it.

The elevator bumped to a stop and the door swung open. "The computer has declared this old body still perfect," joked Pete. Quickly they stepped out and crossed a narrow hallway to a monorail car that looked like it might have come from Disney World. Four deeply padded bucket seats lined each side. Corbin and his granddaughter entered first and slid into the second row, securely fastening their seat belts. Pete took the right front seat. He touched a control panel and the car accelerated rapidly into the pitch black tunnel. Whoever designed this secret subway system had certainly not been afraid of the dark.

"I take it this tunnel parallels the metro," shouted Corbin over the din of the monorail.

"That's right," replied Pete. "We had it installed when they dug the subway. Very convenient. Technically, it's a utilities tube."

The noise echoing from the nearby walls discouraged conversation. Professor Corbin reached across the aisle and found his granddaughter's hand. They rode in silence.

Suddenly, light seemed to explode around them. The monorail slowed, and then stopped. "We're here," said Pete. For a few seconds, they sat and blinked, letting their eyes adjust to the light. Then, with Pete in the lead, they stepped from the capsule and onto the raised platform of a subway station.

Perhaps two dozen people, all dressed in identical beige jumpsuits and white caps, moved purposefully across the platform, some leaving and some arriving. Just to their left, three men stood quietly, apparently waiting for the next car. Corbin tapped his friend on the arm. "More security, Pete?" he asked.

"Very observant, Bill," replied Pete. "I'm impressed."

A young woman stepped from a doorway and strode briskly across the platform, directly toward them. She stopped in front of Pete, and saluted. "Welcome back, Major Smith. The general is expecting you."

"Lead on, Lieutenant," Pete replied in an official voice. "Can't keep the general waiting." Then he chuckled, his formality melting away. "Oh, by the way, let me introduce Professor Bill Corbin and his granddaughter, Susie. Folks, this is Lieutenant Jean Jackson."

Jean blushed, then smiled. "Professor Corbin. It's a pleasure to meet you, sir. I've read several of your books. Before you leave, could you autograph one for me?"

"Certainly, Jean," replied the professor. "I'd be glad to."

The lieutenant turned to Susie. "It's nice to meet you too, Susie. Welcome to SMF."

"Thanks," Susie said, with a grin. "It's nice to be here."

"We're wasting time," growled Pete.

"Right you are, Major Smith," agreed Jean. "Follow me, please. The general doesn't like to be kept waiting."

Lieutenant Jackson led the group through the entryway and into a wide corridor. A series of identical, glass-paneled doors lined both sides; behind them, Corbin knew, lay identical, rectangular offices. "One of these yours, Pete?" he asked.

"Third one on the left," replied Pete, gesturing toward a door. "Nothing to write home about—four walls and a desk."

"I remember using one of these offices about eight years ago. I think we were working on the insurance fraud case. Whose office was that, anyway?"

"You have a good memory, Bill. That was Custer's."

"Oh, yes. G. Armstrong Custer. What ever happened to him?"

"You're on your way to see him right now. He's the general."

"You're kidding. General Custer." Corbin laughed. "Son of a gun. Our mission will be led by General Custer."

"He hasn't changed much, Bill. Still blunt, abrasive, and competent as ever."

"He's a good man, Pete; we could do a lot worse. Tell me, though—what does the G stand for?"

"Gerald."

"Gerald! Why does he insist on G. Armstrong? Does he enjoy being linked to a military disaster?"

"I think he does. You have to admit that people recognize a name like General G. Armstrong Custer. He must be doing something right; he's a general."

"You have a point, Pete."

As they walked on in silence, Corbin thought back to his very first miniaturized mission. Vividly he remembered shrinking to microbe size. An image of the world as seen from that unique perspective would stay with him forever. Perhaps he would once again have an opportunity to return to the miniature universe. He hoped so.

At the end of that long corridor, a single door faced them. The nameplate read:

GENERAL G. ARMSTRONG CUSTER
DIRECTOR, S.M.F.

Lieutenant Jackson knocked. Abruptly, the door swung open and a tall, thin, grim-looking man in a military uniform stepped out.

"General Custer," said Pete. "This is Professor Corbin. I understand you've been waiting for us."

"We've met," replied the general in a low, rumbling voice. "Nice to see you, Professor." They exchanged a rather formal, diplomatic handshake.

"My orders," he continued, "are to brief you and deliver you to the White House as soon as possible. We're running late, so let's get going."

Glancing at the party, he noticed Susie for the first time. "Who's she?" he growled.

"General Custer. Let me introduce my granddaughter, Susie. She's with me."

"Professor, we don't have time for this."

"General Custer, Susie's parents are on vacation and, at the moment, she's my responsibility. My *primary* responsibility. If we don't have time for her, then I'm afraid I don't have time for you. I'm sure Pete wouldn't mind flying us back to Mount Pocono. I must remind you, however, that I am here at the request of the President—your commander in chief, if I remember correctly. I leave it to you to tell him why I'm not available." Corbin's words were cold and chipped, his anger just below the surface.

"She can't go on the mission, Professor."

"Of course not. But unless she is well cared for, neither can I, General."

The two men glared at each other, the tension almost tangible. Then Lieutenant Jackson broke in. "I'm currently between assignments, General," she said. "If Professor Corbin approves, I'd be glad to look after Susie."

"Thank you, Lieutenant," snapped Custer. Pivoting on his heel, he marched back into his office. "This way, Professor. You too, Major Smith. Damn civilians," he muttered, under his breath, shaking his head.

Pointedly ignoring the general, Corbin approached his granddaughter and hugged her. "Susie," he said, "I don't know how long this is going to take—maybe an hour, maybe a day or two. Lieutenant Jackson will be in charge while I'm gone, so you pay attention to her. Maybe she'll take you on a tour of the city. I'll see you later, okay?"

"I'll be fine, Gramps. I'm old enough to take care of myself." She kissed him on the cheek and then turned to Lieutenant Jackson. "Do you think we could see the White House?"

"We'll try, Susie," replied Jean, with a smile. "Don't worry, Professor, we'll take care of her."

"I'm sure you will, Jean, and thanks. Fortunately, not all military people are like Custer."

"I can't comment on that, sir."

"I know you can't." He paused, and then continued. "Jean," he said, "when the good Lord made horses, he had a bunch of rear ends left over. Most of them ended up here in Washington." Laughing, he bent to kiss his granddaughter again. "You be good, Susie."

"Aww, Gramps. Mom leaves me by myself all the time. Don't worry."

"I won't, kiddo."

After one last hug he walked through the door and entered a reception area. A secretary's desk blocked his path. Behind it and to the left lay a private inner office. To the right, the general's aide stood near another door that led to a conference room. "This way, Professor," he called. Corbin followed him into the room and took a chair. As he did, General Custer began speaking.

"Let me introduce my staff, Professor." His gesture took in the three officers seated around the table. "You've already met my aide, Colonel Holtzworth." The general indicated a dark-haired, slightly overweight man with a military bearing that matched his own. Corbin nodded.

"This," continued the general, pointing to a tall, slim man with a droopy handlebar mustache, "is Captain Statler. In addition to being a fine officer, he's a computer expert."

"Excellent," said Corbin. "It's a pleasure to meet you, Captain." He reached across the table and they shook hands.

"I'm looking forward to working with you, Professor," said Captain Statler. "Maybe when this is over we can have a few beers."

"Sounds great."

"The last member," the general went on, indicating the lone woman in the room, "is Lieutenant Cortez. She's a recent computer science graduate."

"Nice to meet you, Lieutenant," said the professor.

"The pleasure is mine," she replied. "It's an honor to meet you, Professor."

"Why, thank you, Lieutenant."

"Sergeant Washington is my secretary," interrupted Custer, almost rudely. "And, of course, you know Major Smith."

"Certainly." Corbin looked directly at his old friend. "Tell me, Pete, when did you get drafted?" he asked impishly.

Pete chuckled.

"He didn't, Professor," said the general, brusquely. "He holds positional rank. It clarifies the chain of command. Shall we begin?"

"Certainly, General."

"Did Major Smith show you the extortion letter?"

"I saw it."

"This Harlequin carried out his threats yesterday." It was a statement of fact.

"I'm aware of that."

"What do you think, Professor?"

"Do I have the whole story, General? Is there anything else I should know?"

"He's had complete control of NECEN for two days now."

Corbin shrugged. "Tell the operator to pull the plug and shut the machine down."

"There is no operator."

"What?"

"NECEN's control room is sealed; the operator runs the show from a remote console. Ever since this Harlequin took over, the system has ignored the real operator's commands."

"You mean you have no physical presence in the room?" Corbin sounded concerned.

"That's right."

"What's been done to gain reentry?"

"We've tried everything, Professor. No luck."

"I assume you've tried breaking down the door."

"Impossible," replied the general. "The door is heavily reinforced."

"Have you considered a bomb?"

"Professor Corbin, the NECEN center is located under Madison Square Garden. A bomb big enough to blow that door would wipe out a big chunk of downtown Manhattan."

"Why not cut the power to the room?"

"We can't. NECEN controls the electric network."

"Now let me get this straight. NECEN is housed in a locked, bomb-proof room, with complete control over its own source of power. If I may say so, General, that's really stupid."

"Oh, come on, Professor! NECEN isn't Frankenstein's monster."

"It's not the machine that concerns me, General. It's the Harlequin. He controls the most powerful computer in the world. I'd feel better if he controlled a missile silo. At least then the potential for disaster would be localized. And we don't even have a fail safe. We can't even pull the damn plug!"

"I see your point." The general's antagonism was fading.

"You have terminals. Have you tried breaking in remotely?"

"Our people have been working around the clock, but no luck yet. This Harlequin is good."

"What about the local terminals?"

"NECEN ignores them. Completely."

"General, I know some of the people who built NECEN. Surely, they have their own private access windows."

"They did, Professor. The windows were closed a month ago, when NETEN came on line. Security."

"Security!" Corbin laughed derisively. "When it comes to computers, General, there's no such thing as security. Breaking in is just a matter of time, skill, and money."

"Do you have any suggestions?"

"We have to get inside the room and disable the machine. If we can't, the Harlequin has us. Either we pay him or we accept the consequences."

"We've reached much the same conclusion, Professor. We can put a team into that room. In fact, we can put the team inside the computer."

"I may be missing something, General. I know SMF can miniaturize people and equipment. I can see slipping a team through a ventilation duct or a crack in the wall. But where do we go from there? How do we get inside the computer?"

"We've made some progress since the last time you worked with us, Professor. Today, we can shrink people down to bit size and put them *directly* inside a computer. Our long-range objective is to infiltrate the Warsaw Pact machines. We're not there yet, but I think we have a means to get at NECEN."

"Fascinating. You mean that human beings can actually move around inside a computer and observe what's happening? What a debugging tool!" Corbin sounded genuinely excited.

"We can do more than observe, Professor. We can change programs and data."

"Ha!" Corbin shook his head in disbelief. "Amazing!"

"Assume we can get a team inside the computer," continued General Custer. "Could they succeed?"

"Certainly! Given the right team and a little luck."

"That's what we want to hear. Let's go see the President." Custer stood and began gathering his papers.

"One minute, General," interrupted Corbin. "Would it help to know who the Harlequin is?"

"Do you know?"

"Yes. Yes I do."

4 *The Harlequin*

"Don't just sit there, Professor," ordered General Custer. "Tell us his name."

"The Harlequin is a former student of mine named Georgie Hacker," replied Corbin.

"Hacker," Captain Statler noted with a grin. "Interesting name. What makes you so sure it's him, though?"

"Several things. His sense of humor, for one. Those curses we heard on the teller terminals this afternoon sounded just like the ones he used to spring on unsuspecting students back in his college days. As for the traffic jams, the subways, and the drawbridges, I can picture him rolling on the floor laughing at tonight's news." Corbin's tone of voice betrayed the affection he still felt for his old student.

"That's hardly conclusive," said Custer, skeptically. He would need concrete proof.

"Oh, I agree, General. But there's more. Not too many people have the ability to break a system as sophisticated as NECEN, but he does. He's the best natural programmer I've ever known. Then there's the extortion note—it's his writing style, I'm sure of it. But the dead give-away is his choice of a name: the Harlequin."

"Why is that?" asked the general.

"Georgie loved science fiction. I remember discussing a favorite story with him. The hero, a guy called the Harlequin, specialized in pulling crazy stunts aimed at embarrassing the bureaucracy. Georgie identified with him. He told me that someday he'd make the establishment look as foolish as the Harlequin had."

"That's still pretty thin," said Custer, shaking his head. He looked at Colonel Holtzworth and frowned. Corbin glanced quickly around the table. Captain Statler doodled, Lieutenant Cortez stared at a spot on the wall. They didn't believe him. At least not yet. "Professor," continued the general, "we'll operate on the assumption that you're right, but I'm not convinced. Give us some background on the guy."

"Certainly, General. I met Georgie about twenty years ago. He was sixteen at the time. Brilliant kid. He'd just aced his college entrance exams, and high school bored him, so he enrolled in our program. His first semester he earned an A in his computer course, but he dropped everything else. He just didn't care about anything but computers. Second semester he did the same thing. He almost failed my course too. Right in the middle of the term he got carried away playing Dungeons and Dragons and disappeared into the campus steam tunnels for about a week.

"I had a talk with Georgie and his father after that incident. His dad flew into town in a private jet—let's just say that the family wasn't hurting for money. After about an hour he announced a cut in Georgie's allowance, and left.

"Georgie took his punishment very well: he got a job. He knew computers, so a local computer store hired him as a technician. He lied about his age, I guess. That's when he discovered hacking.

"He started with a simple salami game. Somehow he got the telephone number of a local bank's computer and poked around in its files. Eventually he learned to transfer money from other accounts into his own—a dollar here, a dollar there, a few pennies from somewhere else. That's why it's called a salami game. You shave a little slice, a little piece of salami, from here, another slice from there, and pretty soon it adds up to a great deal. Georgie was living well."

Captain Statler chuckled. "Sounds like a very enterprising young man," he said. General Custer glared at him.

"That he was, Captain," continued Corbin. "He probably could have gone on forever, but he made a rookie mistake. He kept tapping the same accounts. Most people don't even bother to check a discrepancy of a dollar or two in their checking account balance, but after three or four months of being just a little off, some customers started asking questions, and the bank didn't have any answers. That's when they called me."

"I didn't know you were a computer detective, Professor," said Captain Statler, looking up. He seemed impressed; he had stopped doodling.

"When it comes to computer crime, Captain, most of my clients insist on no publicity."

"I assume you caught the young man," interrupted Lieutenant Cortez. Her attention, too, now focused on Corbin.

"Yes. He had a lot to learn. We put a few traps in the system and he blundered into them. The police arrested him two nights later. Of course, the bank wasn't about to admit that a kid had broken into its computer and messed around with its customer accounts, so the charges were dropped. I can't explain why, but I really liked the young man. I became his advisor, and spent quite a bit of time with him over the next few years.

"He kept right on hacking, though. During his sophomore year he started playing with the school's registration system. In those days everybody wanted computer science, but we didn't have nearly enough teachers to meet the demand, so students frequently found themselves closed out of critical courses. We actually had a few seniors register for classes they didn't need and then sell their spots to the highest bidder. It was a mess.

"Anyway, a friend of Georgie's couldn't get a course he needed for graduation, so Georgie broke into the computer, bumped another student, and added his buddy to the class list. Word got around, and pretty soon he started charging a fee. It almost reached the point where if you wanted to take a computer science course, you had to check with Georgie first, just to make sure you didn't get bumped. He had a regular protection racket going.

"Then he made the mistake of bumping a young woman who just happened to be dating a 250-pound defensive tackle. In those days Georgie was about five-foot-eight and weighed maybe 120 pounds. Needless to say, she got back into her class.

"Unfortunately, Georgie didn't stop there. For some reason, he and this Neanderthal developed a friendship, and a few weeks later Georgie had a chance to help his new friend. It seems the young man's midterm grades included two Fs. Flunk two courses at our school, and you didn't play football. But Georgie had a solution: he broke into the registrar's files and changed the grades. Again word got around, and another new business was born. I understand that Ds cost twenty-five dollars, Cs fifty dollars, and Bs a hundred dollars. He wouldn't give anybody an A; he had his principles.

"Eventually, the administration got wind of what was going on and asked me to investigate. I put my usual traps in the system, but they didn't work. Georgie had learned a great deal. I'll admit I was frustrated. Then, his girlfriend, a super kid, tipped me off about a series of planned grade changes. Wheh you know what to look for, it's easy."

"Why did she turn him in?" asked Colonel Holtzworth.

"Unlike Georgie, she had a sense of ethics, and she felt that changing grades was wrong. I think she really loved him, but he never quite forgave her."

"That's sad," said Lieutenant Cortez.

"I agree. Georgie felt he couldn't trust anybody. His father ignored him. His girlfriend turned him in. And I caught him. The college placed him on disciplinary probation and denied him access to the computer. He tried a few other courses, but he either flunked them or dropped them—boredom, I guess. About a year later, he quit school.

"He never paid attention to the prohibition against using the computer, of course. Right before he left the campus he manufactured himself a transcript under the name Hacker. Before that he'd been Georgie Hackman. He told me he'd decided to bury his past. He wanted to be a hacker, so that's what he called himself.

"Using that manufactured transcript he got himself a programming job with an insurance company. Six months later a routine check exposed his phony credentials, so they fired him. The week after he left, the master policyholder's file disappeared. It cost the company almost a million dollars to re-create it."

"Georgie again," suggested Lieutenant Cortez, fascinated.

"That's right," continued Corbin. "A classic Trojan Horse. He buried a routine in the middle of an accounting program. Each time the program ran, his routine checked the personnel file. As long as his named appeared, nothing happened. One day, however, Georgie Hacker's name wasn't there, so the program erased every policyholder's master record and replaced it with some very interesting garbage. The company almost went bankrupt. For two weeks it couldn't verify claims or payments, and its cash flow just about stopped."

"What was so interesting about that garbage, Professor?" interrupted Captain Statler. "Garbage is garbage, isn't it?"

"I hoped someone would ask that question," Corbin replied. "After Georgie's program ran, each master file record contained the phrase: 'The Harlequin was here'."

No one said a word, but suddenly the professor's story had gained credibility. Georgie Hacker *was* the Harlequin. No one doodled now. No one stared at the wall. Corbin had their attention.

"Then I lost track of him for a while," he continued. "I ran into him again a few years later while working on the VIRUS/VACCINE scam."

"Isn't VIRUS just a legend, Professor?" asked Lieutenant Cortez, skeptically.

"Certain computer manufacturers would like to have you believe that, Lieutenant, but VIRUS was real, and Georgie created it."

"Go on, Professor," said the general.

"VIRUS started as a prank, a clever little program that, basically, dialed telephone numbers. Most of the time, it got a regular telephone and simply hung up. But it kept dialing, again and again, until, eventually, it linked with another computer. Once it made contact, the program copied itself into the new computer's memory, erased the original copy, and went on dialing numbers from the new machine. Picture this little program moving from computer to computer to computer, like a tapeworm. Most computers are underloaded, so it really didn't hurt anything. Besides, VIRUS only resided in a given machine for a day or two before moving on.

"But just before Georgie left the insurance company, he modified the program, deleting the instructions that caused it to destroy itself. It worked just like the earlier version, but with an important difference. Now when it made contact with another computer, it simply reproduced itself; both the new machine and the old one were infected. Soon VIRUS had spread to four computers, then eight, then sixteen—an epidemic.

"A few big computer centers noticed that something was sucking up resources and managed to isolate and remove VIRUS, but, almost inevitably, they were reinfected. That's when the ad appeared in most of the computer magazines. I think I still have a copy." Corbin pulled out his wallet, searched through it, removed a folded sheet of paper, unfolded it, and started reading:

Troubled by VIRUS?
Get VACCINE.
Satisfaction guaranteed by the Harlequin.

"There's a post office box number too; I won't read that." He handed the clipping to Lieutenant Cortez. "You can see for yourself."

"You mean VACCINE *cured* VIRUS," commented Captain Statler.

"You got it, Captain," answered the professor.

"Ha!" Captain Statler smiled broadly. "That's pretty good."

"There's the Harlequin again," remarked Lieutenant Cortez as she carefully studied the newspaper clipping. "Do you think Georgie placed this ad?" she asked.

"I *know* he did," replied Corbin. "I negotiated an agreement between him and a certain computer manufacturer—the big one. They bought exclusive rights to VACCINE and installed it in all their systems. End of the epidemic. End of Georgie's poverty, too."

"That's blackmail!" exclaimed Colonel Holtzworth.

"It's more like extortion, Colonel. Protection rackets have been around for centuries. This one just happened to involve computers. Why would the company pay? If you were a computer manufacturer, would you want to publicize your own equipment's security weaknesses?"

"I see your point, Professor," said the general. "Is there any more we should know?"

"Apparently, a few years ago, Georgie did some work for the syndicate."

"The syndicate!" Suddenly General Custer seemed interested.

"That's right, General," continued Corbin. "Big time. A Miami family needed some drug money laundered, so he tapped into an electronic funds transfer system and disbursed it all over the world. I'm sure that's what he plans to do with his billion dollars. Once he gets the money, it's gone. We'll never trace it."

"Why *shouldn't* we just give him the money, Professor?" asked Captain Statler. "Maybe he'll be satisfied. If somebody gave me a billion dollars, I'd fine a nice place to retire."

"Don't underestimate him, Captain. I don't think he's in this for the money. He and I often talked about politics, and, frankly, some of his ideas scared me. He's an elitist. He believes that the country should be run by a handful of it most intelligent citizens, and he counts himself among that group."

"You can't be serious," said Colonel Holtzworth. "I've seen these computer junkies. They may be good at communicating with machines, but when it comes to dealing with people, they're lost. The idea of one of those characters running the country is absurd."

"Georgie doesn't fit the stereotype, Colonel. He's a very capable, very persuasive young man. He has what the politicians call charisma. Besides, when he talks about an elite running the country, he means indirectly. He doesn't want to *be* president, he wants to control the president from behind the scenes. With NECEN, he can, and that's what scares me."

"How do you propose beating him, Professor?" asked Custer. "You couldn't nail him when he was changing grades back in college. He's probably better now."

"I'm sure he is. But he's not Superman. He won't expect an attack from inside NECEN. If we can penetrate the system we can beat him.

We have the advantage of surprise, General. He doesn't know about the Small Missions Force."

"It's *Special Miniature* Force, Professor," said the general, gruffly. Then he managed a slight smile. "But I'll forgive you this time. What would you like my staff to do while you're talking to the President?"

"We'll need a map of the telecommunication network, General. Have your staff trace a route from here to NECEN. A set of schematics for the computer would help too. Also, we'll need a way to change data inside the machine."

"A laser gun should do the trick," said Captain Statler.

"Any suggestions on the composition of the team, Professor?" asked the general.

"Yes. If she's available, start with Sylvia Potter as pilot. I've worked with her before; she's good."

"She is good. We'll see if we can get her. Who else?"

"We'll need a hardware expert and a software expert, preferably people who know NECEN."

"Consider it done. Anything else?"

"Not at the moment, General."

"Fine. Sergeant, I assume you've been taking notes."

"Yes, sir. We'll have a complete transcript within an hour."

"Good. See that the FBI gets a copy. Colonel Holtzworth, you are in charge of planning for the mission. Have the team assembled when we return. Pending presidential approval, miniaturization will commence at 0900 tomorrow."

"Got it, sir."

"Okay, Professor. You, Major Smith, and I are going to visit the President."

5 The President

The room looked familiar. Corbin had spent many long hours at that massive, mahogany conference table. The Vice President sat to the President's right; the President's chief advisors, McClaren and Montanti, the "M & M" boys, sat behind their leader. Corbin nodded a greeting; they signaled a reply. They had been allies during the fight against NECEN.

"Glad you could make it, Bill," began the President. "We've been waiting for you. Have a seat."

"Sorry to keep you waiting, Mr. President," Corbin apologized, selecting a chair. Pete and the general found two seats along the wall, directly behind him.

"Sorry we had to drag you back to Washington, Bill, but I need your help." The President's sweeping gesture covered the entire room. "Is there anyone here you don't know?"

Corbin looked around the table. He recognized the secretaries of defense and commerce. Charles Martinez, the treasury secretary and NECEN's chief proponent within the President's inner circle, sat to their right. To his right were the chairman of the Federal Reserve Board, the budget director, and the attorney general.

Next, Corbin's gaze settled on the fat, jowly face of an old antagonist, Senator Tompson. Years ago, oil money had bought him a seat in Congress; today, computer money paid for his senatorial campaigns. How a technical illiterate like Tompson could claim leadership of the technocrats defied belief, but just four years before he had led the fight to override the President's threatened veto of the NECEN project. With Tompson and Martinez in the room, Corbin looked forward to a rough day.

General Gantt, the chairman of the Joint Chiefs of Staff, sat next to Tompson. To his right were the directors of the CIA and the FBI. They were old, familiar faces. Corbin remembered another meeting in this very room when he alone had argued against NECEN. Patiently, he had explained the security risk. But they had twisted his arguments. Once again he felt the sting of their ridicule. Well, events had proven him right, but he wouldn't gloat. They seemed ready to listen to him now; the Harlequin had gotten their attention.

Then Corbin spotted an unfamiliar face. "I'd read that you'd appointed Ms. Jackson secretary of state, Mr. President, but I've never had the pleasure of meeting her."

"Of course." The President gestured, in turn, to each of them. "Madam Secretary, Professor Corbin. You can shake hands later; let's get down to business." His gaze settled on Ms. Jackson. "Madam Secretary, bring Professor Corbin up to date."

"Certainly, Mr. President." She flipped through several pages of notes scrawled on a legal pad, then set them aside. "I think I can summarize very quickly, Professor. I assume you've been briefed."

"General Custer did his usual thorough job."

"Excellent. We seem to have two choices: negotiate or hang tough." Her tone of voice betrayed her bias.

"The consensus is to negotiate, Bill," interrupted the President, "but I don't buy it. Unfortunately, we have no alternative plan. That leaves the next move to the Harlequin, and I don't like that. I hoped you might have some fresh ideas."

"Mr. President," interrupted Secretary Martinez," I really can't see *any* options. As long as this Harlequin controls NECEN, he can disrupt banking, Wall Street, the Federal Reserve, in short, our entire financial system. The billion dollars he wants is nothing compared to the damage he can do. We're talking about a potential financial disaster, sir."

"But we can't negotiate with an extortionist, Mr. President," responded General Gantt.

"You don't have a plan, General," said Senator Tompson, matter-of-factly. "We can't just ignore the Harlequin and hope he goes away. If we don't negotiate, how do we recover NECEN? The consensus of this body is clear, Mr. President. We favor negotiation."

"Assume you negotiate, Senator," countered General Gantt. "Assume you pay his blackmail. How do you know he'll surrender NECEN? And if he does, how do you know he won't take it back again?"

"Once we regain control," replied the senator, avoiding the question, "we'll find out exactly how the Harlequin penetrated the system and plug the loophole. He won't get in again."

When would they ever learn? Time after time, people who should have known better continued to imagine that the removal of one final bug guaranteed a perfect system. Invariably, fixing that "last bug" did little more than reveal the next one. The senator, Corbin realized, had learned nothing from this incident.

"Enough!" The President's sudden outburst quieted the group. "I'm getting tired of hearing the same arguments repeated over and over again." He gestured toward Professor Corbin. "It's your turn, Bill."

No one said a word. Slowly, Corbin stood and cleared his throat. "Thank you, Mr. President. Let me respond to the negotiation option first. The Harlequin is a former student of mine named Georgie Hacker. If you think you can negotiate with him, you're dead wrong."

"How can we be sure this Hacker fellow is the Harlequin?" interrupted Secretary Martinez. Respectfully, Corbin noted the tactics of a skilled debater. The secretary favored negotiation. The President sought an option, and Corbin might supply one. Martinez knew that, and his question threatened to subtly sidetrack the discussion. Corbin knew he had started badly. How could he pull the discussion back on track without seeming to dodge the secretary's question?

"Professor Corbin has convinced *me*," volunteered General Custer. "We'll have a transcript of his briefing in less than an hour."

"Mr. President," snapped Secretary Martinez, brusquely. "I object. We're supposed to accept this absurd claim without . . . "

"Mr. Secretary." The President glared at him. "You've had your say." He looked back toward Corbin. "Please continue, Bill."

"Thank you, Mr. President." An air of restrained hostility permeated the room, and Corbin sensed that he stood almost alone. Well, it didn't matter. He wouldn't compromise today. He would tell them exactly what he thought. If they bought it, fine. If not, NECEN became their problem.

"You're dealing with an individual, not a government," he went on, confidently, aggressively. "The Harlequin won't play by your rules. If you give him a billion dollars, he'll laugh and demand another billion. If you negotiate him down to a million, he'll laugh and demand another million. You see, the money isn't the point. It's control. Right now, he has it, and he's not about to give it up. The only way we're going to recover NECEN is to *take* it back. Our only real choice is to fight him."

Suddenly, two secret service agents burst into the room. With practiced precision, each grabbed an arm of the President's chair. Quickly they whisked him through a doorway. Two more agents approached the Vice President; he, too, disappeared. Another agent stepped through the door. "We have an emergency," he said, calmly. "Follow me, please."

What had happened? Had World War III begun? Silently, without a word of protest, this gathering of the most powerful men and women in Washington stood almost as one and filed quickly from the room. Crossing a hall, the group entered an elevator and descended beneath the White House.

The elevator bumped to a stop. The doors opened to a large bomb shelter. Somberly, these secretaries, directors, and generals stepped out and selected seats around the edges of the room. Finally, Secretary Jackson broke the silence. "Would you mind telling us what is going on?" she asked, stiffly.

"I'm sorry, Madam Secretary," responded the agent, politely. "Radar detected an airplane headed directly for the White House. A terrorist attack is always a possibility. I'm sure you understand the need for quick action."

Suddenly, the agent's radio receiver beeped. "Excuse me," he said, as he placed the receiver to his ear. The transmission lasted only a few seconds. Putting the radio away, the agent turned back to the group. "Everything is under control," he said, calmly. "You can return to the conference room now. Follow me, please."

One by one, they filed back into the conference room and took their seats. The incident had sobered them. They sat quietly, waiting. The Vice President entered, clearly shaken. Finally, the President arrived. He stood behind his chair, his eyes flashing anger.

"I just came within seconds of shooting down a passenger jet," he began, his voice tight with tension. "Almost two hundred people were on board. All Americans. The plane strayed from its flight path and seemed headed directly for the White House. As I am sure you all know, antiaircraft missiles were installed here some time ago. Had I given the order, the plane would have been blown from the sky. Fortunately, the pilot took corrective action.

"The jet strayed off course because the air traffic computer told it to," continued the President. "That computer is linked to NECEN. Apparently, the Harlequin is playing tricks again."

A new sense pervaded the room. Perhaps it was anger. Perhaps, for the first time, the problem had hit home. "I am determined *not* to pay his blackmail," continued the President. "If there is even the slightest chance for success, we *will* fight him." He looked around the room, defying anyone to disagree. "Professor Corbin was about to reveal his plan before we were interrupted. The floor is yours, Professor." The President sat down, his anger barely contained. It was Corbin's turn.

Corbin stood and nodded toward the president. "As you all know," he began, "I've been briefed by General Custer. He tells me he can put a team inside NECEN. If we can gain access to the computer, we can plant a Trojan Horse in its memory. Once we've done that, the rest will be easy."

"You're going to have to explain this Trojan Horse idea, Bill." The President took a sip of water. "And don't forget, I'm a computer illiterate. Start from the beginning."

Corbin pushed back his chair, stood, and walked across the room to an easel board. Grabbing a marking pen, he turned to face the conference table. All eyes locked on him, watching for the slightest slip, the slightest sign of weakness. He cleared his throat and began.

"Stop me if I'm going too fast," he said. He turned to the easel and drew a simple sketch (Fig. 5.1). "A computer is a machine whose function is to process data into information. Data are facts: numbers, addresses, values. By themselves, data are useless. But when we organize them they become very useful. When we organize data we get information. Information has meaning."

Corbin had intentionally chosen a most elementary starting point. Data, information, processing—they knew those terms. Subtly, he commented on the state of their computer knowledge. Politely and diplomatically, he insulted them, and it bothered him not a bit. In fact, he rather enjoyed it.

He moved back to the easel and added to his sketch. "Data—facts—enter the computer through an input device. They are processed inside the computer. Then the information is output.

"Internally, a computer contains two main components: a processor and memory." He flipped to a new page and started a new drawing (Fig. 5.2). "When data enter the computer, they are stored in memory. The processor gets the data from memory, manipulates them, and stores its results back in memory. Finally, the results—information—are sent from memory to an output device. Every computer works basically the same way. Memory holds data, and the processor manipulates them."

Corbin paused briefly and glanced around the room. Everyone

FIGURE 5.1 Professor Corbin's first sketch illustrated the basic data processing pattern.

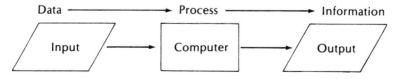

seemed attentive, even Tompson. He noted a slight reddening of the senator's jowls, however; the senator was losing patience. Still, if they were to understand his plan, he had to provide a bit more groundwork.

"A calculator does much the same thing," he continued. "With a calculator, you enter a number, effectively storing it in memory. Then you select a function key—add, for example—and push it. As a result, the data are processed. With a calculator, *you* provide the control. It's up to you to decide what button to push next. With a computer, a program stored in main memory provides control."

He sketched a third diagram (Fig. 5.3). "A program is a series of instructions that guides the machine through a process. Given a program, a computer can manipulate data automatically, with no need for human intervention. A calculator requires a human being to provide direct, step-by-step control. A computer, on the other hand, controls itself by following a program stored in its own memory.

"Picture a piano. Like a calculator, it requires human intervention at each step. In other words, some human being must make a conscious decision to play each note, and then strike the key. A player piano is different. Once a roll is installed, it plays a piece automatically, without human intervention.

FIGURE 5.2 "Internally, a computer contains two main components: a processor and memory. When data enter the computer, they are stored in memory. The processor gets the data from memory, manipulates them, and stores its results back in memory. Finally, the results—information—are sent from memory to an output device."

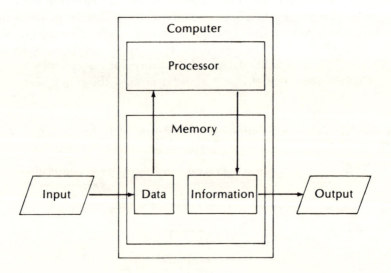

FIGURE 5.3 A computer is controlled by a program stored in its own memory.

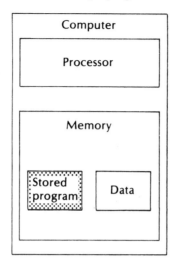

"Of course, it takes time to prepare a player piano roll. Someone must carefully define and encode every single note before the first one is played. Likewise it takes time and effort to prepare a computer program. Someone, a programmer, must carefully define every single step—every addition, every subtraction, every comparison—before the first data can be processed. We don't play all our music on player pianos. We don't process all our data on computers."

"Come to the point, Professor," interrupted Senator Tompson.

"Certainly, Senator," replied Corbin. "I realize that much of what I've said so far is obvious to many of you, but bear with me for one more minute. Just to make sure that we all understand some basic terms, I want to define two more: hardware and software. The equipment—the input and output devices, the memory, the processor, the piano—are examples of hardware. They're physical. The hardware adds, subtracts, and compares. The hardware plays the music. The software—the programs, the piano roll—tells the hardware what to do. The hardware does the work, the software controls the hardware. Without hardware, software is useless; without software, hardware is useless.

"Software is composed of instructions. Change the roll, and the piano plays a new tune. Change the program, and the computer performs a new data processing task. Software is flexible and easy to change. Hardware is more permanent.

"Enough definition. Now I'm going to tell you what the Harlequin did, how he did it, and how we intend to recapture the computer. If you have any questions, jump in." This was what they wanted to hear. He had their attention.

"We start with NECEN." Corbin sketched yet another diagram (Fig. 5.4). "It's a big computer, a mainframe. Unbelievably fast, with thousands of input and output devices attached to it. I won't even try to identify them all.

"This afternoon, the Harlequin showed us, rather graphically, that by controlling NECEN, he could affect, at the same time, New York's traffic lights, Washington's subways, and all the East Coast's teller terminals. Since a computer needs a program to do anything, it follows that programs to control the traffic signals, the subways, and the teller

FIGURE 5.4   The NECEN computer is so big and so fast, that it can run hundreds of programs concurrently.

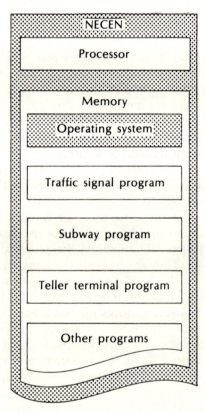

terminals all resided together in NECEN's memory." He added the programs to his diagram.

"Let me get this straight, Professor," said Secretary Jackson. "Are you suggesting that NECEN ran all those programs at the same time?"

"Not quite, Madam Secretary. NECEN has only one processor, so it can do only one thing at a time. But it's so fast, and the input and output devices are, relatively, so slow, that while it's reading data for program A, it has plenty of time to switch its attention to program B. So it really doesn't run them all at the same time; it just switches from program to program to program, and, at any given instant, may be in the process of executing dozens of them."

"That's hard to believe."

"Yes, it is. One of the most difficult things for a human being to grasp about a computer is its time frame. We think chemically. We react, at best, in a thousandth of a second. Computers work electronically; they react in millionths of a second, and the big machines, like NECEN, function in billionths of a second! We can't picture a billionth of a second any more than we can picture a million years. Both concepts are abstractions. Take my word for it—NECEN is fast enough to work on many different programs concurrently.

"Of course, keeping track of all those programs presents a problem. That's why NECEN has an operating system." He added yet another block to his developing diagram. "The application programs process data into information. The operating system allocates resources to the application programs and decides which one gets to control the processor next. It's a control program, an electronic traffic cop. Nothing happens on NECEN without the operating system's blessing. No application program runs. No input device copies its data into memory. No output device copies its information from memory."

"I may be a step ahead of you, Professor," said General Gantt, "but if I wanted to take over that computer, I'd attack the operating system."

"Precisely, General." Once again a jabbing index finger accented Corbin's point. "That's exactly what the Harlequin did. He found a weakness and exploited it. Note that the operating system is software. There is no way the Harlequin could have affected NECEN's hardware, but software is relatively easy to change. Once he gained access, he modified the operating system, reprogramming it to ignore the regular operator's commands and accept his commands instead. Once he had accomplished that objective, he could do whatever he wanted. He's probably still changing the system. We won't recognize it when we regain control."

"Then you plan to counterattack through the operating system?"

"That's right. But it's going to be more difficult for us. He's been probing that operating system for weaknesses ever since the new telecommunication network came on line. I'm sure he's closed the obvious loopholes. We'll have to be very inventive."

"Give us an overview of your plan, Professor," said Secretary Martinez, still skeptical.

"My plan is an electronic variation of the old Trojan Horse strategy," said Corbin. "The first step is to gain entry. We'll disguise ourselves as a typical message, a traffic control signal, for example. Like the Trojans, NECEN should willingly accept us.

"Once we're in main memory, we'll build the Trojan Horse by modifying a portion of the operating system. Like the Greeks' gift, our new software routine will sit in memory, waiting, until we activate it. When we do, in effect it will open the door and give control back to the real operator."

"How do you propose getting into NECEN?" asked the secretary of commerce. "I understand the system ignores our terminals. Besides, won't the Harlequin be watching for any sign of attack?"

"Yes. But . . ."

"Mr. Secretary," interrupted the President, "the plan involves top secret information, and believe me, sir, you don't want to know."

"Fine, Mr. President, I'll accept that. Let me ask a different question. How would you rate your chances of success, Professor?"

"How much time do we have?"

"You have until noon tomorrow, Bill," said the President.

"Realistically, I'd set our odds at about 1 in 4."

"You've never been a cheerleader, have you, Bill?"

"No, Mr. President. And I'm too old to start now."

"Professor Corbin, thank you for your input." The President paused for another sip of water, leaned back in his chair, put his hands behind his head, and glanced around the table. He sighed, deeply. The decision rested with him. "General Custer." He looked directly at the general. "I'm authorizing you to proceed with Professor Corbin's plan. You'll have until noon tomorrow. At that time I will authorize Treasury Secretary Martinez to begin the process of transferring funds to meet this Harlequin's demand. At the same time, I will authorize the secretary of state to begin negotiations. Of course, the FBI will continue its ongoing investigation. Any questions?"

No one moved.

"Fine. Good luck, Professor. We're depending on you. This meeting is adjourned."

6 *The Team*

He would have his chance, but could he beat the Harlequin? Did he want to? That question gnawed at Corbin. Did he really *want* to win? His warnings had been ignored, his expertise ridiculed. But with a single act, Georgie Hacker had captured their attention. No longer could NECEN's vulnerability be denied. If a Harlequin, a clown, penetrated NECEN's security, why not a band of terrorists or a foreign enemy? If he were younger, if he had the brashness of his former student, he could think of no better way to make his point.

Then Corbin remembered Georgie's dream—government by a technological elite. Unthinkable! Georgie was no ordinary hacker; he had to be stopped. Of course, there were risks. No clown, this Harlequin would prove a brilliant and dangerous adversary. There were political concerns, too. Success would stamp him NECEN's savior; failure meant that he would be Tompson's scapegoat. Either way, he'd lose. But the Harlequin had to be stopped.

Slowly, the sound of Pete's voice dragged him back to reality. As he opened his eyes he found himself sitting in a captain's chair in a corner of a small, square room, staring across a desk at a framed picture of "Custer's Last Stand." It must be the general's private office, he decided. He hadn't remembered entering the room, so deeply had he been lost in thought. Like an injured fighter clearing the cobwebs, he shook his head. Finally, his mind focused on the conversation.

"General, I don't want this mission," said Pete. He sensed anger in Pete's voice. "I know nothing about computers. I'll be in the way."

"I need you, Major Smith. The team we've assembled is composed of amateurs. They need a leader. They'll provide the computer expertise, you'll provide the leadership."

"Professor Corbin is no amateur, General," argued Pete. "Put him in charge."

"No. We need you."

"Why don't you give me the real reason, General."

General Custer leaned back and sipped slowly from a cup of coffee. Pivoting in his chair, he stared briefly at the picture of his namesake's final moments. Then his gaze swung back to Pete. "Okay. We have reason to believe the Harlequin has an agent within our organization. We're worried about sabotage."

"Any idea who it might be?" asked Pete.

"No."

"Has it occurred to you that I might be this saboteur?" interjected Corbin.

Startled by the sound of his voice, Pete and General Custer fell silent for a moment. Pete recovered first. "Welcome back, Bill," he said, smiling. "I don't know where you've been for the last twenty minutes, but welcome back."

"Professor Corbin," said the general, "I've heard rumors about your powers of concentration, but I must admit I didn't believe them. Most impressive. In answer to your question, no, we don't suspect you."

"Perhaps you should," replied Corbin. He looked directly at Pete. "I assume you've decided to come."

"Yes. I'll be there."

"Fine," said General Custer. "That's settled. Now let's go meet the crew."

The door from the general's office led into the conference room. Three new people had joined with the general's staff. One looked familiar. As he entered, Corbin could see only a portion of her profile, but he knew he'd seen her before. He stepped around the table for a better look. There could be no doubt! The high cheekbones and deep-set eyes, the little girl features framed by a short, boyish haircut—it had to be her. "Ada?" he asked.

She looked up from her work and immediately recognized him. "Professor Corbin, how nice to see you again," she said. Quickly she pushed back her chair and walked toward him. She might have passed for a twelve-year-old, she was so tiny, but she exuded self-confidence and independence. Corbin felt a sense of pride in his former student.

"Ada Byron," he said. "It's been years." They shook hands, warmly. "You were, without question, the best student I ever had. It's great to see you again."

"That's a very nice compliment, Professor." She smiled. "Thank you. You were my favorite teacher. Data structures, architectures, operating systems—you taught me a great deal."

"I assume you know each other," interrupted the general, brusquely.

"Yes, we do," replied Corbin. He turned back to Ada. "I had no idea you were working for SMF."

"I've been here for three years," she replied. "I understand we're going to have a chance to work together. I'm looking forward to that." She shook her head and laughed softly. Then she grasped his hand in both of hers. "It really is great to see you, Professor."

Once again the general interrupted. "The President has approved our mission. Miniaturization will commence at 0900 hours tomorrow. We'll have until 1200 hours to recover or disable NECEN." The general motioned toward Pete and continued. "Major Smith will be in command. Colonel Holtzworth, introduce the rest of the team."

"Certainly, General. I'll start with the pilot, Captain Potter." He indicated a middle-aged woman standing near one end of the table. Corbin was shocked! Sylvia! He hadn't recognized her. No more than five years ago he'd known her as a young woman. In that five years, she had aged fifteen! "Captain Potter is our most experienced pilot," continued Colonel Holtzworth. "If anyone can get you into NECEN, she can.

"Our hardware expert," he went on, "is Ned Lud." The young man to Captain Potter's right briefly looked up from his work, and then returned to the circuit diagram he'd been studying. His hair had the wild, unkempt appearance of one who simply did not care. His thin, angular face was dominated by thick glasses and a humorless expression. A plaid shirt, looking like it had been worn one day too many, fell open at the collar. A coffee-stained tie hung loosely around his neck. The stereotypical computer jock. A classic nerd. "Mr. Lud helped design NECEN; he knows the hardware inside and out. He'll serve as your navigator.

"Our software expert is Ada Byron." As the captain introduced her, she smiled, squeezed Corbin's hand, and walked back to her place at the table. "She's a system programmer. She worked on NECEN's operating system. Her expertise should prove invaluable once you gain entry.

"Finally," continued the colonel, "we have Professor Bill Corbin. He's your technical advisor." They all knew Corbin. His books had helped educate most of the country's young computer scientists. He enjoyed an unsurpassed reputation as a teacher, a lecturer, and a consultant, and had pioneered the most significant mass market break-through since the development of the microcomputer: voice-input word processing. The respect they all felt for him was almost tangible.

"Thank you, Colonel Holtzworth," said Custer. "Captain Potter, brief the group on our electronic miniaturization experiments."

"Yes, sir." Sylvia pushed back her chair and strode to the front of the room. She still had a presence that commanded respect and attention. She cleared her throat. "For some time now, SMF has been able to shrink a vehicle to byte size and introduce it into a computer. The vehicle can hold as many as eight people; the computer sees each person as a 1-bit.

"We can maneuver inside the machine in either of two ways. Our basic mode is to simply 'go with the flow.' In essence, we become a byte of data, and the computer moves us through its regular circuits. When necessary, the miniaturization craft can fly from circuit board to circuit board. Power is limited, though, so we can't do too much of that. Most of the time, we go where the computer takes us.

"We've tested the craft on a number of microcomputers and it works very well. We've never tried it on a mainframe before, but I anticipate no problems. Basically, that's it. I'll pilot the craft and get you into the machine; the rest is up to you. Any questions?"

"Yes." Ned Lud hardly raised his head as he spoke. "One for the general. We need a communication expert." His manner suggested he'd stated an "obvious fact." "If we're limited to five people," he continued, disdainfully, "we could replace Major Smith. He doesn't seem to have any technical background."

"Major Smith provides leadership, Mr. Lud," said Custer. "He will *not* be replaced."

Ned stared at the general for an instant before turning back to his circuit diagram.

"Professor Corbin." The general was angry, but he tried not to show it. "Give us a brief overview of your plan."

"Certainly, General." Corbin leaned back in his chair. In spite of his personal doubts, his words exuded confidence. "The first step is to penetrate the computer. We'll disguise ourselves as a signal that NECEN will accept." He gestured toward the young hardware expert. "We'll leave it to Ned to prepare an acceptable message format."

"Certainly, Professor," said Ned. Even he respected this man.

"It doesn't matter where we enter memory," continued Corbin. "Once we're in, though, Sylvia—excuse me, Captain Potter—will take off and fly us to the operating system. Ada," he gestured toward her, "you'll have to tell us where that is."

"No problem, Professor," she responded.

"And Ned, you'll have to tell us how to get there."

"Right," responded Ned.

"The Harlequin changed the operating system to accept only his commands. We have to change it back. Timing will be crucial. He's awfully good, and he'll be watching for us. I think our best bet is a Trojan Horse. We'll plant it in the operating system, and then make our escape. The routine should recognize a message from outside, immediately override the Harlequin's commands, and give control back to our operator." He glanced at his former student. "Ada, that's your job. Think you can do it?"

"I have some ideas," she said. "How much time do we have?"

"It's now almost 2100 hours," answered General Custer. "We begin miniaturization at 0900, sharp. That gives you roughly twelve hours. Any more questions?" There were none. "Fine. Let's get going. Major Smith, you're in charge now. Good luck, sir."

"Thank you, General." Pete snapped to attention and saluted. "We'll need it." The general returned his salute, did an abrupt right face, and strode from the room.

Pete turned to face his crew. "We have a lot to do, but we're all professionals and we'll get it done. Let's start by dropping the formalities. It saves time. I'm Pete."

He looked directly at Sylvia. Little in his glance suggested anything but a professional relationship, but Corbin knew Pete too well. There was deep concern in that glance—concern for her well-being. "Sylvia, I know you have premission details to attend to. We'll see you in the morning."

"Right you are, Pete." Her smile betrayed her feelings. Corbin wondered why they'd never married. "See you in the morning." She waved as she walked from the room. He and Ada returned her gesture; Ned ignored it.

"Ned. Ada. You both know what you're doing. If you need anything to help you stay awake, let me know. Professor Corbin."

"It's Bill."

"No. You're the Professor," said Pete. "We have some planning to do. Let's go to my office."

Small and stark, Pete's office consisted of little more than four walls, a desk, two chairs, and a filing cabinet. A cheap calendar hung on one wall. The room felt temporary, unused, a place to wait between real jobs. The two old friends sat in silence. Pete, his feet on the desk and his hands behind his head, stared into space, distracted by something.

After a few minutes, Corbin broke the silence. "It's obvious that you didn't want this mission, Pete. Why?"

"You've always been very observant, Bill," Pete replied. He fell silent again, then, suddenly, started talking. "I feel like a complete idiot when I'm around computer people. Bits, bytes, parity—I don't know what any of it means. How can I command a mission when I won't even know what my crew is talking about?"

"Use me, Pete. If there's anything you don't understand, just ask and I'll translate."

"I know I can depend on you, Bill. And I don't include you in my general denunciation of computer people. But Lud—he acts like I'm illiterate."

"He's a jerk, Pete. And you are clearly not illiterate. Why worry about him?"

"Because I'm supposed to be in charge of the mission. A commander must have the respect of his people."

"Lud doesn't respect anybody."

"He respects you; that's why you're *Professor* Corbin. If I can control him by taking advantage of his respect for you, I'll do it."

"I wondered why you made such a big deal about not calling me Bill."

"You don't mind, do you?" asked Pete.

"No. Of course not. If you think it's important, fine."

"Thanks. I owe you one. Let's get back to technology, though. You know, it just occurred to me that I'm about to become a bit, and I don't even know what a bit is."

"A bit is a binary digit," said Corbin seriously. Then he laughed.

"Thanks for clearing that up," Pete replied, beginning to relax. "Now really, what's a bit?"

"Do you know what a digit is?" asked Corbin.

"Sure," replied Pete, "1, 2, 3, . . ."

"Right. What's the difference between the 3 in thirty and the 3 in three hundred? They're both the same digit, aren't they?"

"They're in different positions. Tens column. Hundreds column. That's obvious."

"Right. Now look at those positions—units, tens, hundreds, thousands. They're all powers of ten—1, 10, 100, 1000. A decimal number is just a series of decimal digits—0 through 9—written in precise relative positions. Seventy-three is 7 tens and 3 ones. Thirty-seven is 3 tens and 7 ones. Same two digits, but because of position, two very different values. Take each digit, multiply it by its place value, add all the sums, and you have the value of the number. The basic idea has been drilled into you since kindergarten. You don't even think about it anymore; it's automatic."

"Fine, Bill," said Pete. "Now what does that have to do with binary numbers?"

"Everything. I said that the value of a number is determined by summing the products of its digit values and its place values. Did I ever say that the digits had to be 0 through 9, or that the place values had to be powers of 10?"

"No."

"They don't." Corbin grabbed a pad of paper and wrote:

2^7	2^6	2^5	2^4	2^3	2^2	2^1	2^0
128	64	32	16	8	4	2	1

"What if I use powers of 2 to define a series of place values?" he asked, as he wrote. "Instead of units, tens, and hundreds, I get units, twos, fours, eights, and so on. I have the framework of a base 2, or binary, number system."

"Okay, I'll buy that."

"Now all we need are the digits. First, we need a zero."

"Why?"

"If you want to write a number as a series of digits in relative positions, you need a way to indicate that there's nothing in a given position. How could I write 30 if I couldn't indicate no ones?"

"Okay, we need a zero."

"A binary zero looks the same as a decimal zero; nothing's nothing. A binary 1 looks pretty much like a decimal 1 too. The pattern changes when we move to 2, however. You can't have a binary digit 2."

"Why not?"

"For the same reason you can't have a decimal digit ten. A ten is one ten and no ones. In binary, a two is written as 10: that's 1 two and no ones. Three is 11—1 two and 1 one. Four is 100—that's 1 four, no twos, and no ones. Five is 101—1 four, no twos, and 1 one."

"Okay, I get it," said Pete.

"The binary digits are 0 and 1. A computer uses combinations of those two digits to form binary numbers, just like we use combinations of the digits 0 through 9 to form decimal numbers."

"Why can't the computer work with decimal, just like we do? Wouldn't that make things easier?"

"For us, maybe, but not for the computer. It's relatively easy to design an electronic device to distinguish two conditions—on/off, pulse/ no pulse, 0/1. It's much tougher to distinguish ten different conditions—not impossible, but difficult. We use decimal because it's convenient for us, maybe because we have ten fingers. Computers use binary because it's convenient for them."

"Okay. So a bit is just a binary digit, right?"

"That's right. In fact, the term bit is an acronym formed from the first and the last two letters in Binary digIT."

"So, what's a byte?"

"Typically, eight bits."

"Why?"

"You can't do very much with one bit—it's either a 0 or a 1. Most of the time a computer uses groups of bits, and it just so happens that eight is a convenient unit to work with."

"So, a bit is a binary digit and a byte is eight of them."

"Exactly."

"Okay, next question. What's this parity they were talking about?"

"Parity has to do with checking for errors, Pete. On a computer, all data are represented as bit patterns. A given bit pattern has to move from an input device into memory. Later, it moves from memory to the processor, and then back to memory again. How is the processor to know that it got the right data from memory? How is memory to know that it got the right data from the input device? Errors are always possible, and if the data are wrong, the answer will be wrong."

"I thought computers never made mistakes."

"Not true, my friend. But one reason why they seem so accurate is because they can spot and correct most of the errors they do make. Parity is part of that process."

"Okay. Explain."

"Well, the exact way parity is implemented varies with the machine and the data type, but let me give you an example that illustrates the concept. Imagine a computer that works with 8-bit bytes. Actually, seven of those bits are all we really need to represent many types of data. The extra bit is the parity bit." He sketched a byte, showing the parity bit's position (Fig. 6.1).

"Now most computers," continued Corbin, "use *even* parity. Even parity means that every byte must contain an even number of 1-bits. Imagine, for example, that we want to store the pattern 0000011." He added the bit string to his diagram. "How many 1-bits do you count?"

"Two," replied Pete.

"Is two an odd or an even number?"

FIGURE 6.1   Under even parity, each byte must contain an even number of 1-bits. The seven data bits are recorded first. The parity bit is then set to either 0 or 1, in order to give the byte an even number of 1-bits.

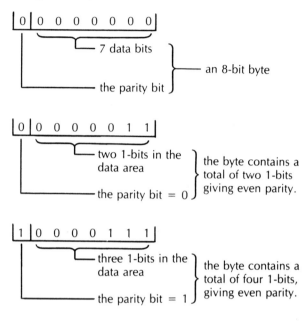

"Even."

"Okay. It's time to set the parity bit. We can set it to either 0 or 1. The only rule is that, after we set it, the total number of 1-bits in the byte, including the parity bit, must be even. We can have zero, two, four, six, or eight 1-bits, but a byte with one, three, five, or seven 1-bits is wrong. You said that the seven data bits in our byte contain two 1-bits. To maintain even parity, should the parity bit be set to 0 or to 1?"

"Zero," replied Pete.

"That's right," said Corbin. "Why?"

"Because if the parity bit were set to 1, the byte would contain three 1-bits, and, according to the rule you just gave me, that's wrong."

"Exactly. Try another one. We want to store 0000111. What value should the parity bit hold to maintain even parity?"

"Let's see. The seven data bits contain three 1-bits. That's an odd number. If I set the parity bit to 1, I'd have four, which is even."

"That's right," said Corbin. "You have the idea."

"I'm still not sure how parity helps the computer identify errors, though," admitted Pete.

"Every time a byte moves from one computer component to another, hardware counts its 1-bits," replied Corbin. "Imagine, for example, that the byte we just discussed is about to move from main memory to the processor. Just to refresh your memory, three data bits plus the parity bit are on—four 1-bits. As the byte moves toward the processor, a sudden flash of lightning causes a brief power surge, and one of the 0-bits flips on. The byte now contains five 1-bits, okay?"

"Okay."

"That can't be right. The rule demands an even number of 1-bits. An error has occurred somewhere. Instead of using that byte, the processor asks memory to send another copy. Let's assume that everything works right this time. We get a byte with four 1-bits. A potential error has been avoided."

"Hmm." Pete scratched his head and smiled. "That makes sense. I understand."

"Great!" said Corbin. "Glad I could help."

Pete glanced at his watch. "It's after 10:00, Bill. We have a long day tomorrow. I'm going to look in on the rest of the team, and . . . Something just occurred to me, Professor."

"What is it, Pete?"

"Our team consists of five members. Sylvia said that each of us will be sensed as a 1-bit. You said that most computers use even parity. Won't that cause a problem?"

"Good observation, Pete. You really do understand. To answer your question, no, it won't. NECEN uses *odd* parity. It's a very unusual machine. That's why we need an odd number of people."

"I see. One more question."

"Shoot."

"What's the difference between a mainframe and a micro?"

"A micro is a small computer and a mainframe is a big one."

"So NECEN is a mainframe."

"That's right."

"And that's all there is to it?"

"Basically, Pete. Terms like microcomputer and mainframe are rather imprecise, but for all practical purposes, small and big are close enough."

"Thanks, Bill. Come on, I'll show you to your quarters." Pete swung his feet to the floor and pushed back his chair, but Corbin didn't move. "Something wrong, Bill?"

"Earlier today, when I was briefing you on Georgie Hacker, I mentioned that he'd had a girlfriend."

"I remember. She turned him in, right?"

"That's the one."

"What about her?"

"She was Ada Byron."

"Our Ada?"

"One and the same, Pete."

"We'd better scratch her."

"No. That would be a mistake. When it comes to raw talent nobody can beat Georgie Hacker, but Ada is the best *performer* I've ever known. She's a good one. We need her. Besides, she's the one who turned him in, remember? She's no saboteur. I'd stake my reputation on that. I just thought you should know."

"Okay, Bill, I trust your judgment. But I'm going to watch her. Now let's get some sleep."

"One more question, Pete."

"Don't you ever stop, Corbin?" Pete asked, with a grin.

"Sylvia."

Pete sat back, suddenly grim. "You noticed."

"Five years ago she was twenty-five. Now she looks forty. What happened?"

"It's this damn miniaturization project, Bill," replied Pete, a hint of bitterness in his voice. "You see, electronic miniaturization is not without its side effects. Inside a computer, a human being functions at computer speed. I can't explain how that affects your metabolism, but your sense of time accelerates—minutes seem like days. And it's not just an illusion. The aging process accelerates, too. They keep sending Sylvia in because she's the best. They never consider what it's doing to her."

"You wanted the general to keep her off the team. That's why you were arguing."

"That's right. It's wrong to send her on this mission, and I told him so."

"Pete, I'm sorry. Had I known, I never would have brought up her name."

"It's not your fault, amigo. You had no way of knowing. Now Custer. He knew."

"You're still in love with her."

"Yeah. We're planning to get married. But inside a computer her biological clock runs fast. One or two more trips and children may be out of the question."

"I'm sorry, Pete."

"I know you are. And it helps to get it off my chest. Thanks for listening."

Corbin glanced at his watch. "It is getting late. We have a big day ahead of us."

"Right. Come on. I'll show you to your quarters."

7
The Mission

As he stared at the roof arching far overhead, Corbin found it hard to believe that the massive SMF operations center lay hundreds of feet underground. The conference room where he stood overlooked the main floor some twenty feet below. Through an observation window, he watched the technicians, dressed in beige coveralls and white caps, scurry across the floor, preparing for the mission.

And there, in the center of the room, resting on a large round, red tile and shimmering beneath the harsh lights, sat the ship that would carry them into the heart of NECEN: *Gossamer*. A train of eight almost transparent bubbles linked by diaphanous, pale blue cylinders, it was well named. Like soap bubbles on a sunny day, the ship seemed to change shape and color as he moved his head. In his imagination, *Gossamer* breathed, like a living thing, its segments shifting rhythmically apart and then back together. It seemed so . . . so insubstantial—eight soap bubbles linked by little more than imagination.

It was not, however, insubstantial. Overall its length approached fifty feet. It stood perhaps nine feet high, and its thickness matched its height. Corbin pressed against the glass for a closer look, and a glint of refracted light from just above the second bubble caught his eye. Helicopter blades! So that was how *Gossamer* flew. Close examination revealed another glint above the next to last bubble. He pictured the two ends moving upward as the middle sagged, limply. *Gossamer* had to be rigid—he knew that. But his senses refused to believe it. How could anything so wispy actually fly? He felt a dull ache in the pit of his stomach. What had he gotten himself into?

A buzzer sounded—0830 hours. General Custer, punctual as usual, called the final, premission briefing to order. Corbin turned his back on *Gossamer* and joined Pete, Sylvia, Ada, Ned, and the general's staff at the conference table. They all wore the same standard SMF beige coveralls he had put on that morning. "Let's run through our assignments one more time," said Custer. "Since the first phase involves the network, we'll start with Mr. Lud."

Ned looked different in his coveralls—better, really. His hair still had that unkempt look, but at least his new uniform was neat, clean, and well-pressed. It destroyed his image; he appeared almost normal.

"Once we pass through SMF's microcomputer," Ned began, "we'll enter the local telephone network and follow it to the Washington area message-switching center. The link between Washington and New York is via satellite, so we'll make a quick trip into outer space. When we return, we'll be in New York's message-switching center."

"Won't we need oxygen equipment?" asked Pete.

"We'll only be up there for a few seconds," replied Ned, impatiently. "You can hold your breath that long, can't you?"

"You're thinking in terms of actual time," interrupted Sylvia. "Once we're miniaturized, we'll function on an accelerated time scale."

"What exactly does that mean?" asked Ned.

"I'm no physicist," replied Sylvia, "so I can't give you a scientific explanation, but as you get smaller, time speeds up. Inside a computer, everything moves at least a thousand times faster, including you. One second of real time seems like fifteen minutes of preceived time, so don't count on holding your breath."

"Good point," said the general. "Colonel Holtzworth, call supply. Tell them to fill all eight oxygen tanks and make sure there's a mask at each station." As Holtzworth hurried to the phone, the general pointed toward Ned. "Continue," he ordered.

"Once we hit the New York center, we're home free," said Ned. "A high-speed line takes us to NECEN. We'll go through a controller and a channel, and hit main memory in less than a second. Piece of cake." He shrugged, a smug look on his face.

"Thank you, Mr. Lud," said Custer. "Ms. Byron, give us a quick summary of your software plans."

"Yes, sir," replied Ada in a soft, confident voice. "We'll take advantage of the way NECEN's operating system handles commands. There are several levels of commands on the system. The main operator can do just about anything—load a program, run a program, cancel a program, change a program's priority, shut the system down—anything. Secondary operators are restricted to a limited subset of commands.

Users are even more restricted. For example, I might be limited to asking the system to load and run one specific program.

"NECEN uses command prefixes to enforce these restrictions. To make it simple, let's say that all main operator commands must be preceded by two ampersands, while my commands need two dollar signs, and the Professor's two slashes. When NECEN receives a command, the operating system checks the prefix. If it isn't on the approved list, the command is ignored.

"Once NECEN has accepted the prefix," she continued, "the operating system turns to the command itself. If I try to issue one that I'm not authorized to use, I'm canceled. Otherwise the operating system searches a table listing all legal commands, finds the routine that carries out the command I've issued, and gives it control.

"When he modified the operating system, the Harlequin must have deleted the main operator's prefix and substituted his own. We have to change that prefix back to one we control. There's some dead space in the operating system; we left room for expansion when we wrote it. We'll use some of that memory for a software routine that will modify the prefix. Then we'll add the routine's name to the command table. The Harlequin won't even suspect that anything has been changed."

General Custer interrupted. "This new program is Professor Corbin's Trojan Horse?" he asked.

"That's right, General," Ada replied. "Note that we won't attempt to recover the computer while we're inside NECEN. That would be too risky. Instead we'll set up our program, steal the Harlequin's prefix, and get out. When we return to SMF Central, the real operator, using the Harlequin's own prefix, will issue a command to run our new program. The command will be accepted, and our Trojan Horse will take over, substituting our prefix for his. Consequently, *he'll* be locked out, and we'll have control again."

"Thank you, Ms. Byron," said the general. "Are there any questions? Professor Corbin, you look troubled. Is something bothering you?"

"Oh, no, General, nothing important. I just hope we're not underestimating our adversary, that's all."

"Would you like to suggest an alternative?"

"No. Ada's plan makes a great deal of sense." Corbin removed his glasses and rubbed his eyes. He was more concerned than he admitted. "It's just that . . . I'm afraid this Harlequin may have modified the operating system more than we can imagine. We might not find what we expect. We'll have to be very observant, and very flexible."

"I'm sure you're right, Professor," said the general. "But I'm equally sure that this team can rise to the challenge." He paused, sipped from his ever-present coffee cup, and locked his gaze directly on Pete. "I want you to understand, Major Smith, that you'll be out of touch with us once you leave our operations center. You are authorized to take whatever action you deem necessary."

"Yes, sir," replied Pete.

"Also, although your assignment is, technically, to regain control of the computer, a course of action that results in shutting down or disabling NECEN is acceptable."

"I understand, General."

"Good. Let's move on. Captain Potter, brief us on *Gossamer.*"

"Certainly, sir." Slowly, Sylvia pushed back her chair and stood, facing them. "Take a good look at me," she said. "I'm twenty-nine years old." Ada gasped. Even Ned snapped to attention, staring. Until now, the idea of accelerated time had been an abstraction; suddenly the implications were all too clear. "You see, you don't just shrink to bit size when you enter a computer—you *become* a bit. Oh, I'll still look like me, and Professor Corbin will still look like himself. Relatively, we'll all be the same. But inside a computer, things happen a lot faster than they do out here in the real world, and we'll be functioning at computer speed. I've logged roughly thirteen days of miniaturized time. Biologically, I'm forty; I was born twenty-nine years ago.

"Communication poses another problem. From the instant we enter SMF's microcomputer, we'll be out of touch with control central. You must remember that, as far as the system is concerned, we'll *be* electronic pulses. We'll move as fast as any message. From wherever we are in the system, we could return to SMF and zip back just as quickly as we could send a message and get a reply.

"There are some pluses, of course. One minute of real time will give us hours of perceived time in which to accomplish our mission. Then there's that miniature universe. It's beautiful. I can't describe it; you'll have to experience it yourselves. But it's worth the price of admission."

"How long will we be under?" asked Ada, shaken.

"Not long, really," replied Sylvia. "It takes about fifteen minutes to miniaturize. Figure a fraction of a second to get to the Washington message center, a few seconds to travel up to the satellite and back, another fraction of a second to get to NECEN—that's about three seconds travel time. Ten seconds inside the machine should be enough. Then we return and deminiaturize. We'll walk back into this conference room about an hour after we leave."

"That's real time," said Ada. "How long will we *think* we've been gone?"

"Let's see. We start in real time, of course. Your time perception changes gradually as you miniaturize. That fifteen minutes will seem about thirty. We figured three seconds to get to NECEN, ten inside, and another three to get back. That's sixteen seconds. At fifteen minutes per second, we'll perceive about four hours of elapsed time. Add another thirty minutes to deminiaturize and you get a total of five hours. The mission will last less than one hour, but we'll think we've been gone for five."

"What if something goes wrong?" asked Corbin. "If my calculations are correct, a minute of elapsed time in the system will seem like fifteen hours. I don't eat as much as I used to, but nature does call."

"We have sufficient provisions for a full week, Professor," said the general. "And lavatory facilities, of course."

"Is that a week of real time, or a week of perceived time?"

"Perceived."

"So, with rationing, we may be able to survive, comfortably, for half an hour or so, real time."

"That's a reasonable estimate, Professor," replied the general.

"And if we're gone much over an hour, we might die of thirst."

"It's possible."

For a moment, as the magnitude of what they were about to do slowly sank in, no one spoke. General Custer, as usual, forced them back on track. "Continue, Captain Potter," he said, quietly.

"Certainly, General. If you haven't yet seen *Gossamer*, take a look." She pointed toward the observation window. "There are eight bubbles, one per person. If you're in your bubble, it's a 1-bit; an empty bubble is a 0-bit. As long as the ship is still, you can move through the connecting tubes from bubble to bubble. When we're moving, however, you pick a bubble and you stay there."

"Do we move in serial or in parallel?" asked Ned.

"Both," replied Sylvia. "On a serial line, we move like a train, with my control bubble at the end. On a parallel line, we move side by side, with my bubble in the low-order position."

Pete looked at the professor, a puzzled expression on his face. An unspoken message passed between them: this serial/parallel business would need explanation.

"Okay," continued Ned. "What about communications? Can we talk to each other while *Gossamer* is moving?"

"Yes," replied Sylvia. "When we're moving in series that poses no problem at all. In fact, although I'd rather you didn't, you can pass from bubble to bubble in series. Parallel motion is completely different. In parallel, each bubble travels on a separate wire. The corridors are designed to allow efficient voice communication across the gaps separating those wires, although voices from the other bubbles may seem muffled.

FIGURE 7.1 To communicate with mission control, the crew members would position themselves in *Gossamer's* bubbles to form bit patterns representing the following coded characters.

CHARACTER	BIT PATTERN								MEANING
	7	6	5	4	3	2	1	0	
									FROM MISSION CONTROL
B	1	1	0	0	0	0	1	0	Begin test
null	0	0	0	0	0	0	0	0	Mission scrubbed
full	1	1	1	1	1	1	1	1	All systems go
									COUNTDOWN SEQUENCE
9	1	0	1	1	1	0	0	1	First countdown code
7	0	0	1	1	0	1	1	1	Second countdown code
5	1	0	1	1	0	1	0	1	Third countdown code
3	1	0	1	1	0	0	1	1	Fourth countdown code
Y	1	1	0	1	1	0	0	1	End countdown
G	1	1	0	0	0	1	1	1	GO—step 1
O	0	1	0	0	1	1	1	1	GO—step 2
									SPECIAL CODES
M	1	1	0	0	1	1	0	1	Mission accomplished
K	1	1	0	0	1	0	1	1	All systems A-OK
W	0	1	0	1	0	1	1	1	Wait for further communication
S	1	1	0	1	0	0	1	1	SOS! Help!
U	1	1	0	1	0	1	0	1	Up. Deminiaturize immediately

However, you cannot leave your bubble when *Gossamer* is moving in parallel."

"Any more questions?" asked the general. "Okay, let's move on. Colonel Holtzworth, pass out the codes, please."

The colonel reached into his briefcase and pulled out a stack of papers. Quickly he distributed the mission codes (Fig. 7.1).

"This sheet lists several coded characters that can be represented by combinations of five 1-bits," said Holtzworth. "Based on your recommendations, we've assumed odd parity. The only way we'll be able to communicate is through these codes. When you've reached full miniaturization, you'll position yourselves inside the ship to form these bit patterns. Captain Potter controls an output button. When she pushes it, your bit pattern will be displayed in the mission control center, at the chief technician's console, and inside the miniaturization input device where you'll be able to visually verify it. Captain Potter's control bubble is always the low-order bit.

"We'll start the countdown process by flashing the letter B. You'll notice that it contains only three 1-bits, so you couldn't possibly generate it from on board. That will be your signal to begin the test. We want you to give us a countdown—9, 7, 5, 3—followed by a Y, the end-test signal. If all goes well, you'll then give us a G and an O—GO. If we're satisfied, we'll flash you eight 1-bits and turn control over to Captain Potter. As soon as she's ready, you're on your way.

"Other characters are to be used if you encounter problems. W means wait. U means up; we'll begin deminiaturization immediately. S means SOS, you're in trouble. When you return, flash us an M, for mission accomplished, followed by a K, all systems A-OK. We can override at any time. A null code—all zeros—scrubs the mission. Any questions?"

"Yes," said Ned. "We'll move from bubble to bubble as we form these characters. Won't you see the intermediate patterns?"

"No," replied Holtzworth, mildly annoyed. "As I said before, Captain Potter has an output button. Your bit pattern isn't communicated to us until she presses it. Also, once she presses the button, your bit pattern display remains fixed until either she presses it again or we change the display." He glanced around the table. "Any more questions?" He paused, waiting. Finally he shrugged. "Back to you, General."

"Fine," said Custer, "I guess we're ready. Captain Potter, Mr. Lud, and Ms. Byron—you're dismissed. Report to *Gossamer* and check out your equipment. Professor Corbin, I'd like to talk with you and Major Smith for a few minutes. Colonel Holtzworth, Captain Statler, Lieutenant Cortez—before you leave for your posts, I want to see you over there by the door. Okay, let's go."

For a moment Pete and the professor found themselves alone. Pete turned to his old friend. "We have a minute or two," he said. "Fill me in on the difference between serial and parallel, Bill."

" It's really quite simple, Pete. A serial line is composed of a single wire. It works like a one-lane bridge. The bits go across one at a time. A parallel line consists of several parallel wires. It's like a multilane bridge. The bits go across side by side."

"Why is that significant?"

"Serial data transmission is simple; parallel data transmission is faster. Picture a one-lane bridge. Say we push one car across every six seconds. That's ten a minute, right?"

"Right."

"Now imagine an eight-lane bridge. If we average one car every six seconds in each lane, that's eighty per minute."

"Okay, a parallel line is faster. But why was Ned so concerned about *Gossamer's* ability to handle parallel transmission?"

"I share his concern, Pete. Serial is easy. *Gossamer's* bubbles follow each other along the same wire, just like a train. Parallel's different. An 8-bit parallel line consists of eight separate wires. Sometimes the wires are molded together in a flat ribbon. Sometimes they're twisted together in a cable. Eight bubbles, linked by connector tubes, will be moving through eight separate wires. Those connector tubes are going to have to be awfully flexible."

"You don't sound convinced," observed Pete.

"I'm not," said Corbin. "But . . ."

"Another question before the General returns," interrupted Pete. "Sylvia said that her bubble will always be in the low-order bit position. What does that mean?"

"What's the low-order digit in the number 152?"

"Two?"

"Sure. The low-order position is always the one with the smallest positional value. With whole numbers, that's the units position."

"In other words, Sylvia is always going to be the rightmost bit in our byte."

"That's right, Pete."

"Final question, Bill. This one might be a little dumb."

"The only dumb question is the one you don't ask," replied Corbin.

"I know computer programs consist of instructions that tell the machine when to add, subtract, and so on. But Ada kept talking about *commands*. What's a command? Is it different from an instruction?"

"Remember the difference between an application program and an operating system, Pete?"

"Sort of. Refresh my memory."

"An application program tells the computer how to perform a specific task, such as compute payroll, analyze statistical data, or format a letter. An operating system manages the computer's resources, determining such things as which application program gets to access the processor next."

"That's right. The operating system is like an electronic traffic cop."

"Good analogy. Let's say that you have an application program to run. The first step is to get the operating system's approval. To do that, you issue a command: RUN MY PROGRAM, for example. In response, the operating system locates your program, loads it into memory, and, eventually, gives it control of the processor. Now, finally, your program's instructions take over, telling the computer when to add, subtract, compare, and so on."

"I see," said Pete. "We use commands to communicate with the operating system. It gives our program control. Then, our program's instructions take over."

"Right."

"But . . ."

"Any last minute ideas on our saboteur, Professor?" interrupted General Custer as he walked up behind them.

"No, sir."

"You're sure it's not Ada Byron?"

"Pete told you?"

"Of course. He said you'd vouch for her, though. Want to change your mind?"

"No. It's not Ada, General. I'd stake my reputation on it."

"Any other candidates?"

"How about me, General?" asked Corbin.

"We do *not* suspect you, Professor."

"I have a history of opposition to this system. How do you know I'm not trying to make NECEN look bad? You have to admit that this incident almost kills the national data bank. If the Harlequin wins, people will say I was right all along."

"He has a point, General," agreed Pete.

"And what about Ned?" continued Corbin. "For all we know Georgie Hacker is his hero—the ultimate computer jock. You know what Ned thinks of ordinary people; you're morons as far as he's concerned. Maybe he sees the Harlequin as a superior mind and this crisis as an opportunity for the elite to take over."

"That's a bit farfetched," said the general. "But I must admit that I don't like the guy very much. Don't trust him, either."

"Next, we consider Captain Potter."

"Oh, come on!" reacted Pete.

"You guys have aged her ten years. You've robbed her of her youth. How do you know she's not out for revenge? Then there's Pete." Corbin pointed toward his old friend. "You know how he feels about Sylvia, General. Are you sure *he's* not out for revenge? It could be any one of us. Don't pick on Ada just because she used to be Georgie Hacker's girlfriend."

"You've made your point, Professor," said Custer. A buzzer sounded. The general checked his watch. "It's 0855, gentlemen. We commence miniaturization in five minutes. You two had better take your posts."

"We're on our way, General," said Pete.

"Good luck."

"Thank you, General," said Corbin. "We'll need it."

8 *Miniaturization*

Corbin stepped onto the main floor and paused. There, directly in front of him, lay *Gossamer*. From the conference room twenty feet above, he'd seen the fragile craft shimmering in the harsh light. Now he found himself looking right through it. Like wet glass, its almost transparent walls distorted his vision, giving the room behind it a ghostlike quality.

He closed his eyes and pictured *Gossamer*'s eight round bubbles, the first one protruding above the others, linked by cylinders. Then he remembered a pulltoy caterpillar he'd given his granddaughter when she was a toddler. The head was a wooden egg with a silly face painted on it. The body segments were slightly smaller wooden balls. The egg and the balls were linked by plastic springs. The body segments bobbed up and down when she pulled it, and she always laughed. Corbin smiled. That's what *Gossamer* reminded him of: a toy caterpillar.

Pete interrupted his daydream. "Ready Professor?"

"What? Oh, I'm sorry, Pete. Just thinking. Corbin looked at his old friend and grinned. "Let's go."

Pete led the way toward the spot where Sylvia sat, apparently suspended about six feet above the floor. She occupied the control module. Its height gave her a clear view in all directions. Near the bottom of her bubble, a temporary stairway led to an open hatch. Pete stooped and entered. Corbin followed. "This," announced Pete, "is bubble 0."

They passed through the connecting tube and entered bubble 1. Ned hardly noticed them as he concentrated on a diagram of the network that would take them to NECEN. Like Sylvia, he sat on an almost transparent chair, his diagram spread over an almost transparent table. Clearly visible beneath the table lay a stack of technical drawings and an oxygen tank; it would be difficult to hide anything on *Gossamer*. His work area filled the bubble's right hemisphere. To the left sat a thickly padded flight chair equipped with seat and shoulder belts. An open passageway down the middle afforded a clear view to the back of the ship.

Bubble 2, Ada's, came next. A mirror image of Ned's, its work area filled the left and its flight chair the right hemisphere. An oxygen tank and Ada's personal equipment lay under her desk. She, too, bent over her work as they entered, but she stopped to greet them.

"Ready, Ada?" asked Corbin.

"I think so, Professor. I don't know when I've ever been so nervous, though. My butterflies have butterflies."

"If you weren't nervous I'd wonder about you," said Corbin. "You'll do fine."

She smiled and turned back to her work.

They passed through another connecting tunnel and entered bubble 3. It contained only a folding table and a small jump seat along the right wall. "Meeting room," said Pete. "We'll all fit in here." He pointed toward the ceiling and Corbin looked up. "There's a hatch up there. It's our access to outside. When you use the laser, you'll stand on the table and poke your head and shoulders through."

They continued on to bubble 4. "This is yours, Professor," said Pete. "I'll be in 5. Number 6 is mostly storage, but there's room to stand in there. If you feel the need, the lavatory is in number 7."

"Thanks, amigo," said Corbin. "But I expect to be back long before this morning's coffee hits me."

"Yeah," said Pete, with a sigh. "Well, I hope you're right. Good luck, Professor." He spun on his heel and walked the few steps to his own bubble.

Corbin's module looked just like the others. His flight chair occupied the right hemisphere. Cautiously, he sat down. The transparent seat felt surprisingly comfortable—firm, but with just enough give. Experimenting, he located the controls on his right armrest. With a touch of a button, he could make the seat rise, lower, tilt, swivel, or recline. Finding a comfortable position, he settled back and tried to relax.

Unfortunately, he found the view outside *Gossamer* disquieting. Through its almost transparent sides, he watched the technicians scurry here and there. Looking up, he spotted General Custer behind one of the observation windows that lined the second level. In fact, he could see *everything*; the ship seemed not to exist. How could it protect him if it wasn't even there? He closed his eyes. "I will not panic," he whispered to himself, over and over. "I will not panic."

He jumped at the sound of the buzzer. Sylvia's voice echoed in his ears: "*Gossamer* ready to commence miniaturization."

"Commence miniaturization," came General Custer's reply. There was no turning back now.

As he stared through his observation window far above the floor, General Custer's attention riveted on *Gossamer*. He saw Captain Potter checking her controls, Ned Lud studying his blueprints, and Ada Byron poring over her program logic. Bubble 3, the meeting room, stood empty; he'd expected that. Corbin sat in bubble 4. He didn't look right. Perhaps . . .

Then the buzzer sounded. "*Gossamer* ready to commence miniaturization," said Captain Potter, her voice echoing loudly through the intercom. It would be their last verbal contact with the control room until the mission ended.

"Commence miniaturization," ordered Custer. A massive, honeycombed disk descended from the ceiling, its diameter exactly matching that of the large, red tile on which *Gossamer* rested. As Custer watched the technicians complete their final preparations, his mind turned to the mission. No denying it, this mission was crucial to SMF. They'd received little or no increase in funding for the past three years. Research had been severely curtailed. General Custer knew that if his team could beat the Harlequin, he'd be a hero. If not, he might be the scapegoat. He'd seen what they'd done to Corbin. He wouldn't have a chance.

The sound of a horn split the air; the miniaturizer had completed its descent. The general focused on *Gossamer*'s first bubble, where Captain Potter flashed the all clear signal. "Activate beam," he ordered. Above the ship, the honeycombs began to glow. They glowed dimly at first; then, gradually, the light increased in intensity, and suddenly, a brilliant red beam engulfed the ship. Slowly, almost imperceptibly, *Gossamer* shrank. As it did, the beam became more and more focused, and the process accelerated. *Gossamer* seemed to recede, moving quickly away toward some distant destination.

As it descended slowly from the ceiling, the honeycombed disk gave Corbin a reference point, a tiny island of visual stability. Intellectually, he knew that it moved toward him, but he pictured himself floating up, toward it. He heard the horn and Custer's command: "Activate beam." He watched the glow develop, and flinched as the brilliant red light exploded around him. *Gossamer*'s sides, glowing from the effect of the beam, seemed more substantial now. Corbin relaxed, his panic subsiding. He'd be fine.

Through a red haze, he could see the SMF operations center. Everything seemed just as before. He leaned to the side and stared straight up the passageway. Sylvia, carefully monitoring her controls, seemed perfectly framed by a supply door that stood open in the operations center wall, her shoulders just touching its sides. Now a few inches separated her shoulders from the door frame—now a few more inches. Either that doorway had grown, or *Gossamer* had moved toward it. Or they were shrinking.

"Amazing, isn't it," said Pete, his words sounding clearly from the next bubble. "Any idea how it works, Professor?"

"Just a vague one," replied Corbin.

"Tell me what you think. I'll tell you if our notes check."

"As I understand it, this red light is a special type of laser originally developed to shrink cancers. It worked, but unfortunately, not without side effects—it tended to shrink the surrounding healthy tissue too. Experimentation stopped, at least as far as the public was concerned. I remember a few technical articles announcing the death of the technology. Then you guys grabbed it and stamped it top secret. Apparently, somebody figured out a way to localize the beam's effect, and the rest is history."

"That's pretty close, Professor," said Pete. "I've heard much the same story from several people. When it comes to the technical details, though, I have no need to know. Any thoughts on how they control the beam?"

"Did you notice the big red tile in the middle of the floor?"

"How could I miss it?"

"It's the same color as this light. I'm just guessing, but I'd imagine that the particular combination of color and texture is impervious to the beam. Everything on the tile shrinks, but because the tile acts as a shield, the beam affects nothing else."

"Why don't they have a similar shield along the sides of the target area?" asked Pete. "Isn't there a risk of spillage?"

"Not with laser light," replied Corbin. "A laser beam can be controlled with a great deal of precision. We don't have to worry about spillage."

Corbin returned his attention to the operations center. There could be no doubt—*Gossamer* had shrunk. The room seemed massive, a small universe. Through it, the shimmering, ghostlike images of gigantic people moved in extreme slow motion. He felt his excitement rising.

General Custer had watched this spectacle many times before, but it never failed to amaze him. A few minutes ago, *Gossamer* had dominated the operations center, stretching from one end of the red circle to another. As miniaturization progressed, more and more of that red circle became visible until it, not *Gossamer*, dominated. Now, seven minutes into the mission, the ship appeared roughly the size of a can of tennis balls. The red glow faded and then disappeared. The large, overhead laser had completed its task. Phase II could begin. When Phase II ended, *Gossamer* would be far too small to see.

A robot rolled onto the red tile. Gently, it inserted two tiny pins into the docking receptacles in both ends of *Gossamer* and lifted the ship from the floor. Slowly, the robot rotated, extending its telescoping arm to a spot just outside the red circle, and deposited the ship on a small, glass-topped table. Gently retracting the pins, it rolled away.

Quickly a technician approached *Gossamer* and stooped to peer inside. He stood and raised his right hand: all clear. "Commence Phase II," ordered the general. The technician moved briskly to a nearby control table and pushed a button. A bowl-shaped hemisphere swung slowly into place and covered the ship. The final phase had begun.

Even without the red glow, the once familiar mission control center now seemed strange to Corbin. Gigantic caricatures of human beings moved in hazy slow motion. To his left, a massive robot advanced, slowly. There was nothing to do but wait. This next five minutes, he knew, would seem like twenty. Then they'd have completed the last phase of miniaturization, and the time differential would really hit home.

Actually, for Sylvia, Ned, and Ada, the change in time perception was a blessing. Seconds of real time would pass, but they would have plenty of perceived time in which to fine-tune their preparations. Imagine, thought Corbin, if college students could have access to the miniaturizer on the night before finals. They could pack a semester's study into half an hour. Remarkable! He smiled to himself and looked back through *Gossamer's* sides. The robot seemed hardly to have moved. I'll just rest, he decided. I'll have plenty to do soon. He closed his eyes and sank into his chair.

With a slight bump, the robot engaged its pins. Eyes still closed, Corbin sensed the ship ascending slowly, like an elevator. Opening his eyes he saw the floor far below. The drop, he knew, was no more than three feet, but it seemed like sixty. For an instant he felt dizzy. He closed his eyes and fought it.

Slowly, smoothly, precisely, the robot swung *Gossamer* across the floor. The ship descended, almost imperceptibly, until it rested on a glass panel in the center of a table. With a slight bump, the robot extracted its pins and swung its arm away.

An immense shape approached, emerging dreamlike from the haze. A technician. Step-by-step, he came nearer and nearer, towering overhead. Finally, he stood right in front of them, so huge that Corbin could see only part of him at a time. The creature stooped, and a gigantic eye peered through the front of the ship. Raising her right arm, Sylvia traced a large circle in the air—the all clear signal. Still in slow motion, the technician withdrew.

For a time, nothing happened. Corbin knew that the technician had to walk no more than fifteen feet to reach the control panel, but it seemed to take forever. Then he felt a slight vibration. Little by little, a bowl-shaped hemisphere, the same color as the circle on the operations room floor, rotated into place and covered *Gossamer*. It grew dark— completely dark. Phase II had begun.

Suddenly, pencil-thin beams of brilliant red laser light emerged from beneath the glass surface on which *Gossamer* rested and engulfed the ship, probing, grasping. It was beautiful! Nothing he had ever seen could match this! If only Susie were here, he thought.

Corbin felt himself being pulled in, falling, faster and faster. Then, abruptly, all was still. A soft, diffused light surrounded *Gossamer*. Outside, he saw a bank of eight lights. Three shone brilliantly, casting their glare through the adjacent bubbles—11000010, they read. That, Corbin realized, was the code for the letter B, their signal from SMF mission control to begin the test. They had made it!

"Prepare for communication," barked Sylvia, her voice sharp and clear. "A reminder before we start. My bubble is 0, Ned's is 1, Ada's is 2, and so on to the last one, which is 7. Okay, our first signal is the digit nine. Pete, move to 7. Professor Corbin, move to 5. Ada to 4. Ned number 3. Let's go!"

Silently, the crew members moved to their assigned stations. "When you hear your name," continued Sylvia, "sound off with your position. Pete!"

"Seven," shouted Pete.

"Check. Professor Corbin!"

"Five," he replied.

One by one, they reported their positions. Satisfied, Sylvia pushed the output button. In an instant, glowing lights flashed their message.

"Verify!" ordered Sylvia. "Pete."

"Seven is on," replied Pete.

"Check. Professor Corbin."

"Five is on." One by one, they verified their status. Five lights should have glowed; five lights did.

"Check," called out Sylvia. "Negative verification. Position 1 is off. Ned, report on position 2."

"Number 2 is off," said Ned.

"Check. Professor, number 6."

Corbin pressed his face to *Gossamer*'s side and stared toward the rear of the ship, expecting to see nothing. But number 6 glowed as brightly as his own light. It *couldn't* be! He shook his head in disbelief, hoping the image would go away, but it didn't. No one occupied bubble 6, he could see that. But still, number 6 was on!

"Professor Corbin! Number 6!" ordered Sylvia, impatiently.

Reluctantly, he replied, "Number 6 is on."

"Did you say *on*, Professor?"

"Affirmative. Number 6 is as bright as a spotlight."

"Pete, confirm," barked Sylvia.

"Affirmative," agreed Pete. "Number 6 is on."

Something had gone wrong. Something had gone dreadfully wrong.

In the control booth, General Custer watched, nervously, as the communication lights winked on. He had the pattern in front of him, 11111001. Mentally, he verified the values, starting on the right with the low-order bit. One, check. Zero, check. Zero, check. One, check. One, check. One, check. One. Wait a minute! Bit 6 is supposed to be zero. Is someone out of position? Sloppy. Oh oh. Bit seven is on, just like it's supposed to be.

Cautiously, General Custer reviewed the bit pattern spread out before him. From the right, he read the values to himself. "On. Off. Off. On. On. On. On. On." Six lights glowed. But only five people had boarded *Gossamer*! Something had gone wrong!

9
The Stowaway

General Custer stared at the lights in disbelief. It couldn't be! He'd watched only five people board that ship. But six lights glowed. What had gone wrong? Perhaps his control panel had failed. He'd need confirmation.

"Mission control," his voice boomed over the intercom. "I have six, repeat six, lights. Do you confirm?"

"Affirmative, General," came the reply. "We read six, repeat six, lights. The pattern is one, zero, zero, one, one, one, one, one."

Something had gone wrong. Reluctantly, Custer issued an order: "Prepare to deminiaturize."

Suddenly Colonel Holtzworth burst into the room. "General Custer! Lieutenant Jackson . . ."

"Not *now*, Colonel. We have an emergency."

"Lieutenant Jackson reports that Professor Corbin's granddaughter is missing, sir."

"What?" Momentarily shaken, Custer hesitated. "Why does bad news always come in clusters?" he asked, rhetorically. "Arrange a search party, Colonel. You are in charge. Check back with me in fifteen minutes. We should have the status of this mission resolved by then."

"Yes, sir." Colonel Holtzworth saluted and hurried off.

Six bits, thought the general, staring at his control panel. He knew what he had to do. Slowly, reluctantly, he moved his hand toward the abort button. Once he pushed it, the mission would be scrubbed, and deminiaturization would begin immediately. It took twenty-four hours to recycle the miniaturizer. If he pushed the button, there would be no second chance; the Harlequin would win. He snapped the protective cover from the oversized red button. His finger felt its smooth, concave surface.

Suddenly, the pattern of lights changed. Once again, the general stared in disbelief at his control panel. It read 11001011. Carefully he counted the five 1-bits. They formed the code for the letter K. Everything was A-OK. Now the pattern changed again, and again: 9, 7, 5, 3, Y, G, O. The correct characters in the correct sequence! With a sigh of relief, he snapped the protective cover back over the abort button, leaned forward, and barked a one-word command: "Launch!"

As he settled back to await the outcome, the general wondered about that extra bit. What had caused it? Probably a transient error. He'd find out when they returned. If all went well, they'd be back in less than a minute. He could wait.

Six bits. Six lights. Impossible! Only five people occupied *Gossamer*. Had the input unit malfunctioned? They'd have time to investigate. SMF control would need several seconds to respond and abort the mission. On board the ship, those several seconds would seem more than half an hour. "Report to bubble 3. Immediately!" ordered Sylvia. They still had time.

Quietly, they all filed into the third bubble. Six lights glowed. They would remain on until Sylvia pressed her output button and changed them to reflect a new pattern. Outside, the light nearest their meeting room glared, casting harsh shadows to match their mood. Something had gone wrong, but what? And could they do anything about it?

Pete took command. "It's obvious that bit number six is on and it's not supposed to be. Any ideas, Sylvia?"

"Not really, Pete," she replied. "We've never encountered this problem before."

"Anybody else?"

"Could it be a mouse, or something like that?" suggested Ned.

"No." said Sylvia. "We've taken mice, rats, and even small monkeys on earlier missions, and they simply don't register. Apparently, any living being smaller than roughly twenty-five pounds doesn't have enough electrical potential to be sensed."

"Maybe a technician loaded a metal oxygen bottle by mistake," suggested Ada.

"That might do it," agreed Sylvia.

"Ned and Ada, you come with me," ordered Pete. "We're going to tear that compartment apart. Sylvia, you go back to your station; when we find out what it is, we may have to move quickly. Professor, you stay here in number 3; we'll pass messages back to Sylvia through you. Let's go!"

It had to be an electrical failure, thought Corbin. There could be no other explanation. Soon he'd be back to full size, the mission aborted, the Harlequin victorious. Somehow, that didn't bother him as much as it should have. In fact, he felt a sense of relief. He'd tried and, through no fault of his own, failed. Georgie Hacker would show the world NECEN's folly. Maybe, he thought once again, the Harlequin should win.

A grim-faced Pete appeared in the passageway, his bulk hiding the rest of the party. As he entered the meeting room, he stepped to the right. "Sylvia," he called, "come on back. We found the problem." He seemed to avoid the professor, his attention focused on the hatch overhead.

Ned entered next, his face expressionless. He stepped to the left, away from Pete, and stared directly at the professor, as though trying to communicate something. Ada came last. She held the hand of a little girl. "My god!" gasped Corbin. "It's Susie!"

"Look what we found curled up in a food box, Professor," said Pete, still not looking at his old friend.

"Susie, what are you *doing* here?" Corbin's tone revealed his deep concern for his granddaughter's welfare. For him, the mission clearly took second place.

"I wanted to come, Gramps," said Susie, her tears just beneath the surface. "I read about the fantastic voyage, and I've always wanted to do something exciting like that. I'm sorry if I caused any trouble."

Ada hugged her, protectively. "It's okay, Susie. We'll think of something."

"Come on, Ada," interjected Ned, gruffly. "Be realistic. The mission's off; we're scrubbed. Even if we go we can't possibly succeed. NECEN is an odd parity computer, remember? Six people means six 1-bits; thats an even number. We'll be rejected as an error."

"What happens if we *are* rejected?" asked Pete. "It seems to me that we have to reach NECEN before the computer can reject us. Once we're there, if NECEN doesn't like us, so what? We just take off and fly to our objective."

"Your ignorance of computers is amazing," said Ned, disdainfully. "I told Custer not to put a technological illiterate in charge."

"Knock it off, Ned," warned Corbin. He turned to face Pete. "The problem *is* serious," he said. "We might be rejected by NECEN, or by either of the two message-switching computers we pass on our way there. The real problem, though, is what happens once we are rejected."

"What's that, Professor?" asked Pete.

"If our byte fails parity," replied Corbin, "the computer dumps us into the bit bucket and asks the source computer to retransmit the message."

"The bit bucket?"

"A ground wire, Pete. For safety, most electrical equipment is grounded, and computers are no exception. If we're rejected, we flow into the ground."

"How is NECEN grounded?"

"I'm not sure, Pete. Do you know, Ned?"

"NECEN is grounded to Madison Square Garden's steel superstructure," replied Ned.

"That superstructure is buried in concrete, Pete," said Corbin. "If we're dumped to the bit bucket, we'll be somewhere inside one of the steel support beams inside one of Madison Square Garden's concrete walls. And current flows one way to the ground; it doesn't flow back. If we hit the bit bucket, that's it. No one will ever see us again."

"I'm afraid he's right," agreed Sylvia as she entered the bubble. "Besides, with six people we can't send SMF the correct signal patterns. If mission control doesn't get the patterns, they'll abort. General Custer is probably about to push the button right now. Unless somebody has a brilliant idea, we're on our way home."

"Sylvia," said Corbin. "You mentioned some experiments with mice, rats, and monkeys."

"That's right, Professor. Little animals didn't register. I don't know what good that does us, though. Susie is clearly over the minimum weight. She's registering as a 1-bit."

"Ned," continued Corbin. "In physical terms, what's the difference between a 0-bit and a 1-bit? We aren't really talking about the absolute presence or absence of a charge, are we?"

"No we're not, Professor," replied Ned. "A 0-bit is a low current or a low voltage that's under a critical level; a 1-bit is above that critical cutoff point."

"So a 1-bit is really a range of electrical potentials, isn't it?"

"That's right," agreed Ned. "So what?"

"Let me pose a question. What whould happen if we put Susie and Ada together in one bubble?"

For a moment, the group fell silent. Sylvia reacted first. "I see what you're driving at, Professor. With a second person in a bubble, we'd just be adding to the electrical potential of that bubble. Two people, one bit. It might work!"

"I'm not sure," said Ned. "Granted a 1-bit is represented as a range of electrical potentials, but there is an upper limit to that range. What happens if we exceed the limit?"

"I don't know," admitted Sylvia. "I guess it depends on how much we exceed it by. It might snap a circuit breaker. It might burn out a circuit."

"Yes," interrupted Corbin, "but Ada and Susie together weigh considerably less than Pete. If our electrical potential is proportional to our mass, the two of them together should fall well within the 1-bit range."

"Are we sure electrical potential is proportional to mass?" asked Ned. "Maybe there's another factor involved. Maybe two little people are worth more than one big one."

"I don't know the answer to that one either," said Sylvia. "We've never tested for the upper limit, only the lower one."

"What if we try and it doesn't work?" asked Ada.

"We'd be no worse off than we are now," said Pete.

"Not necessarily," argued Ned. "Let's say that any two people, taken together, exceed the range for a 1-bit by enough to blow out a circuit. We might not ever get back."

"I don't think that's a danger," said Sylvia. "The deminiaturizing circuits are separate from the bit-sensing circuits. If anything fails, deminiaturization is automatic."

"What do we have to lose?" asked Ada. "If we don't try, the mission is aborted. If we do try and it doesn't work, the mission is aborted. If we try and it works, we have nothing to worry about. We can't lose."

"Okay," decided Pete. "Let's try it. Sylvia, return to your pilot's chair and direct us. Mission control is probably wondering what's going on in here, so let's start with an A-OK signal. Then we'll run through the countdown sequence."

Corbin turned to face his granddaughter, placing his hands on her shoulders. "Susie," he said, gently, looking directly into her eyes. "You were told to stay with Lieutenant Jackson. You disobeyed me."

"I'm sorry, Gramps." She struggled to keep from crying.

"How did you manage to sneak on board, Susie?" asked Ada. Perhaps because Ada was herself so tiny, her question seemed to calm the child.

"It was easy," answered Susie. "This morning I heard some people talking in the hall outside my room. They mentioned something about the miniaturizer, and then somebody else came and told them to go back for oxygen bottles."

"That must have been during our briefing," concluded Ada. "Go on, Susie."

"Well, I peeked out and saw a cart loaded with supplies right next to my door. I didn't see anybody around, so I took some food from one of the boxes and climbed in. When the people came back, they just loaded me on board."

"The general and I will have to discuss this security breach," said Pete. "I can't believe they left a cart unattended."

For a moment, no one spoke. Then Susie realized they were waiting for her to continue. "It felt kind of strange. Somebody picked me up and then dropped me. Then they must have stacked other boxes on top of the one I was in, because I couldn't get out. For a while it felt like I was on an elevator. Then it felt like I was falling. Next thing I knew, Pete found me. I didn't mean to cause any trouble. Honest!" Again, she blinked back a tear.

"I know, honey, but . . ."

"Just put me off, Gramps," she sniffed. "I'll go to my room and wait there until you come back. I won't get in any more trouble. I promise."

"We can't, Susie," replied Pete, with a sigh. "We've already been miniaturized."

"You mean—I'm tiny? I don't feel tiny."

"We're all tiny, Susie," said Pete. "And time is running out. Professor Corbin," he continued, "if you insist, we'll go back. I understand that you might not want your granddaughter along on this mission. But make up your mind right now while we still have time."

Corbin felt confused. The mission could be dangerous, but Susie might never have an opportunity like this again. Besides, to go back now meant surrendering to the Harlequin, and despite his reservations, Corbin knew that Georgie Hacker had to be stopped.

"Let's go for it," he said. "Susie, you stay with Ada."

"Okay," she agreed, smiling.

"And you do *exactly* what she tells you," he warned, sternly.

"Pete, bubble 7," interrupted Sylvia. The test had begun.

"Professor, 6." One by one, Sylvia positioned them. Then, just to be sure, she double-checked.

"Pete!"

"Seven," he replied.

"Check. Professor."

"Six."

"Check. Ada."

"Three. Susie is with me."

"Check. Ned."

"One."

"Check." She pushed the output button. In an instant, they would know if their experiment had worked. The lights seemed to take forever to change, but finally, their pattern emerged: 11001011. Five 1-bits! Only five! And they formed the correct pattern—the code for the letter K, the A-OK signal. They'd done it! A cheer echoed through the corridor.

Step-by-step, the crew formed the remaining bit patterns in the mission countdown sequence. The digit 9 came first. Following Sylvia's directions, they moved to their assigned bubbles. As she hit the output button and their bit pattern emerged, they counted five 1-bits. It was working! Next came a 7, then a 5, then a 3. Finally, they formed, in turn, the letters Y, G, and O. Only one question remained: Had they acted in time?

10 *The Microcomputer*

The countdown had ended. In a few seconds, *Gossamer* would leave
SMF Control Central and enter the microcomputer. On board the ship,
however, each of those seconds would seem like fifteen minutes. As he
entered the meeting room, Corbin wondered if the others sensed the
time differential as deeply as he did.

He noted with satisfaction the photograph that lay on the table
(Fig. 10.1). It showed the microcomputer's insides. Ned, he knew, pre-
ferred schematics, but Pete would find a picture much easier to follow.

Ned leaned over the table, his attention focused on a diagram (Fig.
10.2). "We're here," he said, pointing to a box marked "input unit."
Corbin showed Pete the equivalent spot on the photograph. "Once we
start moving," continued Ned, "we flow across this cable and enter the
interface board." His finger followed a straight line, stopping on a box
marked "interface." Corbin found it on the photograph. "The interface
passes us on to the bus line." Again Ned traced *Gossamer*'s expected
path. "Then it's straight to main memory."

"Thanks, Ned," said Pete. "Any questions?"

A sudden change in the light distracted them. "That's the signal,"
announced Sylvia. "All eight lights are on. Time to go."

"Back to your stations," ordered Pete. "Susie is with you, right,
Ada?"

"That's right," Ada answered.

Corbin stepped toward Susie. "Are you ready, honey?" he asked.
She nodded. He sensed her excitement; in fact, he shared it. For the
first time, he honestly *wanted* to defeat the Harlequin. He reached for

Figure 10.1 A photograph of the inside of the SMF microcomputer.

1. The input unit is not shown in this picture. It lies outside the computer, and is plugged into the interface board.

2. The interface board marks Gossamer's point of entry to the computer.

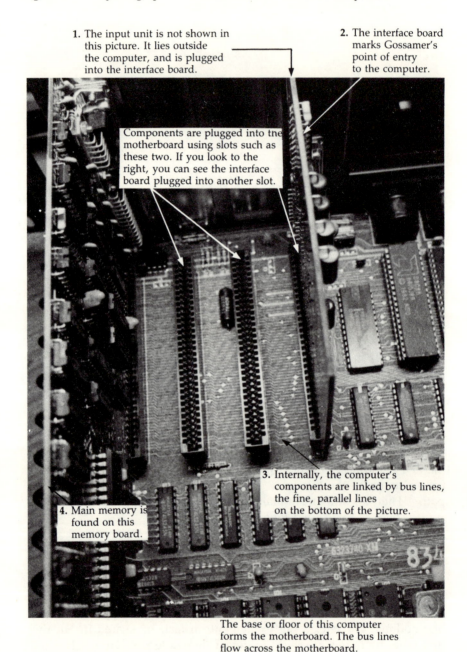

Components are plugged into the motherboard using slots such as these two. If you look to the right, you can see the interface board plugged into another slot.

3. Internally, the computer's components are linked by bus lines, the fine, parallel lines on the bottom of the picture.

4. Main memory is found on this memory board.

The base or floor of this computer forms the motherboard. The bus lines flow across the motherboard.

her hand and squeezed it. "You go with Ada," he said, not quite willing to let her go. "And do *exactly* what she tells you." Reluctantly, he released his grip.

"I will, Gramps." With a crooked smile, Susie turned and walked away.

"You should be in your seat with all belts fastened," called Sylvia from her control module. "When you hear your name, please verify. Pete."

"Ready," he replied.

"Professor."

"Ready."

"Ada. Susie."

Ada glanced across the aisle to where Susie sat in the work area chair. Susie snapped her shoulder harness into place and, her face glowing, smiled in answer to an unasked question—yes, she was ready. Ada checked her own belt. "Ready, Captain," she replied.

"Ned."

"Ready."

"Okay—here we go!" Slowly, smoothly, Sylvia pulled back on a

Figure 10.2 A diagram of the inside of the SMF microcomputer. *Gossamer*'s path into main memory is identified.

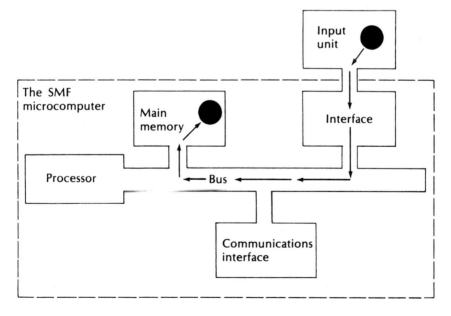

control lever. Almost imperceptibly, *Gossamer* moved. Then, abruptly, like a rocket, it accelerated. The force pushed Corbin back into his chair, but only for an instant. Almost before he knew what had happened, the ship reached operating speed and entered the input cable.

Gossamer drifted near the center of a beautiful, perfectly round, apparently endless copper tunnel. It seemed as though the golden dome of a cathedral had been stretched to infinity and wrapped around them. Soon, however, the true nature of their surroundings became more clear. The ship floated in a cylindrical sea of tiny golden balls—copper atoms. Much as dust particles in the air refract the sun's light to give the sky its pale blue color, the myriad copper atoms refracted whatever light entered the wire, producing the golden glow.

But how, wondered Corbin, could light enter a solid copper wire? It didn't, he realized. The light came from *inside* the cable. Electricity does not flow unimpeded; instead, the wire offers resistance. Because of this resistance, a wire absorbs some of the electrical energy and converts it to heat and light. Thomas Edison use that principle when he invented the electric light bulb. Impurities—non-copper atoms—offer even greater resistance, absorbing more energy than the copper atoms. Those impurities, dull red glowing spots mixed in the the copper atoms, marked *Gossamer*'s passing.

"Wow!" whispered Susie.

Ada smiled. "It is beautiful, isn't it?" she whispered. Hearing no response, she loosened her harness and leaned across the aisle. Susie sat mesmerized. Ada understood. She had studied computers for years, but she had never imagined such beauty. Never again would she look at a circuit diagram in quite the same way. Unfortunately, her years of training had left her almost too familiar with a computer's internals, and she found herself translating everything she saw into a physical reality. Susie carried no such burden. Her imagination could soar free.

But Ada had a job to do. There would be time for sightseeing on the return trip. For this crew to regain control of NECEN, her Trojan Horse routine had to work perfectly. There would be no second chance. Carefully, she retraced her logic, again and again. Had she forgotten something? In spite of the fascinating sights streaming by just outside *Gossamer*'s walls, she forced herself to play computer, mentally executing the program over and over, instruction by instruction, step-by-step.

Sylvia leaned back and relaxed. This phase of the journey called for little action on her part. She had experienced the microscopic universe many times before, but its strange beauty never lost its appeal. Still, like any experienced pilot, her attention remained fixed on her ship's control panel. Almost unconsciously, she monitored the various controls and gauges. Everything appeared normal. Fuel consumption, energy loss, temperature, pressure—all fell within expected limits. Yet she knew that the unexpected could occur at any time.

"Any surprises, Ned?" she asked.

Ned's bubble lay directly in front of her. He sat hunched over a schematic diagram, carefully tracing *Gossamer*'s path through the microcomputer. Reluctantly, he glanced toward Sylvia, hardly noticing her or the great beauty that lay just outside. "No," he said. Almost at once, his attention returned to the diagram. Sylvia smiled. Ned was impossible, but at least he seemed competent.

Without warning, the cable turned silver. "Where are we, Ada?" asked Susie.

"We're in a pin," replied Ada. "It links the cable to the interface board. We shouldn't be here long."

Almost as she spoke, the silver pin dropped behind, and *Gossamer* floated onto a lake of pure gold! The diffused light filtering through the slots and openings in the computer's casing illuminated the inside of the machine with a soft glow that made the gold shimmer. It took her breath away!

"Is this gold?" asked Susie.

"Yes it is," answered Ada, softly, as though reluctant to speak in the presence of such beauty.

"Why gold?"

"This board has to be connected to other boards. The gold tabs are used to attach the wires."

"But why gold?" Susie asked again.

"Oh, I understand what you're asking. Gold is an excellent conductor of electricity, Susie. And it won't rust or corrode."

"Is that all?" Mildly disappointed, Susie drifted back to the world of her imagination.

Gossamer crossed the fingernail-shaped golden tab and, at its highest point, entered a narrow, silver channel. The channel led to what looked like a small, silver pond. Crossing the pond, the ship joined a threadlike canal. Overhead, a pale green curtain filtered and colored the light.

"How come everything is green?" asked Susie, returning from wherever her mind had taken her.

"We're on a circuit board," replied Ada. "We're following a line that lies just beneath the surface. That green haze you see overhead is a protective coating."

"Why is this interface board necessary, Professor?" asked Pete, picking up on the conversation.

"It links the input unit to the computer," answered Corbin. "Most microcomputers use one interface board for each peripheral device."

"Why one per device?"

"Basically because for any given computer there can be hundreds of input, output, and secondary storage devices, and each type is different."

"In what way?"

"Well," replied Corbin, "outside the computer, data take many different forms. For example, have you ever noticed the strange black characters on the bottom of a check?"

"All the time," said Pete. "Never paid any attention to them, though."

"They're printed with a special magnetic ink called MICR. Each character is represented by a unique magnetic pattern. The characters are read by a device that senses those patterns."

"Last year in school we took a basic skills test," said Susie, rejoining the conversation. "We had to mark the answers by filling in little circles with a pencil. The teacher said the forms were graded by a computer."

"That's right, Susie," continued Corbin, pleased with his granddaughter's interest and insight. "White paper reflects more light than a black mark. The scanner reads the pattern of marks and no marks and converts it into a pattern of ones and zeros. Another device you may have seen is a supermarket scanner. It reads the bar code printed on most packages. Here's another one, Pete. You're old enough to remember punched cards, aren't you?"

"Sure. Do not bend, fold, spindle, or mutilate."

"That's it. On a card, characters are represented by a pattern of holes punched in a column."

"I understand everything you're telling me, Professor," said Pete, "but I still don't see why we need an interface board."

"The key, Pete," Corbin went on, "is that, outside a computer, data can take many different forms. The letter A, for example, might be represented as a magnetic intensity, a spot on a sheet of paper, two parallel bars, a key on a keyboard, dots on a screen—anything. However, inside the computer, an A is *always* represented as the same pattern of eight bits. Outside it depends on the device; inside it's always the same pattern. The interface board accepts the external device's signals and converts them to the computer's internal form."

"I see," said Pete. "Several starting points, same objective."

"That's right. Because translating bar codes is different from translating keystrokes or magnetic pulses, we need a different interface board for each device. On a computer . . ."

Suddenly, without warning, the light disappeared. "What happened?" cried Susie, a bit frightened.

Ada smiled; she'd expected this. "Don't worry, Susie," she said, calmly. "This won't last long. We're inside the board right now, that's all. We'll come up soon. A circuit board is like a sandwich with lots of layers. Holes drilled through the board are filled with pins that connect the layers. We just followed a pin to an inside layer where no light can penetrate."

"But," argued Susie, regaining her spunkiness, "we had plenty of light inside the cable."

"That's a good point," admitted Ada. "Remember all the little copper-colored balls in the cable?"

"Sure," replied Susie.

"They were copper atoms. When we moved through them, they tried to resist our progress. That resistance caused them to absorb some of our energy and give it back as light. This line is so fine, and the material is so pure, that we encounter very little resistance. That means little or no lost energy, and very little light."

"Oh." Susie seemed satisfied. She leaned back and stared out at the darkness.

As promised, the ship quickly joined another pin and broke the surface again. The light returned abruptly. From the pin, *Gossamer* crossed a fine, hairlike wire to the surface of a chip and continued down a wide boulevard lined, on both sides, with row after row of perfectly square circuit elements separated by narrow cross streets. The chip reminded Corbin of a small prairie town.

Bubble 7 made a sharp left turn and entered a cross street. One by one, the others followed. "My drill sergeant would have loved this," joked Pete. Then, simultaneously, all eight bubbles turned to the right. Now they traveled on separate streets, in parallel. Corbin watched, fascinated, as the tube linking his bubble to Pete's oozed through the tiny square that separated them.

"Pete," he called.

"I'm still here," came the reply, muffled and distant. In spite of their separation, they could still communicate.

"*Gossamer* is amazing, Pete. Any idea how these tubes work?"

"Nope. And I'm not about to find out either. Keep your hands in your own bubble, amigo."

"Sounds like good advice."

Once again *Gossamer* left the chip and plunged into the board's interior. An instant later the bubbles rose, side by side, and entered yet another chip.

"What does this circuit do?" asked Pete.

"We are about to have our parity checked," replied Corbin.

"Hey!" cried Susie.

Startled, Ada looked across the aisle. Susie's hair stood on end, and her own scalp tingled! Of course. To check parity, the computer read each bit. How else could it determine if their byte contained an odd number of 1-bits? To read bits, the computer passed them through an electronic field and sensed the change in that field. "Nothing to worry about, Susie," Ada said. "We're being read. But you sure look funny with your hair sticking out."

Susie giggled. "So do you, Ada."

"Yes, I'll bet I do."

Once again, the ship crossed a hairlike wire, joined another pin, and plunged beneath the board's surface, emerging, instants later, its bubbles floating, side by side, on eight identical silver ponds. Evenly spaced, the bubbles passed through eight parallel silver channels and entered eight identical golden lakes. Near the far end of each lake, a tiny silver pin led to a thin wire, one of sixteen parallel wires embedded in a flat, multicolored ribbon. *Gossamer*'s bubbles flowed, side by side, through the rightmost eight.

"I assume this is the bus, Professor," called Pete.

"That's right," replied Corbin.

"What exactly is a bus?"

"Remember how data move between the processor, memory, and the input and output interfaces? Well, the bus is the electronic path that links those components."

"I notice we're moving in parallel," said Pete. "Is that common on a bus?"

"Oh sure, Pete. It's almost a rule; bits move in parallel inside a computer. This bus we're on now is a ribbon containing sixteen side-by-side wires. That's a common design."

"Why?" asked Susie.

Surprised that his granddaughter still listened, Corbin hesitated briefly before continuing. "Speed," he said, finally. "You can move more bits per second over sixteen parallel wires than you can over a single series wire."

"But why sixteen?"

"We're moving through a 16-bit microcomputer," answered Corbin. "On this computer, all the internal components are designed to work with 16-bit units. The processor adds 16-bit numbers. Memory stores and retrieves 16-bit words. Since the bus lines link the internal components, they carry sixteen bits at a time." He wondered if his explanation had been too technical for his granddaughter.

"How many bits can NECEN handle at a time?" asked Susie.

"Sixty-four."

"That's why it's so fast, right?"

"That's the major reason, Susie." Corbin smiled, impressed with his granddaughter's reasoning ability. There would be no need to talk down to her.

"You know, Professor," said Pete, "I've looked inside computers before, but I never really paid much attention to them. Suddenly a lot of things make sense. Do me a favor, will you?"

"Sure. What is it?"

"Remember the photograph we looked at earlier?"

"You mean the one that shows the inside of this computer?"

"That's the one. I have a copy in front of me (Fig. 10.1). Go through it and explain how the pieces fit together."

"Glad to." Corbin found his copy and studied it briefly. "Let's assume we're going to assemble the system from scratch. We start with a metal framework called a motherboard. You can see it in the background." He pointed to a casing near the bottom of the picture, barely visible beneath the circuit boards. "It's basically a series of slots. Think of it as a chest of drawers with all the drawers removed."

"Okay. I can picture that."

"Good. Now imagine that at the bottom or back of each slot is a plug."

"Like an electrical outlet?" asked Susie.

"Basically. But a standard wall outlet has two or three openings. These have sixteen."

"Because this is a 16-bit computer."

"Exactly, Susie. Now, take circuit boards and plug them into the slots. One board might contain main memory. Another might be an interface that links an input device to the system. A third might be another interface unit for an output device. Given the interface boards, input and output devices can be plugged into them."

"So to add components, you just plug them into the motherboard," concluded Pete.

"That's right," agreed Corbin. "You got it."

"What about the bus lines?" asked Susie.

"The bus lines run from slot to slot. They connect the components."

"That makes sense," said Pete.

By now *Gossamer* had traveled much of the computer's width. Suddenly it seemed to leap from the main bus, joining the eight identical golden lakes that marked the entrance to a memory board. Moving quickly across the board, its bubbles still in parallel, the ship passed row after row of identical chips before finally selecting one and coming to rest in main memory.

"Another question, Professor," called Pete. "There had to be hundreds of identical chips, and thousands of identical spots on each one. How did the system know to drop us here?"

"Remember bytes, Pete?"

"How could I forget? I'm part of one."

"The byte is the basic unit of memory on this machine. Each one is assigned a unique number: the first byte is 0, the second one is 1, the third one is 2, and so on. The numbers are called addresses. An instruction told the processor to read us and put us at this address, so here we are."

"I'm not sure I understand," admitted Pete.

"Picture memory as a bank of mailboxes," said Corbin. "Number each one, starting at the top left—0, 1, 2, 3, 4, and so on. If I handed you a letter and asked you to put it in box number 100, could you do it?"

"Sure. Just find the box numbered 100 and slide the letter in."

"Exactly. Later, if I asked you to retrieve the letter stored in box number 100, could you find it?"

"Certainly."

"The numbers represent each box's address. Conceptually, the only difference between the sequentially numbered mailboxes and the sequentially numbered bytes inside a computer's memory is that memory is electronic. We tell the computer to store a byte of data in memory location 100. Later, we tell it to retrieve the data stored in memory location 100. The byte's number is its address, and each byte has a unique address. That's all there is to it."

Sylvia's voice sounded again. "We're scheduled for a brief rest stop here. We'll have time to get together and review the next phase of our mission. I'm setting a timer. When the buzzer goes off, get back to your stations. See you in the meeting room."

11 *The Local Network*

Corbin knew all about memory. At least he thought he did. He'd designed memory circuits. He'd held memory chips in his hand. As a programmer, he'd used memory. But now he experienced it from a new perspective. Tiny squares, each big enough to hold one bit, stretched in endless replication as far as he could see. Narrow pathways separated the squares. In the distance, the pathways crossed wider avenues.

Gossamer occupied random access memory, or RAM. He pictured its structure in his mind (Fig. 11.1). The ship covered the eight bits of one byte—more specifically, byte number 1025. This 16-bit microcomputer manipulated and stored 16-bit words. Byte 1024 and *Gossamer's* byte combined formed a word. When they moved, the two bytes would move together.

Slowly, showing his age, Corbin swung his feet to the floor and stood up. He stretched. Then he looked toward bubble 3, the meeting room, where Ned, waiting impatiently, had already claimed the table for another diagram (Fig. 11.2).

Ada stood nearby, a faraway look in her eyes. Corbin had seen that look many times. She was, he realized, mentally exercising the Trojan Horse logic, analyzing her routine, instruction by instruction, bit by bit, playing computer, her mind almost totally preoccupied. To a nontechnical person, she might have appeared absentminded or lost in a world of her own, but Corbin knew better. Good programmers are rare; few jobs demand such complete concentration. Still, this meeting could be important. Intentionally, he brushed her arm as he entered the room. "Something wrong, Ada?" he asked.

FIGURE 11.1 The microcomputer's random access memory (RAM) was organized into 8-bit units called bytes. Each byte had a unique address. Groups of two bytes, called words, moved together between the computer's internal components. *Gossamer* occupied byte 1025, which together with byte 1024 formed a single word.

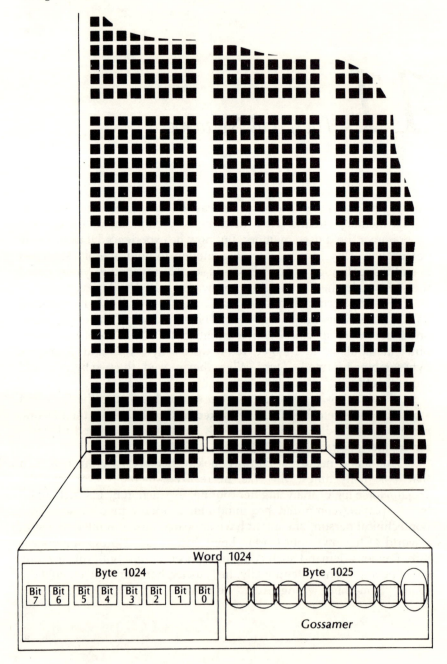

FIGURE 11.2 From the SMF microcomputer's main memory, *Gossamer* will flow over the bus line, through a communication interface, through a modem, over a telephone line, through another communication interface, over another bus line, and, finally, into the message-switching computer's main memory.

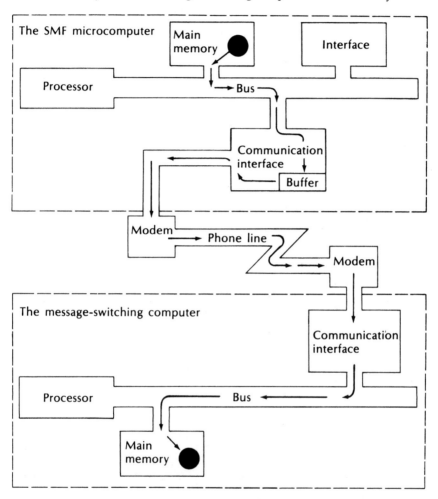

"What?" She seemed startled. "I'm sorry, Professor, just day-dreaming."

"Those circuit diagrams have taken on a whole new meaning, haven't they?"

"They certainly have," she replied. "I never realized the inside of a computer could be so beautiful."

"Yes it's very beautiful," said Susie. She stood near Ada. The two of them might have passed for sisters. "Especially that big tunnel. It felt like we were on a space ship, and we had just gone past warp speed. That's the speed of light," she explained, seriously. Corbin started to smile, but Ada's gesture stopped him. "Everything curved around us," continued Susie. "It looked like another universe. You could just about see the red suns as we flashed past. Then everything turned silver and we landed on a golden lake. That was something!"

Ada nodded her agreement.

"We have about five minutes," interrupted Pete as he walked in. "Ned, give us an overview of the next phase."

"Let's continue this later," whispered Ada to Susie. "I'm really interested in your impressions." They turned their attention to the work table.

"We're here," said Ned, pointing to the SMF microcomputer's main memory (Fig. 11.2). "When the processor issues a data fetch, we move back to the bus." Step-by-step, he traced *Gossamer*'s intended path on the diagram. "From the bus, we enter the communication interface. Inside the interface we sit in a buffer while protocols are exchanged, then we follow our message characters through a modem and over a telephone line. Finally, we pass through another modem and another communication interface, and enter the message-switching computer's main memory."

Pete wore a puzzled expression. "Any questions?" he asked. Ned's explanation, an almost unbroken stream of technical buzzwords, approached overkill. He hadn't understood a word of it.

"I assume the telephone line is analog," said Corbin, introducing yet another new term.

"That's right," agreed Ned.

"Has *Gossamer* ever been tested on an analog line?"

"No, Professor," answered Sylvia. He hadn't noticed her before, but she stood just behind Susie and Ada. "We're pioneers."

"Well, I guess it's too late to turn back now," reflected Corbin, nonchalantly. Inside, however, his mind churned. No human being had ever crossed an analog line before. *Gossamer*'s crew was about to become the subject of an experiment. The line might be safe; it might be deadly. No one knew. That, he realized, was what bothered him: the unknown. He'd never wanted to be a pioneer. He forced himself to shake off his nagging fear. Perhaps he'd seen too many B movies.

By unspoken consent, the meeting had ended. As he and Pete walked back toward their bubbles, Corbin noted that his old friend seemed uncharacteristically quiet. Perhaps some of Ned's technical terms needed translation, but which ones? He hesitated to ask, not wanting to underscore Pete's lack of knowledge. Then Susie called. "Gramps."

"Yes, Susie." Corbin looked toward bubble 2 and saw Ada once again lost in thought. Maybe his little granddaughter just wanted someone to talk to.

"What's analog?" she asked, seriously.

Corbin smiled. Her question solved his dilemma. Through her, he could translate for Pete without calling attention to Pete's limited technical expertise. "Do you know what an analogy is, Susie?" he asked in reply.

"Sure," she answered. "An analogy is when you explain something by comparing it to something else. Like when I compared the cable to a big tunnel."

"That's right," replied Corbin. He'd have to be careful not to talk down to her—she wouldn't stand for it. "An analog is a physical analogy. For example, the position of a needle on a car's speedometer represents the car's speed. A thermometer is another good example. We can't measure temperature directly, but we can represent it by measuring the height of a column of mercury."

"That tuner on your old radio is analog, isn't it?" she asked, thoughtfully. "On my radio, I just set the numbers to 102.7 to get my favorite station. On your radio, a needle moves across a dial and I have to guess where 102.7 is."

"Good example, Susie. The needle's position represents the frequency in analog form. Your radio's tuner displays the frequency in digital form. The difference between those two types of data is important. When you switch your radio from 102.7 to 102.8, you go directly to 102.8. There's nothing between those two settings; digital data are discrete. With the analog dial, however, there are any number of possible settings between 102.7 and 102.8. Analog data are continuous."

"Why is that important, Gramps?"

"Let me give you an example you can visualize, Susie. Imagine a computer that runs on water. Each 1-bit is a drop of water. A 0-bit is a dry spot. Each bit is discrete. It's either a 0 or a 1; there's no other possibility. That's digital data.

"We want to send some data through a hose to another computer. It's tough to push individual drops through a hose, so we'll start with a continuous stream of water. Normally, the water pressure is constant. To transmit data, we vary the pressure: for each 1-bit we increase the pressure slightly, for each 0-bit we decrease it. At the other end of the line, changes in pressure are sensed as bit values. Using such a scheme, we could take a pattern of bits in one computer and reproduce it in another. Variations in water pressure represent the digital data in analog form.

"Right now we're stored inside a real computer. The computer sees us as independent, discrete pulses of electric current. Like those drops of water, we're in digital form. Unfortunately, the telephone line can only transmit analog data."

"You seemed concerned about that, Professor," observed Pete, finally joining the conversation. "Why?"

"Think back to my analogy. We're like discrete drops of water. To get from our computer to another one, we have to dive into a continuous stream. When we enter the stream, will we still be discrete drops, or will we be part of the stream? For the system to send us over the telephone line, it has to convert us from digital to analog form, and I have no idea how that will affect us."

"Obviously, we're not going to join a stream of water," said Pete. "Explain the nature of this analog signal."

"Local telephone systems transmit a continuous electronic wave; you'll hear it as a steady hum. Data, or sounds, are superimposed on the wave by interrupting the pattern. A higher than normal frequency might be a 1-bit, while a lower than normal frequency might be a 0-bit. We'll all be part of that wave."

"Sounds exciting," said Pete, facetiously.

"I'm sure it will be," agreed Corbin. "Any more questions?"

"Several," said Pete, suddenly aware that his ignorance could have far worse consequences than any embarrassment he might feel. "We're waiting for data fetch. What's that?"

Corbin paused for a moment, collecting his thoughts. Pete needed a complete answer, but not a course in computer internals. "Let me put it in context for you," he began, finally. "When data enter a computer, they're stored in main memory. Memory just holds the data. To process them, the computer has to move them. To perform arithmetic, for example, the data have to move to the processor. On output, the data have to move to an interface. The processor controls this movement. When it needs some data, it sends a signal to memory, and the memory controller gets them. That's data fetch."

"So we're waiting for a signal from the processor."

"Exactly, Pete. Right now we occupy byte 1025; we're part of word 1024. Our destination is another computer, NECEN, so we have to move from this microcomputer's main memory to a communication line. Sometime soon, the processor will tell memory to fetch word 1024 and transfer it to the bus; that's data fetch. Once we reach the bus, we'll flow to the data communication interface."

"What's a data communication interface?" asked Susie.

"Remember the interface board we crossed on our way in here?"

"Sure."

"It linked the input unit to the computer. The communication interface is another board that links the computer to a communication line. The input unit's interface accepted input signals and converted them to computer signals. The communication interface accepts data in the computer's internal form and converts it to the form required by the communication line. At the other end of the line, another communication interface will convert us to the message-switching computer's internal form."

"Interesting," said Pete. "Is that related in any way to protocols?"

"Hmm." Corbin thought for a moment, scratching his head. "Let me use another analogy to illustrate that one. Imagine that I'm trying to place a telephone call to you. First question: How do you know I'm trying to call?"

"I'm not sure what you mean," admitted Pete.

"The phone rings," suggested Susie.

"Exactly," said Corbin, pleased with his granddaughter. "What do you do when you pick up the phone?"

"Say hello."

"Sure. Then you identify yourself, I identify myself, and the conversation begins. That's a protocol. The phone rings. You pick it up and say hello. I identify myself. You identify yourself. It's a social protocol, but it's still a protocol. Until we get through the preliminaries, we can't start communicating.

"An electronic protocol has the same objective," continued Corbin. "The SMF microcomputer wants to establish communication with a message-switching computer. First, the two machines exchange a set of predefined electronic signals. Once they identify each other, communication can begin."

"I see," said Pete. "Are message characters part of the protocol?"

"In a way," answered Corbin. "Imagine that we've already established contact with another computer by exchanging protocol signals. We're about to transmit a message—a string of numbers, perhaps. Message characters are placed at the beginning and at the end of the message. When our data stream reaches its destination, the message characters arrive first. They alert the target computer that the data are coming. The end-of-data characters tell the target computer that the message has ended."

"You mean they're just markers?"

"That's a key function. On some systems, however, the message characters also carry such information as the message's source and destination, too."

"I see," said Pete. "Now, what's a modem? I've heard the term before, but I've always ignored it."

"Remember the difference between analog and digital signals, Pete?"

"Sure. We just discussed it."

"Inside a computer, data are stored in digital form. Local telephone lines use analog signals. Electronically, analog and digital signals are different, so we have to translate from one form to the other. The process of converting from digital to analog is called modulation. The process of converting back is called demodulation. The device that performs that function is called a modulator/demodulator, or modem for short."

"That's all there is to it?"

"That's right, Pete."

"Last one, Professor. What exactly is this message-switching computer we're headed toward?"

"The best way to explain that term is through an example," replied Corbin. "We're on our way to the Washington, D.C., message center. Hundreds of local lines flow through it. Other lines link Washington to dozens of other major cities. When our message arrives on a local line, the computer will scan our message characters, determine our destination, and switch us to the right high-speed, long-distance line. At the other end of that line, another message-switching computer will accept the message and switch it to a local line so it can go to its ultimate destination—in our case, NECEN. That's essentially all a message-switching computer does: it routes messages."

A buzzer sounded; data fetch had begun. In the control module, Sylvia once again became as one with her controls. In the next bubble, Ned sat anticipating the ship's every move, his left index finger marking *Gossamer*'s current position on a circuit diagram, his right index finger tracing the next stages of the journey through the system.

Abruptly *Gossamer* accelerated toward the wide avenue that bisected the chip. Reaching it, the bits executed a sharp right turn and moved on in parallel. The avenue led to a set of fine wires, each of which led to a tiny pin. Quickly the ship dropped into the darkness beneath the board's surface, its bubbles emerging, instants later, in identical silver ponds. Now the bits passed through identical silver canals, sailed across identical golden lakes, and joined a bus line. The bus led to a communication interface board. *Gossamer* stopped.

"Where are we?" asked Susie.

"We're in a buffer," replied Ada. The sudden movement had broken her concentration, and, at least for the moment, she had set her program logic aside.

"What's a buffer?"

"Temporary storage. We're about to move from the computer to the communication line, so we're on hold for a while."

"Why?"

"The computer is much faster than the telephone line, Susie," answered Ada, "and the buffer helps to bridge the gap. The computer dumps us into temporary storage at a few million bits per second. Later, when it's ready, the line reads us from the buffer at a few *thousand* bits per second. Because we move either at computer speed or at line speed, we don't have to worry about accelerating or slowing down, and that's a lot easier for the equipment to deal with."

"How long will we be here?" asked Susie.

"Not long," replied Ada. "Right now, we're waiting for our computer to exchange signals with a message-switching computer. As soon as the link is established, we'll go."

As he waited, Corbin pictured an electronic signal called a token, moving silently from the message-switching computer, across a communication line, and into a microcomputer. Now the token rejoined the line and flowed to the next microcomputer. Eventually, he knew it would reach the SMF microcomputer's communication board.

The SMF micro shared the line with perhaps a dozen other computers. Passing the token was part of the protocol. If two or more machines tried to use the line at the same time, their messages would interfere with each other, so only the computer holding the token could transmit. Soon it would be their turn. *Gossamer* surged ahead.

"See," said Ada, "I told you."

Like a column of soldiers, *Gossamer*'s bubbles left the communication interface and entered a cable. Remembering Susie's description, Ada tried to picture herself flashing through space at the speed of light, but a loud hum shattered her fantasy. The ship had entered the modem.

Steadily, the hum's intensity increased. Soon it became almost unbearable. Concerned for his granddaughter, Corbin strained against his shoulder harness. He saw her sitting there, two bubbles away, her hands pressed tightly against her ears, a look of pain on her face. He tried to call out to her, to tell her everything would be fine, but the hum drowned out his voice. He had to reach her. He removed his seat belt and stepped into the aisle.

Suddenly, the floor seemed to drop from beneath his feet. Now it rose to meet him. He felt like a kid on his first roller coaster ride, with no bar to hold onto. *Gossamer*, he knew, had joined the analog wave, but his mind refused to discount what his senses reported. He felt out of control, out of phase. Nothing seemed right. His mind spun, the ship moved at an impossible angle. He had to make it stop! He felt himself falling.

The floor whipped up and down, like a small boat caught in a thunderstorm. His legs turned to jelly. He began to panic. Desperately he searched for something to hold onto. Finally he grabbed a table leg. He stared at his feet. For an instant, they appeared far above his head. He grasped the table tightly to keep from slipping backwards. Now his feet dropped below him; he pitched forward. His sense of up and down disappeared. He closed his eyes, fighting nausea.

He heard Susie—"Gramps!" she called. No, that wasn't her voice. He sensed her thoughts! Pete's too. And Ada's. In some way, they all shared his terror. Perhaps this continuous wave they all rode linked them in some mysterious way. Fascinated by this new phenomenon, Corbin relaxed his grip. He felt himself drifting, falling free. An intense pain exploded in his side. Then everything went blank.

12 *The Satellite*

Slowly, Corbin regained consciousness, his mind a jumble. Had there been an accident? His head ached. He struggled to get up, but a powerful weight pinned him down. He had to get up!

"Take it easy, Professor." The calm, soothing voice penetrated his rising panic. He opened his eyes and saw Pete. "Calm down," Pete said. "Take it easy. You're okay. It's all over."

Corbin forced himself to relax. He was, he realized, safely on board *Gossamer*, inside a computer. *Safely?* He shook his head. "I'm okay," he whispered. With Pete's help, he sat up and looked around. "What happened?" he asked.

"You blacked out," replied Pete. "I found you on the floor."

"Where are we?"

"Inside the message-switching computer."

"Are we still in Washington?"

"Yes. We're waiting to leave for New York."

"I don't know what hit me. I remember being concerned about Susie. I guess I took off my seat belt and stepped into the aisle. After that, everything went crazy."

"I saw you. In fact, I felt like I was inside your head." Pete wore a puzzled expression. "What an eerie feeling. To tell you the truth, Professor, I don't care if I ever ride an analog line again. Are you hurt? When *you* fell, *I* felt something pop."

"I don't think so." Corbin's side throbbed but he wasn't about to tell anyone. "Where is Susie?"

"I'm right here, Gramps," she replied, stepping around Pete. "You scared me. I didn't know what happened to you."

"I scared myself, too. Guess I'll have to remember to stay in my seat next time. Are we missing the meeting?"

"There is no meeting," said Pete. "We don't know exactly when this computer is going to decide to move us." He relaxed his grip. "Let me give you a hand."

"That won't be necessary," protested Corbin as he slowly struggled to his feet. "You don't want to be in here when we start moving, Pete. You really should get back to your station. You too, Susie." Painfully, he pulled himself into his flight chair. He reached across his body to fasten his seat belt, and the pain intensified. It felt like a broken rib. He must have hit the chair when he fell. He'd just have to tolerate it. He found a comfortable position and lay still.

"Gramps," called Susie from her own bubble.

"Yes, honey," he replied.

"What happened on the telephone line? It felt strange. I knew what you were thinking, Gramps."

"I sensed your thoughts, too. In fact, I shared everybody's thoughts." For a moment, Corbin turned reflective. "Maybe, because we were all part of the same wave, we weren't discrete and separate anymore," he mused. "We were joined in some strange way. SMF will have to investigate that phenomenon." Suddenly he snapped out of his mood. "Anyway, it's a good thing you stayed in your seat, Susie."

"Yes," agreed Pete. "It's a good thing we all did. And that analog phenomenon will be investigated." His voice suddenly grew louder. "SMF will want a full report, so please record your observations at your earliest convenience," he announced to everyone. His voice dropped back to a conversational level. "Tell me, Professor," he said, "are all telephone lines analog?"

"No, Pete." Corbin hesitated. His side throbbed. He shifted to a new position and then continued. "Early telephone technology wasn't sophisticated enough to transmit digital signals, so the first communication networks used analog. Today, most new lines are digital. They're much more efficient. In fact, the local networks are about the only place where analog data transmission is still used."

"If digital is so much more efficient, why haven't all the local analog networks been replaced?"

"Economics," replied Corbin. "The telephone company has billions of dollars invested in the old equipment, and ripping it out would cost more than it would save. Besides, the old stuff still works pretty well."

"Interesting, Professor," said Pete. "It's good to know that technology doesn't drive everything. There's still room for good, old-fashioned money. What about the network we're about to join, though? Is it digital or analog?"

"It's digital, Pete," answered Corbin. "It's a packet-switching network."

Pete breathed an exaggerated sigh of relief. Then he grinned. "I suppose you're going to explain packet-switching now," he surmised.

In spite of the pain, Corbin chuckled. "I'd hate to disappoint you, my friend," he joked. "Packet-switching is a high-speed data communication technique. The best way to explain it is through an analogy. Imagine a convoy of seven or eight cars headed for the office picnic via the freeway. Given traffic conditions, there's no way all the cars can stay together, so the drivers agree to split up and reassemble later. There's a break in traffic, so the first car joins the flow. A little later, the second car moves out. Eventually, all the cars are on the freeway, widely separated but headed in the same direction. When they reach their exit, they all get off, reassemble the caravan, and continue toward their destination.

"A packet-switching line is like a freeway. A message is like the caravan; pieces of the message, called packets, are like the cars. When a message enters a message-switching computer, it is broken into packets. Under computer control, the packets are placed on the line wherever they fit. Later, at the other end of the line, the message is reassembled by another computer and sent on its way."

"You mean . . ."

"Our message characters are moving," interrupted Sylvia. "We're in the second packet, so make sure your seat belts are fastened. Ned tells me the next phase will take us into outer space, so put on your oxygen masks. New York, here we come!"

This time, *Gossamer*'s acceleration hit Corbin like a fist. Intense pain washed over his entire body. He felt lightheaded and nauseous. He pressed his left arm tightly against his side, easing the pain a bit.

"Are you okay, Professor?" called Pete, concern in his voice.

"Just bumped my side," answered Corbin through clenched teeth. "I'll be fine." His words were intended to convince himself as much as Pete. With a deep sigh, he settled back, slipped on his oxygen mask, and tried to relax.

From the message-switching computer's main memory, *Gossamer* followed a bus line to a communication interface board, entered a cable, and then, instants later, emerged. Brilliant light surrounded the ship. Corbin rubbed his eyes, blinking them again and again. Everything was blue. Then he looked down.

Directly below him lay a gigantic, weblike structure. From a rounded point in the center, eight spokes fanned outward. A series of concentric circles linked them. An antenna! He watched the antenna grow smaller and smaller. Now a building appeared. Soon, all of Washington lay spread out beneath him. Mentally he drew a line from the Capitol, through the Washington Monument, to the Lincoln Memorial, and used it to orient himself. *Gossamer* climbed to the southeast. The satellite's orbit lay to the southeast; the ship followed the correct path.

As *Gossamer* climbed, the city faded into the surrounding countryside. Soon the entire Chesapeake Bay could be seen, its numerous tiny inlets penetrating the surrounding land. There, to the north, the Susquehanna River emptied into the bay. Directly below, the Potomac glinted in the morning sun. Still *Gossamer* climbed. Now the Delaware Bay came into view. Between it and the Chesapeake, the Delmarva peninsula jutted into the sea.

Gradually, as the East Coast receded, Corbin's field of vision expanded. He could make out the distinctive shape of Long Island, and there, to the south, lay Cape Hatteras. Soon he could see the entire coast. At this height details grew fuzzy, but Florida stood out clearly. The ship drifted southward. The communication satellite, he knew, orbited directly over the equator.

Gossamer's bits moved in series now, with Sylvia's control module at the end. Corbin's gaze settled on their pilot. In spite of the awesome spectacle surrounding the ship, her attention never wandered from her controls. Watching her work, oblivious to all distractions, he remembered why he had suggested her to General Custer: she was the best. Just knowing that Sylvia controlled *Gossamer* helped him to relax.

Next he focused on Ned. Like Sylvia, he, too, seemed to ignore his surroundings. Hunched over a drawing, he continually monitored *Gossamer's* position, occasionally calling out its coordinates. Apparently, the opportunity to translate a physical reality into abstract marks on a sheet of paper fascinated him, as he rarely looked up from his schematic diagram. Ned may be strange, thought Corbin, but he's a pro too.

Ada and Susie occupied the next bubble. Through *Gossamer's* transparent walls, they seemed to float in space. Susie's chair faced the control module, looking backward. She sat motionless, her attention fixed on the earth far below. Corbin tried to imagine what must be going through her mind. He longed to be her age again. He missed the thrill of a young imagination.

Ada leaned back in her flight chair, a stack of program coding forms in her lap. Once again she reviewed her logic. In spite of the great beauty surrounding her, she stuck to the task at hand. Another professional, Corbin decided. All in all, this crew ranked with the very best he'd ever known.

Still *Gossamer* climbed. Clearly outlined, far below, lay much of North, Central, and South America. His gaze swung past Pete toward the lead bubble, number 7.

As *Gossamer* approached the limits of the earth's atmosphere, the brilliant blue of the summer sky faded gradually to black. Then, suddenly, directly ahead, the satellite appeared. At first it seemed just a bright spot in the sky, but quickly it grew into a gigantic balloon floating against the blackness of space. Still *Gossamer* went on, until the satellite dominated the field of vision. Then the ship plunged inside.

Like a spider web trapping an insect, the satellite's outer skin captured the ship. Wires led from the skin to a small computer at the satellite's exact center. *Gossamer* followed one and soon rested in main memory. Once the computer determined the ship's destination, *Gossamer* would be on its way back to earth.

"Professor," called Pete. "The air pressure seems to be holding. I think we can take off our masks. Pass the word. Masks go back on as soon as we start moving, though."

"No need to pass the word, Professor," answered Sylvia from her control module. "I heard Pete loud and clear."

Corbin relaxed. While his side still ached, the pain seemed less intense here in the weightlessness of outer space; as long as he remained relatively motionless, he could bear it. He decided to remove his mask. That felt good. He had always hated those things; they never fit quite right.

He heard Susie and Ada talking, and settled back to listen, pleased that they had become friends. "Why do we need communication satellites, Ada?" asked his granddaughter.

"As long as we can run a wire between a message's source and destination, we don't," replied Ada, "but sometimes, it's more convenient to bounce the message off a satellite."

"How do the messages get up here?"

"We use microwaves. The sending station points an antenna at the satellite and transmits the signals. The satellite accepts them, checks their message characters, determines their destination, and sends them back to the receiving station's antenna."

"Why can't we just send a signal from Washington to New York? Why do we have to come all the way up here and then go all the way back down?"

"That's a good question, Susie. These microwaves we're talking about can only travel in a straight line. The earth is round—it curves.

Because the earth curves, a radio signal aimed from Washington toward New York would go right over the top of the city and disappear into space. Unless, of course, we had an antenna tall enough to catch it."

"As tall as the Empire State Building?"

"Oh, much taller than that. Actually, we might be able to transmit from one tall building in Washington to another one in Baltimore, but that's about the limit. That's where the satellite comes into play. It's visible from almost anywhere in our hemisphere. If we aim a message from Washington to the satellite, we can bounce it to New York, or almost anywhere else in the country. The earth's curvature isn't a problem anymore."

"What if I wanted to send a message to Japan? That's over on the other side of the earth."

"You're right. We couldn't transmit directly from this satellite to Japan. But we could transmit from here to another satellite, and go from there to Japan."

"I see," said Susie.

"Replace your masks," ordered Sylvia, ending the conversation. "We're next in line."

Abruptly, *Gossamer* moved from memory, crossed the satellite, and leaped into outer space. The earth lay spread out far below. There, like a gigantic, deep blue bowl, Corbin saw the Caribbean, and to the north, the Gulf of Mexico. He focused on the Florida peninsula and gently closed his eyes, dreaming of his winter home on Sanibel Island. When he opened them a few seconds later, the peninsula seemed much larger. *Gossamer* fell quickly. Much too quickly, it seemed.

Corbin swung his chair back toward the control module. Ada, Susie, and Ned seemed strangely immobile. Even Sylvia, their pilot, did nothing. Why, he thought, isn't she struggling with her controls? He knew *Gossamer* rode a beam, but somehow he couldn't convince his falling body to accept that logic.

There, again, lay the Chesapeake Bay, the Delaware Bay, and Long Island. Now the islands comprising New York City came into view—Manhattan, Staten Island, Long Island's western edge. A network of roadways appeared, then the buildings, then the automobiles and the boats crossing the waterways. Faster and faster they fell, the ground drawing ever closer! Corbin felt dizzy. *Gossamer* was going to crash! Sweating, he sank back into his chair, exhausted, his side throbbing.

13 *The Objective*

Still *Gossamer* dropped, plummeting toward lower Manhattan. Corbin sank deeper into his chair. The steady acceleration and gravity's increasing pull seemed to conspire against him. His side felt ready to explode. He'd never experienced such pain before. When would it end?

Again he stared down *Gossamer*'s corridor at the world outside. By now individual buildings could be identified. The ship's destination, the twin World Trade Towers, dominated his vision. He spotted a tiny, white dot on the rightmost tower's roof: an antenna. The smooth, white bowl grew larger and larger. He felt like a bullet approaching its target. Now a dark shadow loomed near the antenna's edge. The roof! Had the signal shifted off center? If *Gossamer* missed the bowl and slammed into the World Trade Towers . . .! The antenna's edge seemed perfectly centered in bubble 7. Safety lay a millimeter to the left, disaster a millimeter to the right. He closed his eyes, afraid to look.

Like an outfielder catching a fly ball, the antenna snagged the falling ship. Crossing the bowl, *Gossamer* entered the antenna's center. A cheer echoed through the corridor. Corbin opened his eyes. A microscopic universe surrounded him. He felt safe now. Relieved, he settled back into his chair and tried to relax.

"Boy!" said Susie. "That was great! Now I know how the astronauts feel."

"Really something, wasn't it?" agreed Ada.

"Yeah!"

"Were you scared, Susie?"

"I was," chuckled Pete. "My knuckles are white. What about you, Ada?"

"I had my eyes closed the whole time," she admitted with a laugh. "What an experience, though!"

By this time, *Gossamer* had left the cable, passed through a communication interface board, and entered a bus line. "Correct me if I'm wrong, Professor," called Pete, "but I assume we're headed for main memory again."

"That's right, Pete." Corbin tried to sound normal, but his words came in short bursts. "We're in New York."

"Where do we go from here?"

"NECEN."

"Do we have to cross another analog line?" Pete suspected something. He knew the answer to that one.

"No. Only old lines are analog." Corbin spoke through gritted teeth. He shifted to a more comfortable position; that seemed to help. "The line to NECEN is brand new," he continued, almost normally. "It's high-speed and digital."

"That's good," said Pete. "I did *not* enjoy my analog experience."

"Neither did I," said Corbin. "Neither did I."

Gossamer jumped from the bus. Joining eight parallel pins, its bits flowed to a memory board. Now the ship rested in the message-switching computer's main memory. "Stay in your seats," ordered Sylvia, before anyone could move. "We should be leaving shortly. Ned has our route, so listen up."

"I placed a diagram of the next phase in each bubble," started Ned. Corbin found his and opened it (Fig. 13.1). "Once we leave here, we enter a fiber optics line that leads to NECEN. The line ends in a transmission control unit." Corbin traced their path with a finger. "We'll enter the control unit through a port and sit in a buffer for a while; we'll check NECEN's circuit diagrams while we're there. Eventually we'll be polled. Then we'll move through the control unit and a channel to main memory."

"The data fetch signal just arrived," announced Sylvia. "See you all in NECEN."

The by now familiar path led from memory, over a bus, to a communication interface. Then, without warning, *Gossamer* plunged into the fiber optics cable. Brilliant laser pulses flashed back and forth, an endless stream of multicolored lights illuminating a perfectly round tunnel. Beautiful! Ordinary laser light shows paled in comparison.

"Gramps," called Susie.

"Yes, honey," he replied, somewhat reluctantly. It hurt to talk, but

FIGURE 13.1 The path to NECEN led over a digital communication line and through a transmission control unit and a channel.

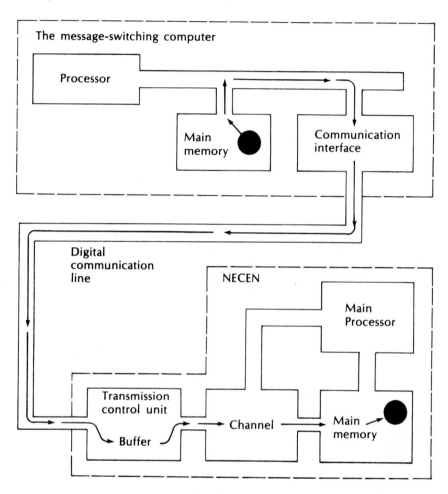

he did feel better. The pain seemed to come and go.

"This doesn't look anything like the cable we went through before. What are all these lights?"

"They're laser pulses. This is a fiber optics line. It uses light to transmit data."

Corbin waited for Susie's next question, but it never came. He turned his attention to a detailed diagram of the transmission control unit (Fig. 13.2). A series of ports lined one side. A single communication line entered through each port. Some of those lines, Corbin knew, transmitted analog signals; their messages would pass through a modem before entering a buffer. *Gossamer* traveled over a digital packet-switching line and thus would pass through a message assembly chip before entering its buffer. Once in the buffer, the message would be eligible for input to NECEN.

As *Gossamer* plunged back into more normal electronic circuitry, the light show disappeared. Then the ship stopped. "We're in the buffer," announced Ned. "We won't be polled for a second or two; that should give us time to go over the circuit diagrams."

"Good idea," agreed Pete. "Let's assemble in bubble 3."

Quickly the crew sprang to life. Entering the meeting room first, Ada dropped the folding table into place. Ned came next, a diagram under his arm (Fig. 13.3). He spread it over the table and waited for the others to arrive.

"Ned," said Pete, informally calling the meeting to order, "tell us where we are and where we're going."

"Okay," agreed Ned. "We're right here." He pointed to the buffer inside a box marked transmission control unit (Fig. 13.3). "We're waiting for NECEN to poll us. Once it does, we'll pass through some additional circuits on the TCU . . ."

"TCU?" interrupted Pete.

"Transmission control unit," snapped Ned. The fact that Pete's knowledge of almost any subject other than computers far exceeded his own mattered not a bit to Ned. Only computers, *his* chosen field, counted. Nonetheless, Pete held his temper.

"The TCU is linked to a data channel," continued Ned, tracing their path through the system. "In the channel we may encounter a slight delay of unpredictable duration; don't get up. Finally, we'll move from the channel into main memory. We'll review the next stage once we get there."

"Any questions?" asked Pete.

"Yes," said Corbin from his flight chair. He hadn't attempted to join the meeting. "You mentioned some additional circuits on the transmission control unit. What are they?"

"Nothing unusual, Professor," answered Ned. "We'll be polled. Then our parity will be checked. Finally, we'll switch back from serial to parallel. I think that's all."

"Other questions?" asked Pete. There were none. "Okay, let's get back to our stations. Next stop, main memory. Ada, we'll expect a software briefing once we get there."

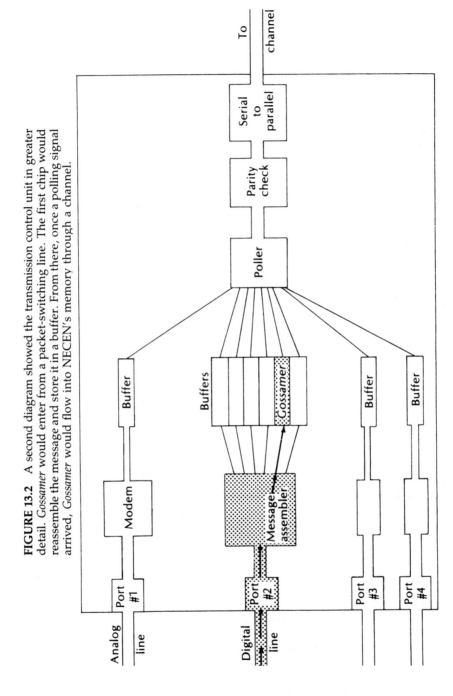

FIGURE 13.2 A second diagram showed the transmission control unit in greater detail. *Gossamer* would enter from a packet-switching line. The first chip would reassemble the message and store it in a buffer. From there, once a polling signal arrived, *Gossamer* would flow into NECEN's memory through a channel.

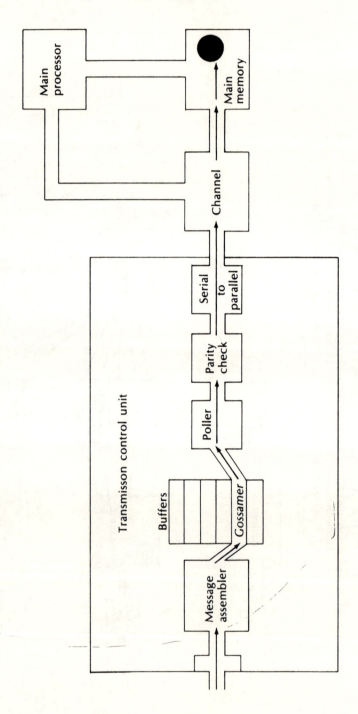

FIGURE 13.3   Once inside the transmission control unit, *Gossamer's* route ran through a polling chip, a parity checker, and a serial to parallel chip, before it passed through the channel and entered NECEN's main memory. However, just after leaving the parity checking chip, the ship took an unexpected detour.

"I'll be ready," she promised.

The meeting over, Pete walked slowly back toward his bubble, stopping near Corbin's chair. "Suppose you tell me what's wrong, Professor," he said, quietly. "You've been hurting since we left Washington."

Corbin settled back into his seat. He wanted to deny the pain, to tough it out, but the look in Pete's eyes stopped him. Pete knew; no sense lying about it. "It's my side," he whispered reluctantly. "I hit something when I fell."

"Let's have a look," said Pete. Slowly, gently, he unzipped Corbin's jumpsuit, revealing a bruised and discolored lower left side. Fortunately, the skin appeared unbroken. "Might be just a bruise, but I'm afraid you broke a rib. Looks like a clean break, though. Let me wrap it."

"Didn't know you were a doctor, Pete," joked Corbin through his pain.

"Our friend Ned may consider me a computer illiterate," replied Pete, "but I do know my first aid. At least I bring something to this mission." He reached under the work table, located the first aid kit, and removed an ace bandage. Gently, he eased Corbin's jumpsuit down over his shoulders and started wrapping. Beads of sweat formed on the professor's forehead as he tried to hold still. "That should help," said Pete, fastening the edge.

"It does feel a bit better," admitted Corbin. Gingerly, he pulled his jumpsuit back up and zipped it. Then, settling into his chair, he smiled. "Thanks."

"That's okay," said Pete. "Let me know if it still hurts." He stepped back into the aisle.

"I'm afraid I'm in no shape to fire the laser," said Corbin. "You'll have to take over that job."

Pete nodded, grimly. Perhaps he feared his lack of computer expertise would cause him to overlook a key target. "I'd better get back to my station," he muttered. Quickly he walked through the connecting tube and swung into his seat.

Corbin raised an arm and stretched, testing his side. A dull ache had replaced the searing pain; Pete had done his job well. Suddenly he noticed Susie standing in the passageway. "How long have you been there?" he asked.

"Just a few minutes," she replied. Silently, she crossed the bubble to her Grandfather's side, stooped, and kissed him on the cheek. "Are you okay?" she asked, looking directly into his eyes.

He nodded, touched by her show of concern. "I hurt my side when

I fell," he said, gently. "Pete took care of it, though. Thank you for asking. You better get back to your bubble now. That polling signal could come at any time, and we wouldn't want you injured, too."

"Okay, Gramps," she said, a tentative smile touching the corners of her mouth. She turned and walked away.

Quietly she slipped into her seat and glanced across the aisle at Ada. The coding forms were gone. "Are you still busy?" she asked.

"No," replied Ada. "Time for a break."

"Where are we?"

"We're in NECEN's transmission control unit."

"What's a transmission control unit? Is it anything like an interface?"

"Almost. On a big computer like NECEN, control units replace the interface boards."

"So we move from here to main memory."

"Not directly," answered Ada. "We have to pass through a channel first. But, basically, you're right. On the other computers, we moved from an interface board into main memory. On NECEN, we'll move from this control unit into main memory via a channel."

"Why is that, Professor?" asked Pete.

"What?" Finally able to relax, Corbin had begun to doze off, missing Ada and Susie's conversation.

"Small computers use an interface board to link peripherals to main memory. NECEN uses control units and a channel. Why?"

"Oh, I see what you're asking," said Corbin, slowly waking up. He felt much better. "Think about that interface for a minute. What exactly does it do?"

"Basically, it translates," replied Pete. "It takes data from inside the computer and puts them in a form an external device can accept. Coming the other way, it takes data from the peripheral and puts them in a form the computer can accept."

"Good. You've described a couple of functions. Focus on input. A scanner reads a bar code and sends it to an interface. The interface translates the bar code to the computer's internal form. A different interface accepts punched card codes and translates them into internal form. Exactly what the interface does depends on the external device."

"Okay, I understand that," said Pete. "Because each device is different, we need different interface boards for each one."

"That's right," replied Corbin. "Now remember, once the data have been converted to computer form, we have to move them from the interface to main memory. Exactly how that is done depends on the computer. In other words, some of the functions performed by an interface depend on the external device, and others depend on the computer.

"Now, on any given system, we may have dozens of different input/output devices, but only one computer. On input, each device sends its own, unique code to its interface, but once the codes are converted to internal form, the process of transferring them into main memory is identical. On output, the process of transferring data from main memory to an interface is the same no matter what the external device may be. Only after the data have reached the interface do the unique requirements of the peripheral device become important.

"On a big computer, the responsibility for transferring data between main memory and the peripheral devices is divided between two components, a channel and a control unit. Some functions depend on the computer; the channel takes care of them. It moves data from main memory to the control unit and from the control unit to main memory. Other functions depend on the external device; the control unit takes care of them. It routes the card reader's hole/no hole pattern through the circuits that convert them into internal binary form. It converts the scanner's bar codes into computer form. This particular transmission control unit takes care of the details of dealing with a communication line.

"Since the control units communicate with the external devices, and since the external devices are, potentially, all different, we need one control unit for each device, or at least one for each class of device. Since the channel communicates with the computer, and all communication with the computer must follow the same form, a single channel can link many control units."

"That makes sense," said Pete. "But why don't micros use channels, too?"

"Cost," answered Corbin. "Channels are expensive. In fact, they're small, special-purpose computers that cost at least as much as a typical microcomputer. Large mainframes like NECEN run dozens of concurrent applications, each of which may involve several different input and output devices. Controlling all those peripherals is a real problem, and the channel relieves the main processor of that responsibility. Channels improve a mainframe's efficiency. Most micros, on the other hand, are used by one person at a time."

"I see," interrupted Pete. "Channels help to efficiently control multiple peripheral devices. Because a microcomputer has so few, the benefit isn't worth the cost."

"Exactly," agreed Corbin.

"What's taking so long, Gramps?" called Susie, impatiently.

"I don't know," responded Corbin. "Ask Ned."

"We're waiting for the polling signal," replied Ned, his tone just a bit condescending. "Sometimes they take a while. It should come any second now. Nothing to worry about."

"So we wait," concluded Pete. "Tell me, Professor, what's a polling signal?"

"Let's go back to the basics, Pete. A computer works by executing instructions, one by one. To put it another way, nothing happens until an instruction is executed."

"Okay. I'm with you."

"Good. That includes input and output. Data are not sent out from memory until the processor executes an instruction telling it to output them. Data do not flow into memory until the processor, in response to an instruction, asks an input device for them.

"On simple devices like keyboards or screens, that's no problem. On a communication system, however, it is. For example, right now, we're just one of hundreds of messages moving through this transmission control unit. We're sitting in a buffer. Over there to our right is another message. To our left is yet another message. Other buffers hold other messages that came in through other ports.

"The next time NECEN decides to accept some input data from its transmission control unit, which message does it get? Polling answers that question. The system starts by checking the first buffer. If it's empty, the second one is polled. If the second buffer contains a message, NECEN accepts it. The next time the system needs some data, it starts with the third buffer. The polling signal moves from buffer to buffer, looking for the first one that contains data."

Suddenly, *Gossamer* lurched forward. "And, unless something totally unexpected has happened," said Corbin, "we've just been polled."

The inside of the transmission control unit, barely visible in the dim light that leaked through its ventilation slots, looked much like a microcomputer, with several boards plugged into a common framework. Even the chips seemed the same. As expected, the first one checked *Gossamer's* parity. Then, suddenly, the ship veered sharply to the left.

"Where are we headed, Ned?" called Corbin, anxiously. "I don't remember this path."

"Probably an error on the diagram," said Ned. "Once we reach the next chip, I'll correct it."

"I don't like surprises," argued Corbin. "I suggest we take off and identify the chip before we go through it."

"What's the point?" countered Ned.

"I believe in being cautious," replied Corbin. For some reason he couldn't explain, he feared that chip.

"I do, too," Pete interrupted. "Sylvia, take off."

"Roger!" she responded. Smoothly, the rotary blades kicked in. With a slight shudder, *Gossamer* pulled away from the circuit line, and rose above the surface. Corbin breathed a sigh of relief. Had they hesitated a moment longer, the ship would have plunged beneath the surface, making flight impossible.

From board level, the ceramic housing that contained the mystery chip looked like a black granite cliff, its sheer walls masking its contents. Finally, *Gossamer* reached the top and started across it. Character by character, Corbin read the chip's identification code: A7325. It couldn't be!

Suddenly, a violent wind caught *Gossamer*. Sylvia fought to regain control. The fragile craft creaked and groaned under the strain. Much more, and it might break apart. The ship drifted closer and closer to the board's edge. The board seemed to block or at least moderate the wind's force. What would happen if they lost its protection?

Wind inside a computer—it seemed impossible. Then Corbin remembered the fan. Of course. All electronic equipment generates heat, and that heat must be dissipated. A fan cooled the transmission control unit. On the board's surface, the surrounding chips had blocked the air flow, but, once it rose above the chips, *Gossamer* had no protection. How could he have overlooked something so obvious? He must be getting old. Why hadn't Ned said something? Later, he'd ask that question. At the moment, however, their lives rested in Sylvia's hands.

The wind had struck as *Gossamer* climbed above a chip. Thus Sylvia fought to escape its force by dropping below chip level. Slowly, under her firm control, the ship lost altitude. Now her concern focused on *Gossamer*'s tail. Steadily, it whipped back and forth, its arc gradually increasing. Calling on her years of experience, she struggled to dampen the swing, but, in spite of her efforts, the tail's arc gradually increased. Then, all at once, it turned too far, and the full force of the wind crashed against *Gossamer*'s side. The control module whipped violently toward the rear. *Gossamer* spun, hopelessly out of control, the board's edge looming closer and closer.

14 *The Belly of the Beast*

Slightly larger than the other bubbles, the control module caught an extra measure of the wind. Like a weather vane, *Gossamer* pivoted about its center. The ship shuddered, spinning out of control.

Wind inside a computer did seem impossible, but it didn't matter. Possible or not, the wind *did* blow, and unless Sylvia found a way to counter it, *Gossamer* would crash. Corbin grabbed his shoulder harness and held on. There was nothing else he could do. His life and the lives of the other crew members were in Sylvia's hands now.

The ship spun wildly, its tail lower than its head. The control module rose higher with each revolution. *Gossamer* seemed almost to dance on its tail. Suddenly, Sylvia cut the engines. The ship hung in the air, balanced precariously, tail down. Corbin held his breath. What was she doing?

For the moment, the wind blew upward through the rotor blades. Slowly, the blades began turning in reverse. Instead of lift, the rotating blades created drag. *Gossamer* dropped. Then, suddenly, the air calmed. Quickly Sylvia engaged the engines. Deftly she landed between two chips. They were safe!

"Report to the meeting room," boomed Pete. "Immediately!"

Where were they? As he unfastened his seat belt and stepped into the aisle, Corbin searched for an answer. The fan had blown *Gossamer* from right to left; thus the ship rested near the board's left edge. Mentally he pictured Ned's map of the control unit. Ahead and to the right lay the tabs that led to the channel's bus. Once *Gossamer* reached those tabs it could simply rejoin the data stream. There was no need to panic.

Slowly, gingerly, expecting another surge of pain, he took a step.

He felt fine. Pete's first aid had relieved the pressure. He staggered slightly, shaken by the near–crash landing. Then, regaining his composure, he walked confidently into the meeting room.

Never one to waste time, Pete had already started analyzing their problem. "We're here," he thundered. "But where exactly is 'here,' and how do we get out?"

"Flying over that chip was stupid," accused Ned. "We should have gone through it." He stared contemptuously at Corbin.

"Let's not waste our time fixing blame," said Pete. By his tone, however, he seemed to agree with Ned.

"There's nothing to worry about," said Corbin, quietly.

"You must know something we don't," snapped Ned, sarcastically.

"I doubt that," replied Corbin. "Think. We're inside a closed box. How do you get wind inside a closed box?"

"A fan!" suggested Ada.

"Exactly. Electronic equipment generates heat. If the heat isn't dissipated, it builds up and the equipment fails. This transmission control unit is fan cooled."

"You're right, Professor," agreed Ned. "The fan blows from right to left, directly across this board."

"Yes, I've studied the drawing. We're near the left edge. If we go straight ahead and to the right, we'll hit the tabs that link the board to the channel's bus. We can rejoin the data stream there."

"You're right again," admitted Ned, reluctantly.

"I may need some help finding it," said Sylvia.

"Think you can serve as copilot, Ned?" asked Pete.

"Yeah. Sure."

"Okay, that's settled. Now, tell us, Professor, why did you insist we bypass that chip?"

"Fair question, Pete," answered Corbin. "First, it didn't show up on Ned's map. The unknown can be dangerous."

"So can unscheduled flights," muttered Ned, darkly.

"As it turns out, the flight was far less dangerous than the circuit," countered Corbin. "We were about to enter a parity changer. We had five active bubbles, five 1-bits. That's okay for odd parity, but the chip would have tried to reset us to even. Bubble 7 would have been hit with a charge strong enough to turn it on. That could have crippled the ship."

"Are you suggesting that a simple electrical charge could disable *Gossamer?*" asked Pete.

"No question about it," volunteered Sylvia. "A strong charge would overload the ship's circuits. If that happened, we wouldn't be able to fly. And that's the minimum impact; the jolt could have killed us all."

"I think you're guessing, Professor," argued Ned. "You can't possibly know that chip would have changed our parity."

"Quite the contrary," replied Corbin. "I'm certain of it."

"How can you be so sure?" asked Pete.

"Just before the wind hit us, I managed to read the chip's code number: A7325. Ever seen one of them, Ned?"

"Yes I have," he admitted. "And you're right," he added apologetically, "an A7325 chip changes the parity bit."

"Exactly," said Corbin.

"But, why?" wondered Ada. "NECEN is an odd parity machine. We're an odd parity byte. It doesn't make sense."

"I can't be sure," responded Corbin, "but I think the Harlequin changed NECEN to even parity."

"Why would he do that?" asked Ada.

"NECEN's odd parity was a security feature," said Corbin. "Everybody assumes even parity. Internal bit patterns look unusual on an odd parity computer, and that confuses potential hackers."

"Come on," challenged Pete. "How could something so simple confuse a hacker? Switching the parity bit seems almost too obvious to work."

"Sure it's obvious," countered Corbin. "So obvious that an expert will likely overlook it." He gestured toward Ada. "You're a programmer. When's the last time you worried about the parity bit?"

"I can't remember ever worrying about it," she admitted.

"Exactly," said Corbin. "That's why changing the parity bit is such a useful security feature. Picture yourself as a hacker. You're trying to read the system's internal codes, but they all look wrong. You search for a sophisticated explanation—cryptography, maybe. When you don't find it, you conclude the security isn't worth breaking and move on to easier prey. Every little hurdle helps. We made NECEN an odd parity machine to confuse potential hackers. The Harlequin switched to even parity to confuse us. He used our own logic against us."

"If you're right, Professor," concluded Pete, "*Gossamer* must now become an even parity byte."

"That's right," agreed Corbin. "While we're inside NECEN, we need an even number of people. Fortunately, there are six of us." He gestured toward Susie. "She can stay here in bubble 3."

Ada draped an arm around Susie's shoulders. "See kid," she said with a wink. "I knew we'd need you before this trip ended. Glad you snuck on board."

Susie beamed. Finally, she felt part of the team—an important part.

"Let's get moving," said Pete. "Ned, you go forward with Sylvia and guide her back to the data stream. Susie, you stay right here. There's a jump seat that folds down from the wall. I'll help you set it up."

As he slid into his flight seat, Corbin thought about the near miss. Ned, their hardware expert, knew about the parity changer. He had to. Had he intentionally left it off his map? Was he the saboteur? He'd seemed unusually quiet during their discussion. Perhaps his reaction stemmed from embarrassment; Ned found it difficult to admit his mistakes. Besides, Corbin couldn't imagine him involved in a conspiracy with anyone.

"Glad you spotted that chip," said Pete, as he entered the bubble. He flashed Corbin a glance. He, too, it seemed, wondered about Ned. "How's your side? You looked like you had it under control out there."

"Much better," replied Corbin. "You missed your calling, Pete. You should have been a nurse. As long as I stay still or move slowly, it's just a dull ache. Sudden movements are something else, though. Don't ask me to do any calisthenics."

"Don't worry." Pete laughed. "We brought you along for your brain, not your body. How about the laser, though? Can you fire it?"

"I don't know, Pete. Maybe."

"I sure hope so, Professor."

Once again Sylvia's voice reminded everyone to fasten seat belts. Pete hurried back toward his own bubble. A moment later, the low whine of the rotor blades echoed through the ship.

Flying low, beneath the turbulence, *Gossamer* skimmed the board's surface. Ned spotted a circuit line and Sylvia followed it, detouring around the chips that lay across the path. Finally, in the distance, a row of golden tabs glinted in the dim light. Sylvia headed straight toward them. Aligning *Gossamer* with the eight low-order bits, she hovered, waiting. Soon, a telltale glow signaled an approaching message. Just as the bits flowed past, Sylvia landed. *Gossamer* had joined a new data stream. It wasn't their original message, but it would get them into NECEN.

Following another bus, *Gossamer* entered the channel and stopped in a buffer. The wait would be brief; no one moved.

"Professor," called Pete.

"Yes, Pete. What is it?"

"I've been thinking about channels. Earlier you said they cost as much as a decent small computer, but I can't understand why. They must do more than an interface board."

"Yes, they do," replied Corbin. "They're special-purpose computers. They relieve the main processor of the responsibility to directly control I/O."

"Could you be more specific, Professor?"

"Sure," replied Corbin. "Input and output are not automatic. There are several logical functions involved in controlling I/O. Imagine we have some data in computer form ready to move into main memory. The bytes are transferred one at a time, usually into contiguous storage locations. In other words, if the first one goes to memory location 2000, the second goes to 2001, the third to 2002, and so on."

"Right. I understand that."

"Fine. Now on most systems, input begins when the processor executes a read instruction. The instruction usually specifies the number of bytes to be input and the main memory address where the first one is to be placed. The programmer sees a single instruction. To the processor, however, input involves executing several microinstructions over and over again. The first byte is moved to the first memory address. Then the second byte is moved to the second memory address, and so on. This cycle continues until all the bytes are input.

"On a microcomputer, the responsibility for computing addresses and counting bytes rests with the main processor," continued Corbin. "How many instructions can a processor execute at one time?"

"One," answered Pete.

"Sure. If the processor must directly control I/O, then it's not available to perform any other task while data are being transferred. On a micro, that's no big deal. Waste a tenth of a second on a micro, and you waste the potential to execute a few thousand instructions. That's insignificant. A large mainframe computer, however, is much faster. Waste a tenth of a second on a mainframe, and you throw away the potential for executing a *million* or more instructions. That *is* significant. It's like the difference between keeping ten dollars or ten thousand dollars in a dresser drawer. The ten bucks we don't worry about. The ten thousand, however, could be earning a great deal of interest, so we make a point to get it into the bank.

"The fact that a mainframe supports multiple users creates another problem too. On the micro, if you have to wait a tenth of a second for data to be read from disk, so what. On a mainframe, however, there might be hundreds of users lined up to access the system. If the first one waits a tenth of a second, and the second one waits another tenth of a second, those delays begin to accumulate. If you're last in line, you could face a very long wait. That's unacceptable.

"That's where the channel comes into play. It's a computer. It has its own memory and, more importantly, its own processor. The main processor still starts input or output, but once it gets things going, it turns control over to the channel's processor. Now the channel takes over . . . Oops. Here we go again."

Gossamer left the buffer and started through the channel toward

NECEN's main memory. By now Corbin had grown accustomed to the ship's almost instant acceleration, and with Pete's bandage supporting his ribs he felt only a small twinge of pain. Perhaps he could fire the laser after all. Time would be short, and Pete might have trouble identifying an appropriate target.

"You were about to tell me what happens when a channel assumes control," Pete reminded him.

"Sorry, Pete," apologized Corbin. "I was thinking about something else. Let's see, where was I." He scratched his head. "Oh yes. The channel takes over. Its processor counts bytes, computes addresses, and copies the data, byte by byte, into main memory. The important thing, though, is that the channel's processor is independent. It works in parallel with the computer's main processor. Consequently, while the channel transfers data, the main processor can turn its attention to some other task. Two different applications receive simultaneous support from the system."

"But didn't you say a computer could execute only one instruction at a time?"

"Yes I did. Let me be more specific, though. Each processor is limited to executing one instruction at a time. With a channel, however, we have *two* processors, the channel's and the computer's. The processors are independent; each one can execute instructions without regard for what the other one is doing. Together, they can execute two *different* instructions simultaneously."

"That makes sense: two processors, two instructions."

"Right," said Corbin. "While the channel worries about controlling input or output, the main processor turns its attention to some other application. We don't waste the main processor's time, and we don't make everybody wait in line while all those slow input and output operations take place."

"I'm beginning to understand why you find computers so fascinating," said Pete. "Thanks."

Corbin's attention drifted to the sights outside *Gossamer*. By now the ship had crossed the channel and entered NECEN itself. NECEN. The most powerful computer ever built. He remembered the 16-bit bus lines inside the microcomputer. NECEN manipulated 64-bit words; thus the ship flowed through an almost unbelievably wide 64-bit bus. Compared to NECEN's bus, the microcomputer's 16-bit lines were like shallow mountain streams running into the Mississippi. The mainframe's tremendous speed and power inspired awe.

Moving along the bus, *Gossamer* glided past memory board after memory board. NECEN contained space for millions of bytes. Finally, the ship left the bus, entered a board, and, selecting a chip near the board's edge, settled into main memory. The crew cheered; their biggest hurdle lay behind them. Nothing could stop them now. It was time to regroup and plan their final attack.

"You okay?" asked Pete as he walked by, laying a hand on Corbin's shoulder.

"Couldn't be better," said Corbin, swinging from his chair. He stepped briskly into the aisle.

"Don't push it, my friend." Pete's concern showed in his eyes. "Believe me, before this mission ends, we are going to need you." He stood still for a moment, blocking the passageway. Together he and Corbin watched the rest of the crew file into the meeting room. For some reason, Sylvia still sat at her console. Finally, she swung her chair around, stepped out, and hurriedly crossed her bubble. Then, suddenly, without warning, *Gossamer* lurched forward. Horrified, they saw her lose her balance and fall, head first, from her elevated platform. She hit the floor *much* too hard. She tried to rise, then collapsed.

"Back to your stations!" ordered Pete as he ran toward his flight seat. "Right now! Ned, make sure Sylvia is completely inside her bubble, then get back into yours. Move!" Reacting quickly, Ada and Ned sprinted toward their stations; no one wanted to be caught in a corridor when *Gossamer* reentered the bus line.

Ned stared down at Sylvia. She lay just inside her bubble, her arm extending almost into his. With *Gossamer* already under way, he couldn't risk entering the passageway. Tentatively, he stretched his hand toward her. He felt resistance. "I can't reach her!" he cried. He pulled back his arm and staggered toward his flight seat.

Gossamer entered the bus line, its destination unknown.

15 *Spooled Out*

Painfully, Sylvia raised her head. She sensed danger. Outside, electronic components raced past. Her arm felt strange. It extended into the tube that linked her bubble with Ned's. A steady pressure seemed to drag her into the gap. She had to break free! She tugged, but the pressure only increased. Inch by inch, the tube seemed to swallow her, moving steadily up her arm. Barely conscious, she rolled away from the opening. Her arm popped free. Exhausted, she collapsed.

Back in bubble 5, Pete watched, unable to help. He saw her struggle, pull free, collapse. She needed him, but as long as *Gossamer* moved, he could do nothing. Frustrated, he slammed his fist against the arm of his chair.

By now the ship had left the bus and entered another circuit board. "Where are we, Professor?" Pete called, concern clearly evident in his voice.

"I think we're in a channel," replied Corbin. He looked toward Pete. For a moment, the scene of an earlier accident flashed through his mind. He pictured his wife, Marty, lying still. He recalled his feeling of utter helplessness. He hurt for his friend.

"We just entered this system. Are we being shipped back out already?"

"No. This isn't the same channel."

"You mean the computer has more than one?" Pete seemed surprised.

"That's right. NECEN has at least five," replied Corbin (Fig. 15.1). "One channel links several transmission control units. Two are for disk.

NECEN uses magnetic tape for backup, so another one serves the tape drives. The fifth channel is for local terminals, card readers, printers, and other slow I/O devices."

"Which one is this?" asked Pete.

"I think we're headed for disk."

"Why disk?"

"I'm just guessing, but I think the message we joined back inside the transmission control unit belonged to a batch stream. If I'm right, we've been spooled out."

"What exactly does that mean, Professor?"

"We're being set aside for future processing, Pete."

"Set aside! For how long?" Though it seemed impossible, Pete's concern had deepened.

"Hard to tell," answered Corbin. He looked at Pete; their eyes met. An unspoken message passed between them. The delay could prove quite lengthy. *Too* lengthy. Their lives were in jeopardy.

Without stopping, *Gossamer* flowed through the channel, crossed a bus, and entered a control unit. Smoothly, the ship followed a fine wire across the underside of a metal framework. Then it turned sharply to the right. A narrow metal rod led to an ultrathin, waferlike read/write head. Just below, a metallic brown landscape spun past. With a jolt, *Gossamer* dropped to the surface. The ship rested on disk.

"Think we can move around, Professor?" asked Pete, impatiently glancing toward Sylvia.

A disk, Corbin knew, spins at thousands of revolutions per minute. He pictured *Gossamer*, pulled by centrifugal force, sliding across the surface. He saw the fragile craft flung from the spinning disk, completely out of control. But he felt only a slight tug; *Gossamer* seemed stable. "Why not?" he said.

Pete leaped from his seat and raced to Sylvia's side. Dropping to one knee, he checked her pulse and her breathing. "Ned," he ordered. "Get the first aid kit and bring it in here. Ada, get some water and some towels." Gently, he touched Sylvia's head, probing for injury.

"How is she?" asked Ada.

"She's breathing," answered Pete. "Pulse seems normal. She hit her head, though. We'll know in the next few minutes." Sylvia groaned and tried to sit up. "Take it easy," whispered Pete. Cradling her in his arms, he checked her eyes for evidence of a concussion. "How do you feel?" he asked. "Are you nauseous?"

Corbin stared through *Gossamer*'s side. Pete, he knew, would handle the medical emergency. Meanwhile, his job was to find a way out of this mess. Clearly, *Gossamer* had joined a batch stream; that seemed

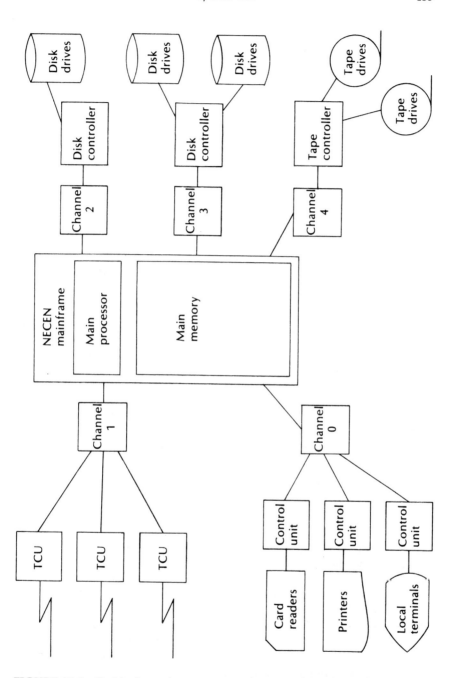

FIGURE 15.1 Corbin formed a mental image of the NECEN system. In it, he pictured the numerous channels and the wide variety of input, output, and secondary storage devices linked to the system.

the only reasonable explanation for what had happened. Batch applications run at regular intervals. Typically, data are collected over time
and held until the batch is scheduled for processing. When might that
be? Minutes from now? Hours? Days? Ada might know.

What about Ada? As their software expert, she should have warned
them about NECEN's batch applications. Why hadn't she? Could he
have been wrong about her? Could she be the saboteur?

He shook his head as if to clear it; he had to focus on the immediate
problem. Eventually, he knew, NECEN would read *Gossamer* back into
main memory, but eventually might not be soon enough. Perhaps, if
he carefully reviewed exactly how this disk drive worked, he might find
an escape route.

He stared at the surface. Mentally, he mapped it (Fig. 15.2). A disk
is a rigid platter that rotates constantly around a central drive shaft. Its
surface is divided into a series of concentric circles called tracks. The
tracks are subdivided into sectors, the basic units of physical storage.
Data move between main memory and the disk's surface a sector at a
time. *Gossamer* occupied one of those sectors.

Again he stared at the surface. In the distance, through a soft haze,
a spot of light glowed brightly. Gradually it faded, then, suddenly, it
winked out. Now it reappeared, dim at first, then, gradually, brighter.
The light, Corbin realized, streamed through an opening in the disk
drive's side. *Gossamer* sat on a rotating surface, first approaching the
light, and then moving away from it. Once each revolution, when the
ship drifted behind the central drive shaft, the light disappeared, only
to reappear an instant later.

He wondered about the haze that seemed to softly filter the light.
What caused it? He sensed a pattern to that haze. To his left loomed a
large arc, to his right a slightly smaller one. Two short, straight lines
connected the arcs. The haze, Corbin realized, outlined the sector. Track
and sector boundaries were visible. He hadn't expected that. It might
prove useful.

Suddenly, unexpectedly, the light flickered. A mass moved overhead: the access mechanism. Analogous to the tone arm on a record
turntable, it carried the disk's magnetic read/write head. He visualized
the process of reading data (Fig. 15.3). First, the disk controller positioned the access mechanism over the track containing the desired sector.
Next, the read/write head hovered, waiting for the sector to rotate to
it. Finally, the head copied the sector's contents from the surface, the
data flowing through the access mechanism, the disk controller, and the
channel, into main memory. It seemed simple enough. *Gossamer* merely
had to reach the read/write head.

FIGURE 15.2 A disk is a rigid platter that rotates constantly. Its surface is divided into a series of concentric circles called tracks, and the tracks are subdivided into sectors. Data are stored in the sectors. They move between main memory and the disk surface a sector at a time.

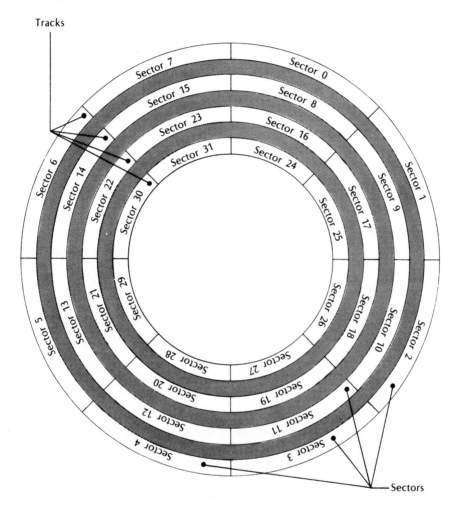

The head, Corbin knew, rode on a cushion of air, mere millionths of an inch above the disk's surface (Fig. 15.4)—tantalizingly close. Compared to that gap, a tiny smoke particle looked like a boulder. There were complications, however; those millionths of an inch might just as well have been miles. A moving target, the access mechanism stepped

FIGURE 15.3 Accessing disk is a two-step operation:
a. The access mechanism is moved to a position directly over the track containing the sector to be read or written.

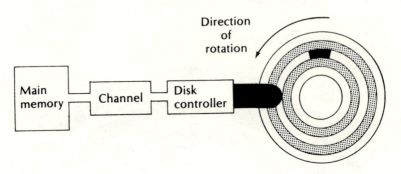

b. When the desired sector rotates beneath the read/write head, the data are transferred.

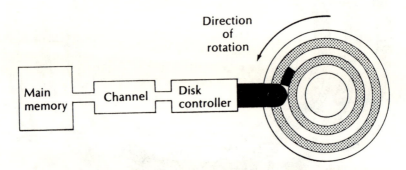

rapidly from track to track, hovering only long enough to read or write a sector. The surface on which *Gossamer* rested also moved, rotating constantly. A powerful fan blew filtered air across the disk surface. Wind and air movement would be a problem, especially around the access mechanism itself, where swirls and eddies could prove tricky.

That wasn't all. To join the data stream, Sylvia would have to position *Gossamer* over exactly the right track at the precise instant when the disk controller activated the read/write head. Since the control unit moved the access mechanism only in response to a signal from the main processor, she could not predict exactly when it would move, or on which of the four hundred tracks it would stop.

And even if she could, that might not be enough. *Gossamer* rested

FIGURE 15.4 A disk's access mechanism rides on a cushion of air a few millionth's of an inch above the surface. With such tight clearances, such pollutants as a smoke particle, dust, or a human hair could destroy both the disk surface and the access mechanism.

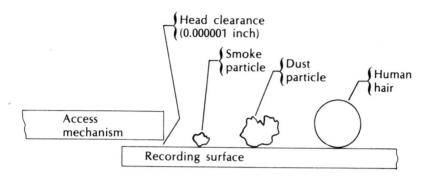

on a disk pack (Fig. 15.5) consisting of eleven disks stacked on a central drive shaft. Data were recorded on the top and bottom surfaces of each disk, yielding twenty recording surfaces (because of the risk of contamination, the pack's top and bottom surfaces weren't used). The read/write heads for all twenty surfaces shared a single, comblike access mechanism; they moved together. Even if Sylvia were to select the correct track, and arrive at precisely the right time, the odds were only one in twenty that the disk controller would turn on this track's read/write head. The situation seemed hopeless.

Of course Sylvia's injury complicated matters even more. Lost in thought, Corbin had almost forgotten about her. How was she? Again he turned to the control module where Pete continued to work on their pilot. Sylvia sat upright now; she seemed much better. Apparently the crew would soon assemble in bubble 3; Ada and Susie already waited there. He listened as they talked.

"We're on a disk, right?" asked Susie.

"That's right," answered Ada. "We're on secondary storage."

"Why do computers need secondary storage?"

"It's an extension of main memory, Susie. Normally, main memory holds only the programs actually being executed and the data actually being processed. Secondary storage holds the rest."

"Why don't we just use more main memory?" Corbin smiled, pleased with his granddaughter's question. Too many people simply accepted computers. She didn't. She wanted to *understand* them.

"One reason," replied Ada, "is that main memory is volatile; when

FIGURE 15.5 The disk surface on which *Gossamer* rested was one of twenty on the disk pack. A single, comblike access mechanism held all twenty read/write heads. Once the access mechanism was positioned over a given track, any one of the twenty heads could be turned on by the disk control unit.

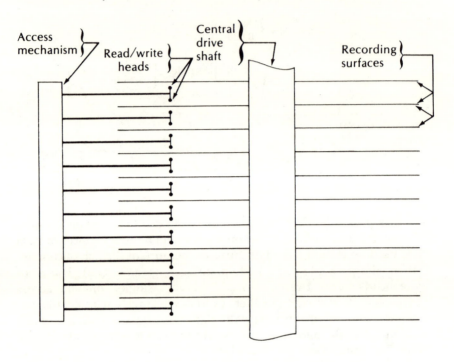

the power is cut, its contents are lost. Disk is nonvolatile; data or programs stored on disk stay there almost forever, no matter what happens to the power. Disk is permanent; main memory is temporary.

"Another reason," she continued, "is cost. Main memory is a lot more expensive than disk. It makes sense to store inactive programs and data on the cheaper device. That's the big reason."

"On my computer, I'm only allowed to have 512K. Why is that?"

"A computer's architecture usually limits its memory capacity, Susie." Ada paused briefly. Was she being too technical? "Do you know what an address is?" she asked.

"Sure. Each byte has a number."

"That's right. When the processor asks main memory for data, it requests the data by address. For example, say we occupy byte 1000. If the processor wants us, it has to ask memory for the contents of byte 1000. That means the address, 1000, has to get from the processor to main memory, right?"

"Sure."

"And the only way anything flows from the processor to main memory is over a bus line."

"The bus links the computer's internal components, right?" asked Susie.

"Exactly," said Ada, impressed. Susie knew more than she thought. "The address is just a number, just a string of bits. Each bit takes up one of the bus line's wires. Let's say the bus contains sixteen wires. That means we can send a 16-bit number over it. The biggest possible 16-bit number is, in decimal terms, roughly 32,000. Since the processor can't send addresses bigger than 32,000, it can't have more than 32,000 bytes of memory.

"Real addressing schemes are more complex, of course, but the idea still holds. A processor can address only so much main memory, so a computer can *have* only so much main memory. If we want to store data or programs that won't fit within that limit, we have to use secondary storage."

"Secondary storage is disk, isn't it?"

"Usually, but not always. Magnetic tape, video disk, and many other media are used, too."

"Is this disk anything like the diskettes on my computer at home?"

"Basically, yes. The idea is the same. The surface is divided into tracks, and the tracks are divided into sectors. An access mechanism moves from track to track and transfers data, sector by sector.

"There are a few differences, though. Unlike the hard disk we're on now, a diskette doesn't rotate constantly. Before data can be accessed, the drive must be brought up to operating speed, and that takes time. Relative to hard disk, diskette is pretty slow. Also, on diskette, the read/write mechanism actually rides on the surface; on hard disk, it floats on a cushion of air."

"Sylvia's coming around," interrupted Ned as he walked into the meeting room. "She and Pete will be here in a few minutes." Ned looked frightened. He understood their predicament. Trapped on disk, *Gossamer* could not escape until the processor asked for their sector, and that request might not come for hours. In real time, the crew had provisions for perhaps half an hour. Marooned on a spinning disk, there was a real danger that they might never get back.

"Any idea why NECEN put us here, Ada?" asked Corbin as he entered from the other side. He watched her carefully, looking for her reaction.

"You told Pete we've been spooled out, Professor. I'm afraid you're right." If Ada was the saboteur, she had nerves of steel.

Slowly, supported by Pete, Sylvia limped into the room. Looking pale and weak, she staggered across the bubble and dropped into Susie's jump seat.

"How is she, Pete?" asked Corbin.

"I've been better," Sylvia admitted, before Pete could speak, "but it's nothing I can't live with. Hit my head. I'm dizzy, but it's clearing. Give me another fifteen minutes and I'll be fine."

"You said we'd been spooled out to disk, Professor," said Pete, getting right down to business. No matter how hopeless the situation, he would never give up. "What does that mean?"

"Spooling is a method for improving the efficiency of batch applications," started Corbin.

"Batch applications?"

"A common data processing technique, Pete. Data are collected and held in a batch. Later, usually at some scheduled time, a program processes all the transactions, often thousands of them, one after another. Payroll is a good example; everybody's paycheck is computed and printed once a week.

"All those input data create a problem. Relative to a computer's speed, most input devices are quite slow. If the computer had to wait for all those transactions to be read, the batch program would run for hours.

"Instead," Corbin continued, "long before the batch program is loaded into main memory, its data are read, transaction by transaction, and copied to disk. Because a computer isn't busy all the time, the data can be transferred during slack periods. Later, when the batch application runs, its data are already on high-speed disk, so the program is completed much more quickly. The process of copying data from a slow device to a high-speed device for eventual input is called spooling. Spooling makes the computer more efficient on batch applications.

"Our initial message would have stayed in memory long enough to allow us to carry out our plan. Unfortunately, back in the transmission control unit, we were blown off course and lost that message. Apparently, the transaction we did join belonged to the batch stream. As soon as we hit main memory, the spooling routine took control and sent us out here."

"Okay," said Pete. "That tells me why we're out on disk. Now, how do we get back into NECEN?"

"That could be a problem," said Ned. "Data move between secondary storage and main memory only at the request of the processor, and it won't ask for us until a program tells it to."

"That's only a matter of time," said Corbin. "Eventually, we'll be read by a batch program. How often do they run, Ada?"

"There are at least a dozen major batch applications on NECEN," answered Ada. "Data collection, long-range data analysis, accounting. Some run daily, some weekly, some monthly, some whenever a politician needs a report. None of them run on first shift, though."

"When does first shift end?" asked Pete.

"Five o'clock, I think," answered Ada.

"We don't have that much time," said Pete.

"Obviously," agreed Corbin.

It was approximately 9:00 A.M., real time. At best, the batch program that would read *Gossamer* into main memory would get control in about eight hours, and the delay could well be longer. Everyone remembered Corbin's words, uttered, it seemed, days ago: "If we're gone much over an hour, we might die of thirst." A sense of hopelessness settled over them. They were, it seemed, doomed.

16 *The Index*

"Often," said Pete, attempting to break through the gloom, "the first step in escaping an impossible situation is to study that situation in detail. All it takes is one little crack."

"You don't understand computers," countered Ned. "We're on disk. We're stuck here until the computer decides to get us, and we have no control over when that might happen. There is nothing we can do; it's hopeless. We might as well spend our time praying."

"I agree with Pete," said Corbin. "We might come up with something. Besides, what do we have to lose? Brooding sure isn't going to help. Ada, why don't you start. What exactly is going to happen when the computer decides to get us?"

"Reading a sector is a two-step operation," she replied, listlessly. "First, the processor tells the disk controller to position the access mechanism over a given track. Once the mechanism is positioned, the processor asks for the data stored in a particular sector. The disk controller accepts the read command, waits for the requested sector to rotate to the read/write head, and then transfers the data into main memory. That's about it."

"Can you be a bit more explicit?" asked Corbin. "For example, do you have any idea exactly where we are on the disk surface?"

"No," she replied. "It really doesn't matter, though. As far as the mechanics of disk access are concerned, one sector is pretty much like any other."

"Do you agree, Ned?" asked Corbin.

"Yeah, I guess so," Ned replied. "Except for the first few, of course."

"What's unusual about the first few sectors?"

"They contain the boot routine."

"What's a boot routine?" asked Pete.

"It's a small program that loads the operating system," answered Ned (Fig. 16.1). "When the operator first turns on a computer, there's no program in main memory. Computers can't do anything without a program, and that includes loading a program. It's a catch-22. Without a program, a computer can't load a program, so how does it get started?

"On most systems," Ned continued, "whenever the computer is turned on, hardware automatically reads the system disk's first few sectors into main memory. They contain the boot routine. The boot, in turn, reads the rest of the operating system. With the operating system in memory, application programs can be loaded and given control.

"But we're wasting our time talking about the boot," he went on, sounding discouraged. "We're not on one of the first few sectors, and even if we were it wouldn't do us any good. The boot routine is needed only during startup. It won't be read again until after NECEN is shut down, and NECEN is *not* going to shut down. It's the most reliable

FIGURE 16.1   The boot routine is used to load the operating system into main memory.

a. As we begin, main memory is empty.

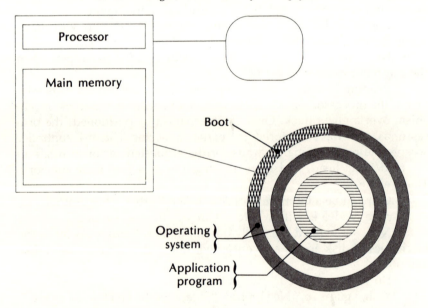

b. When the power is turned on, the boot is copied into main memory, and its instructions are executed.

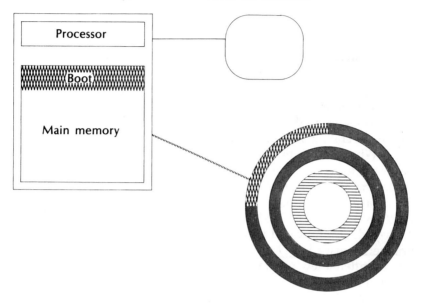

c. The boot reads the operating system into main memory.

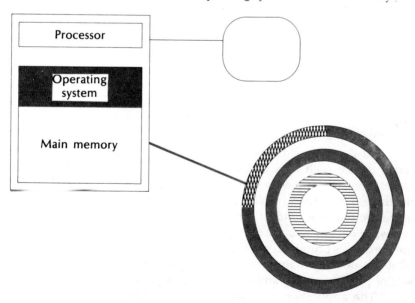

computer ever built, so a hardware failure is unlikely. The Harlequin isn't about to shut it down for us, and if the government people could do it, they wouldn't need us. Even if we were able to reach one of the first few sectors, we'd just sit there. We're better off here."

"Ned's right," agreed Corbin. "Let's try a different line of reasoning. Let's make an assumption: we're on track 50, sector 25. Exactly how does the system find us, Ada?"

She thought for a moment before replying. "The process starts with an application program," she said, finally, her tone demonstrating little confidence in this exercise. "It requests the data at track 50, sector 25. The operating system gets control, and . . ."

"When I write programs, I just say 'read'," interrupted Susie. "I never ask for track 50, sector 25. Before today, I never even knew what tracks and sectors were."

"Susie has a point," said Sylvia, quietly. Surprised to hear her voice, everyone turned to look at their pilot. Though still not quite fully recovered, she appeared much better. That was a good sign; the mood brightened just a bit. "I'm no computer expert," Sylvia continued, "but I *have* written a few programs, and I never requested data by track and sector either."

"Susie does have a point," admitted Ada, "but she's thinking about logical I/O. We have to focus on physical I/O."

"Why?" asked Corbin. Sometimes a technical expert can know a subject so well that he overlooks the obvious. Susie's question would never have occurred to him, or Ned, or Ada. She had opened a whole new line of reasoning. "Let's follow this idea a bit further. Explain what you mean by logical and physical I/O, Ada."

"Okay," she agreed. "I'm an application programmer. As far as I'm concerned, I want a particular record and I don't care how the system finds it. That's logical I/O. That's what Susie and Sylvia were talking about."

Susie nodded her agreement.

"At the other extreme," Ada continued, "is physical I/O. An external device such as a disk drive—more accurately, the drive's controller—can perform a limited number of functions. With disk, we can list three. First, the controller can seek—move the access mechanism to a specific track. Second, it can read a sector from that track. Finally, it can write data to a sector on that track. That's it. Those three functions are the drive's primitive operations: seek, read sector, write sector. That's all it can do. The main processor controls the disk drive by sending it sets of primitive commands—seek/read or seek/write.

"The application programmer doesn't have to worry about the

FIGURE 16.2 A programmer requests logical I/O: for example, "Get me the next record." An external device requires specific, primitive, physical commands, such as "Seek to track 50, read sector 25." The access method translates.

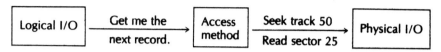

primitives. Instead, there's a special software module that accepts the programmer's logical request for the next record, and sets up the primitive commands that actually get it. On this computer, that software module is called an access method.

"Basically, the access method translates," she continued (Fig. 16.2). "The programmer issues a logical request: get me the next record. The access method converts the request to a specific location on disk: track 50, sector 25. Then it tells the operating system to get that sector, and the operating system issues the primitive commands. And I'm beginning to think this whole exercise is a waste of time."

The group fell silent again. It did seem hopeless. As any expert knows, the main processor controls everything that happens on a computer system. Until the processor encountered an instruction that told it to get their sector, *Gossamer* would remain trapped on the disk's surface. They could not change the bottom line. They might know everything there was to know about how disk worked, but escaping the surface depended on an event totally beyond their control.

"How does the access method know it needs track 50, sector 25?" asked Susie, unexpectedly. For a moment, everyone stared at her.

"Your grandfather made it up," snapped Ned.

"Now, wait a minute," cautioned Pete. "That question hadn't occurred to me, but come to think of it, I don't know the answer. Fill us in, Ada."

"The access method computes the location of the desired record relative to the beginning of the file," said Ada. "I really don't see the point . . ."

"I think we're onto something," interrupted Corbin, abruptly. Once again, little Susie, the crew's least expert member, had opened a new line of thought. "I don't know exactly how NECEN's access method works, but let me ask some questions. First, Ada, explain what you mean by relative to the beginning of the file."

"Okay," she agreed, and quickly drew a sketch (Fig. 16.3). "Assume we have a file containing several hundred records. Number each record: 0, 1, 2, 3, 4, 5, and so on. The first one is at the start of the file

FIGURE 16.3   Ada sketched the records in an imaginary file. She assigned each one a number that defined its position relative to the beginning of the file.

RELATIVE RECORD NUMBER	THE RECORD	PHYSICAL DISK ADDRESS Track	Sector
0	First	50	25
1	Second	50	26
2	Third	50	27
3	Fourth	50	28
4	Fifth	50	29
5	Sixth	50	30
6	Seventh	50	31
7	Eighth	50	32
8	Ninth	50	33
9	Tenth	50	34

plus 0 records; the second is at the start plus 1—those are relative record numbers."

"Fine," said Corbin. "Now, if the file actually starts at track 50, sector 25, its first record, relative record 0, is stored at track 50, sector 25, and its second record is at track 50, sector 26, right?"

"Usually," agreed Ada. "Actually, the records can be spread all over . . ."

"Let's ignore that complication for the moment," interrupted Corbin, gesturing for Ada to stop. "Assume we're dealing with a nice, clean file. To find any record, I just add its relative record number to the file's start address. For example, let's say I want relative record 4. The file starts at track 50, sector 25. Record 4 must be stored on track 50, sector 29, right?"

"That's right, Professor."

"So, given the disk address of the first sector, I can compute the location of any other sector, right?"

"That's right." Ada stared at her old professor, a quizzical look on her face. She grinned. He'd used this approach many times in class. He was leading her to a conclusion, but what was it? "What are you driving at?" she asked, finally.

"Bear with me a bit longer," he replied, with a wink. "Where does the address of the first sector come from?"

"I'm not sure what you mean."

"A typical disk pack contains hundreds of files, and each file contains hundreds, maybe even thousands of records. You want a record on a particular file. How does the system find the start address of your file?"

"I think I see where you're headed, Professor," said Ada. She spoke more rapidly now, her negative attitude gone. "Each disk contains an index listing, by name, every data file and every program stored on that disk. Among other things, the index shows the file's start address. Before the file can be accessed, it must be opened (Fig. 16.4). When the open module gets control, it reads the index, searches it for the file name,

FIGURE 16.4 Before any file can be accessed, it must be opened. The open module reads a disk's index to find the track and sector where the file begins. Given this starting point, the actual physical location of any record can be found by using its relative record number.

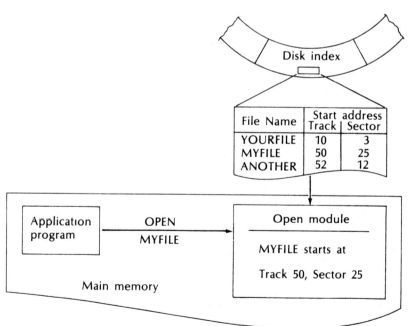

and gets the file's start address. Using relative record numbers, all the file's sectors can be found relative to that starting address."

"How does the operating system find the index?" asked Corbin.

"It's always in the same place," volunteered Ned. "Earlier I said that the first couple of sectors on the disk are set aside for the boot. On NECEN, it's the first three. The rest of track 0 holds the index. Data storage starts at track 1, sector 0." Ned drew a map of the disk surface (Fig. 16.5).

"In other words, the index starts at track 0, sector 3," Corbin added.

FIGURE 16.5 Ned sketched a map of the disk's surface. The first three sectors on track 0 hold the boot; the rest of track 0 holds the index. Data and programs are stored beginning with track 1, sector 0.

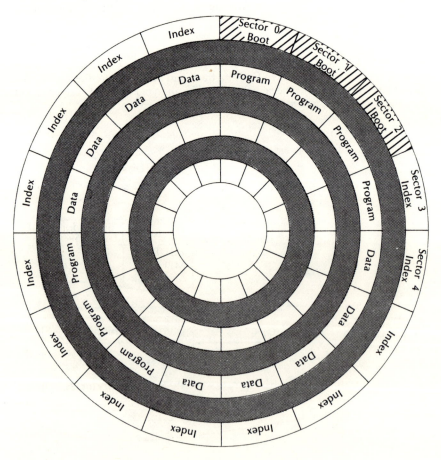

"That's right," agreed Ned. "It always starts there."

"Now, correct me if I'm wrong, Ada," continued Corbin, "but I'm assuming any time one of the hundreds of application programs serviced by NECEN wants to access data on this disk, it must first ask the operating system to open the file."

"That's right," said Ada.

"And opening a file implies reading the index."

"That's right," she agreed again.

"How often does that happen?" he asked.

"Every time a new file is accessed," she answered. "On a system as active as this one, probably every few seconds."

"So, if we could get to the disk's index, we could expect to be transferred into main memory within a few seconds, right?"

"Yes," agreed Ada. "Certainly no more than a minute. That's real time, of course."

"Right," said Corbin. "We'll probably sense a delay of an hour or so. But that's certainly better than what we face here."

"I agree," said Ned. "But how do you propose getting there?"

"We can fly," interjected Sylvia.

Once again, the crew fell silent. Of course, they could fly! More than just ordinary bits in a computer, they had a source of power. In a few short seconds, they'd be sitting in the index waiting for the operating system to read them. Once in memory, they'd immediately take off, find a safe landing place, and plan their next move. They still had a chance.

"Do you feel up to it, Sylvia?" asked Pete. Once again he checked her pulse. "You were out for quite some time. Flying across this surface could be rough." He tilted her head back and looked at her eyes. "Any sign of nausea?" he asked.

Mildly annoyed, Sylvia good-naturedly tolerated Pete's excessive concern. He finished his examination. She looked at him and smiled. "No, Pete," she said, finally, "I am *not* going to throw up. I've had concussions before; I do *not* have one now. Take my word for it—I feel fine. I can do it."

"Let's not forget the wind," said Corbin, with a chuckle. "It almost finished us last time."

"Yes," said Ned, seriously. "There's a fan in here, too. It blows air across the disk surface."

"We might be able to take advantage of the wind," suggested Sylvia. "Do you know its direction, Ned?"

"Not without a reference point," Ned replied.

"Take a look at that flashing light over there," said Corbin, pointing through *Gossamer*'s side. As the crew watched, the dim light winked out only to reappear a moment later. Gradually it grew brighter. "I noticed it when the rest of you were working on Sylvia." The light grew dimmer and, suddenly, winked out again. "We just passed behind the central drive shaft." The light reappeared. "Now, we're rotating back toward it." The light grew brighter again.

"That defines our direction of rotation," said Ned. "Now, if we can identify one reference point, I'll know where the fan is."

"Would the access mechanism do?" asked Corbin.

"Certainly," replied Ned.

"Once, while I was watching the light, just before *Gossamer* passed behind the drive shaft, the access mechanism blocked it."

Ned stood up and faced the light. It winked off. *Gossamer* had just passed behind the drive shaft. "That means the access mechanism is to my left," he concluded.

"I agree," said Corbin.

The light winked back on. "The light source is the fan," said Ned, confidently.

"Are you sure?" asked Pete.

"Of course!" Ned seemed surprised that anyone would question his technical opinion.

"I'll take off as we're approaching the light," said Sylvia. Her self-assurance had returned; she really had recovered. The crew's mood brightened. "We'll fly with the direction of rotation until we clear the drive shaft. Then, we'll cut across the surface, pick up a tail wind, and follow a straight line to the index."

"Won't we cross the access mechanism's path?" asked Corbin.

"Sure," said Ned. "So what?"

"If it moves while we're in its way, we're in trouble. Why not fly against the direction of rotation? Then we'd avoid any risk of being hit."

"But," countered Sylvia, "with the air flowing one way and the surface moving the other, we'd encounter a great deal of air turbulence. We'd use twice as much fuel, and, as we've already discovered, *Gossamer* isn't at its best in rough air."

"How serious is our fuel problem, Sylvia?" asked Pete.

"It's tight," she replied. "We're not critical yet, but one more emergency and we may not be able to complete our mission."

"That settles it," decided Pete. "We go with the rotation. Any more comments?"

"Yes," said Ned. "Suppose we fly this route. How do we recognize the first track? In fact, how do we recognize any track? You can't see them."

"Look outside," said Corbin. "Focus on the light." He paused and pointed toward it. "Look closely. Down near the disk surface, it shines through a haze. I think the haze marks our sector's boundaries."

"I see it," said Susie. She pointed toward one corner. "There's a long curve." Facing *Gossamer*'s side, her back to the drive shaft, she traced the arc. "Then a straight line." As she traced it, she turned to face the drive shaft. "Then a shorter curve, and another short line." She'd returned to her starting point. Corbin chuckled to himself. Track and sector boundaries are invisible, every "expert" knows that. Consequently, Ned and Ada would never have seen the pattern to that haze. But Susie lacked the expert's blinders. Now everyone saw the sector's boundaries. Like a magician's tricks, they became obvious once someone pointed them out. Ever since the mission deviated from plan, Susie had become more and more valuable.

"Assume we find track 0," said Ada. "It contains both the boot and the index. How will we know we haven't hit the boot?"

"There are at least one hundred sectors on the first track," said Corbin. "The odds of our landing in the boot are only about three in one hundred, and that's not bad."

"But it could happen," she argued.

"Yes, it could," agreed Corbin. "But we can read the bit values from inside *Gossamer*. Look through the floor and you'll see what I mean." Sure enough, a close examination revealed subtle patterns on the disk surface. "Bits are recorded on disk as magnetized spots," he continued. "A magnetized spot is formed by aligning just enough surface molecules to create a magnetic flux. The lines running perpendicular to the direction of rotation are 1-bits. The bits are recorded at fixed intervals. An open space is a 0-bit. Given the bit pattern, you and Ned can easily distinguish an index entry from a boot routine."

"No problem," boasted Ned.

"If we land on the wrong sector, we'll fly to the next one," concluded Corbin.

"That's that," decided Pete. "We take off as soon as everyone is strapped in. I'll move up to Ned's bubble just in case Sylvia needs help. Ned, you drop back to my place for the time being. We'll switch back after *Gossamer* reaches the index. Let's move." He paused. "Are you going to be okay, Sylvia?"

"I'm fine," she replied. She and Pete exchanged a glance. "Really, Pete," she insisted. Corbin smiled. Once upon a time, he and Marty had shared a similar, unspoken language.

Spirits lifted by a plan that just might work, the crew members scrambled back to their stations. Carefully, Sylvia checked her instruments. "Ready to depart," she said. Slowly, smoothly, *Gossamer* rose. As the disk's metallic brown surface spun beneath them, the ship seemed, for a time, almost stationary. Gradually, Sylvia turned to the left and, with the wind at her back, followed a straight-line course across track after track toward the index.

As *Gossamer* approached the point where its path intersected the access mechanism's, Corbin held his breath. Should a seek operation occur now, he knew it could destroy the ship. Suddenly he noticed a dark shadow approaching from just overhead. "Watch out!" he cried.

The access mechanism moved with surprising speed. Quickly, inexorably, it bore down on the fragile craft. The air became turbulent. A sudden current directed the ship under the advancing read/write head. Given perfect conditions, Sylvia might have slipped between the head and the surface, but conditions were far from perfect. Buffeted by winds, *Gossamer* brushed the whirling disk surface, and, spinning out of control, crashed on an unknown sector.

17 *Stranded*

With a sickening thud, *Gossamer* slammed into the disk surface and skidded to a stop. For a moment, no one moved. Then Pete pushed himself to his feet. "Anybody hurt?" he asked, softly. No one answered. "We'll meet in bubble 3," he said.

Grimly, the crew filed into the meeting room. No one spoke. They all sensed the danger. *Gossamer* might be damaged. They were lost, and maybe out of options.

When faced with a crisis, most people panic, but Pete was not like most people. He seemed to improve in an emergency, his mind sharp and precise, his thinking clear and analytical, his attitude positive. The others, even Ned, sensed this, and looked to him for leadership. "Our first order of business," Pete began, "is to assess damage. Sylvia and I will inspect *Gossamer*. Meanwhile, I want the rest of you to work on finding a way out of here. I'll leave you in charge, Professor." He reached up and opened the hatch.

"Okay," agreed Corbin, "we'll see what we can do."

"What's the point?" interjected Ned. "If *Gossamer* can fly, we can still make the index. If it can't, we're finished."

"I don't buy that," countered Pete. "We're not finished until we're finished. I expect you to find a way out, Ned. You're an expert. At least that's what they told me. Now's your chance to prove it." He stared at Ned for a moment. Without another word, he grasped Sylvia by the waist, lifted her through the open hatchway, and, pulling himself up, joined her outside the ship.

Angered, Ned glowered at Pete. That dressing down, Corbin feared, may have been a mistake. Ned, he knew, might react by withdrawing into a shell. If he did he'd be useless for the rest of the mission, and they needed him. In some way, he'd have to be placated.

"Any idea where we are, Ned?" Corbin asked, hopefully.

"Sure," Ned replied, sullenly. "We're on disk. But good old Pete will save us."

"Come on, Ned," urged Ada. "Pete was right. We can brood or we can think. Personally, I'd rather think. Brooding isn't going to get us anywhere."

"Don't lecture me," countered Ned. "If anybody can find a way out of this mess, I can."

"Good," said Corbin. "I hope you're right. Can you be a bit more precise on our location?"

"Not really," said Ned, his attitude still negative.

"Eventually," suggested Ada, "every sector on this disk will be transferred into main memory; it's only a matter of time. We may actually be in better shape than before."

"Is there any way to predict when this sector might be read?" asked Corbin.

"If I knew what was stored here, I might be able to make a reasonable guess," she answered. "It's a long shot, though."

"We have some bad news," interrupted Pete as he and Sylvia dropped back through the hatchway. "One of the front rotor blades is bent. Assuming the engine still works, we can fly, but only in short hops. We'll never make the index. You people have any ideas?"

"A glimmer," said Corbin. "If we knew the exact contents of this sector, Ada might be able to figure out something."

"What are you waiting for?" asked Pete. "You can read the bits, can't you?"

"Yes," said Ada.

"Okay. Ada, you and Ned go outside and record them."

"Is that possible?" asked Ned. "The surface is pretty slick. Given the centrifugal force, we could slide off."

"Sylvia and I were just outside," answered Pete. "We made it back."

"Obviously," countered Ned. "But you stayed with *Gossamer*. We'll have to walk a considerable distance from the ship."

"You have a point," agreed Pete. "You better wear lifelines. I'll get them." His manner conveyed an order: be ready when I return. He hurried through the passageway toward the supply room in bubble 6.

"Actually," said Corbin, "the real danger isn't the disk's rotation. What happens if this sector is read while you're out there?"

Ned paled. "I hadn't thought of that," he admitted, quietly. Corbin sensed Ned's fear. Still, the risk had to be taken.

Pete returned carrying two ropes. He tossed an end of one to Ned and fastened the other end to an eyelet near the hatchway. Then he repeated the process for Ada. He tugged on the ropes, testing the knots. "Ready when you are," he said.

"Ready," replied Ada. "Give me a hand, Pete. I can't reach the hatchway." With a grin, Pete grabbed the tiny woman around the waist and lifted her straight overhead. A steady wind whistled through the opening. Ada pulled herself out and stood atop *Gossamer*, the wind whipping her jump suit.

"There's a ladder to your right," called Pete. "Be careful. It's hard to see."

"I found it," she answered. "Coming, Ned?"

"Yeah, sure," he replied. Rejecting Pete's offer to help, he jumped, caught the edge of the hatch, and pulled himself through. "Shall we record hex or binary?" he asked Ada as they stood together.

"Hex," replied Ada. She turned and started down the ladder. Ned followed, close behind. Corbin watched as they took their first tentative steps onto the disk surface.

"What is hex?" asked Pete. Corbin, his attention focused on Ada and Ned, didn't respond.

"What is hex?" Pete repeated.

"Hex is short for hexadecimal, the base 16 number system," replied Corbin. "It's used as a shorthand for recording or displaying binary values. For example, this sector contains 256 bytes. Each byte contains eight bits, so there are 2048 ones and zeros stored here. When Ned and Ada read the bits, they'll record them using hex shorthand. Each hex digit is exactly equivalent to four binary digits, so those 2048 bits equate to only 512 hexadecimal digits. With fewer symbols, Ada should be able to spot a pattern, assuming there is one, much more quickly."

"That makes sense," said Pete. He turned to Sylvia. "We have work to do." Then he laid a hand on Susie's shoulder. "You can help with the tools, Susie. Professor Corbin, I hate to leave you alone, but I'm going to. Put your mind to work on this one, my friend. We need a way out."

Corbin nodded. He would try.

"By the way, how's your side? Are you holding up?"

"No problem, thanks. It still hurts when I move suddenly, but since you wrapped it the pain is tolerable."

"Good." Pete swung back to Sylvia and Susie. "Lets go," he said. Determined, they trudged off toward the control module.

Gossamer would, of course, escape the disk surface. Corbin firmly believed that. He had confidence in Ada, Ned, Pete, and Sylvia; they'd find a way. His mind moved beyond their current predicament. Once the ship reached NECEN's main memory, what could they do? Clearly, *Gossamer* could not fly through the mainframe. They needed a new plan.

Then he recalled the general's words: "A course of action that results in shutting down or disabling NECEN is acceptable." Maybe, if they couldn't control the machine, they could break it. But how? Suddenly an idea flashed into his mind. Of course! In their weakened state they couldn't fight NECEN, but, like martial arts experts, they might be able to use the machine's own power against it. The idea lacked elegance, and it offended his sense of sportsmanship, but it just might work! Once again he entered a trancelike state, his mind totally focused on NECEN's internal structure.

Outside, Ned and Ada crept tentatively across the slick surface, squatting to lower their centers of gravity, fighting the centrifugal force that tugged at them. Soon they reached the sector's high-order bits. Ada began reading values aloud; Ned recorded them. Bit by bit, they moved across the sector toward the low-order position. Now Ned read the values and Ada recorded them. Slowly, carefully, they worked their way back to the high-order position. They stopped to compare notes. Their notes matched. Satisfied, they headed back toward *Gossamer*.

Meanwhile, Pete approached *Gossamer*'s control panel. Beneath it lay a cabinet. He pulled open the door, revealing the engine compartment. Stooping, he looked inside. Gages and wires hung from the top. He and Sylvia would have to slide in, on their backs, side by side. The engine itself, he assumed, lay behind all those wires.

"Ready?" asked Sylvia. He nodded. They lay down, and, grasping flashlights, slid under the cabinet. Beyond the wires, the opening narrowed. Sylvia went on alone. Reaching the engine, she switched on her flashlight. Almost immediately she spotted the problem: a broken gear. Made from a hardened version of the same material that formed *Gossamer*'s skin, the gears were quite brittle; they failed frequently. Fortunately, *Gossamer* carried a spare.

Sylvia called for a wrench. Susie selected one and handed it through the opening. Pete passed it along. Sylvia positioned the tool around a nut and tugged. Suddenly, she felt dizzy. That blow to the head still bothered her. She slid from the cramped engine access area. "Dizzy," she said, quietly. "Nothing serious. The wrench is on the nut. Take over, Pete."

His concern for Sylvia's well-being would have to wait. Without a word, Pete slid into the work area, grabbed the wrench, and turned it. The broken gear came loose. "Got it," he said, sliding back out.

Taking the broken gear from Pete, Sylvia handed it to Susie. Replacements lined a shelf inside the cabinet door. She selected one and gave it to Pete. Again he slid into the engine compartment. Deftly, he dropped the gear into place; it fit perfectly. He tightened the nut. Finished, he tugged on the wrench to remove it. The wrench stuck. He tugged harder. Suddenly, unexpectedly, it pulled loose. His hand hit something solid just over his head. The wrench flew from his grasp. He heard it clatter against other engine parts as it fell.

"What happened?" called Sylvia.

"I dropped the stupid wrench," Pete replied, embarrassed. Twisting his body in the cramped space, he aimed his flashlight toward where he thought the wrench might be. He spotted it and reached for it, but it lay just beyond his grasp. "Can't reach it," he muttered, sliding out to where Sylvia waited.

"We have to get it," she said, stating the obvious. "A loose wrench could jam the engine. I'd better go."

"No way!" exclaimed Pete. "Nobody else can pilot the ship. If you pass out, it doesn't matter whether we find it or not."

"But you're too big," she argued. They stopped and looked at each other. Of course! Susie!

"Professor!" interrupted Ada as she dropped through the hatchway and hurried into his bubble.

"What?" With a start, Corbin awoke from his trance. "Oh, it's you, Ada. I'm sorry. I was working on an idea. When did you get back? Did you and Ned find anything?"

"We'd better get Pete and Sylvia. We have a real problem."

"We're on our way," called Pete from the control module. "We heard you. Thanks to Susie, we're finished. We'll be right there. Start talking, Ada."

"Okay. First, the bad news. We're on a deleted sector."

"What exactly does that mean?" asked Pete as he entered the bubble. Overhead, Ned dropped through the hatchway, pulling it closed behind him.

"Basically, two things," Ada replied. "First, this sector will never be read into main memory. Second, this sector is a candidate to be destroyed. If the system needs space, it can write new data over us. We have to move."

"How do you know it's deleted?" asked Sylvia, following right behind Pete, her arm draped over Susie's shoulder. So far, Susie's decision to stow away had been the mission's one stroke of good luck.

"The first byte contains all 1-bits," Ada replied. "That's how the system flags deleted sectors."

"What's the good news?" asked Corbin, hopefully.

"I recognize this code," she replied. "We're sitting in the middle of a sort program. This sector contains the instructions for part of a common sorting algorithm. Obviously, the code has been modified. Otherwise, we wouldn't be sitting on a deleted sector. But . . ."

"Why is that good news?" asked Pete.

"Programs are stored in consecutive sectors," answered Ada. "That means the rest of the program is nearby. If *Gossamer* can fly at all, we should be able to reach an active sector. If we can, we'll be inside main memory in no time, because the sort routine is easily the most active application program on the system."

"Can we jump two sectors, Sylvia?" asked Pete.

"Probably," she replied. "What choice do we have?"

"None," answered Corbin.

There was nothing else to say. Silently, the crew members filed back to their stations and strapped themselves in. An air of quiet desperation pervaded the ship. Sylvia started the engine. It sputtered and coughed, but, finally, reluctantly, the rotor blades grabbed at the air. Hesitantly, *Gossamer* lifted from the surface and hovered just above it. The disk rotated beneath them. Sylvia counted one, then two sectors. With a groan, the ship dropped to the surface again.

"It's active!" called Corbin. "I read the first byte on the way in."

"I agree," said Ada. "I read it, too."

"And now for the bad news," interrupted Sylvia. "I felt something give when we landed. I think the other rotor may be damaged."

"Let's check it out, Sylvia," suggested Pete. "Susie, you come with us; we may need you again. Meanwhile, the rest of you see if you can come up with an alternative plan. Is there anything we can do if *Gossamer* can't fly?" By the time he finished talking, he had already entered bubble 3 and pushed open the hatchway. Quickly, Susie and Sylvia joined him. One at a time, he lifted them through the opening. Then he, too, slipped out.

For a time, Ada, Ned, and Professor Corbin sat silently, thinking. Then Ned spoke. "It's hopeless," he said. "If we can't fly, we don't have a chance. If we can find a way out of NECEN, we should grab it before it's too late."

"Are you suggesting a retreat?" asked Ada.

"Exactly," said Ned, much more willing to talk with Pete out of earshot. "If you can't win, you may as well retreat and fight another day."

"But," countered Corbin, "we don't *have* another day. The Harlequin's deadline is today at noon."

"Why not let him win this time?" argued Ned. "We can always attack again tomorrow."

"Given *Gossamer*'s condition, we won't be ready tomorrow," said Corbin. "Besides, I have an idea."

"What is it, Professor?" asked Ada, with interest.

"Remember, during our last briefing, when the general said that damaging or disabling NECEN would be an acceptable outcome?"

"Yes," replied Ada. "I remember that."

"I think I know how to blow down the system."

"How do you propose doing that, Professor?" asked Ned. "NECEN is the most reliable computer ever built. I know; I helped build it." Clearly, the idea of anyone threatening to harm his creation distressed him.

"Every machine has a weak spot," answered Corbin. "I think we can find NECEN's."

"Good luck," said Ned, doubtfully.

"Tell me, Ned, what exactly does NECEN do when a hardware component fails?"

"They don't fail," he answered.

"Nonsense," countered Corbin. "What if I took an ax to a bus line?"

"Major damage like that would obviously shut the system down, but we can't do that much damage."

"Okay, I agree. Let's cut back on the amount of damage. What if we were to sever one of the fine wires that ties a chip to its carrier? We could do that with the laser, couldn't we?"

"Probably," agreed Ned, reluctantly.

"If we did, how would NECEN respond?"

Ned counted off the steps on his fingers. "First," he said, "the system would pause. Next, it would figure out an alternate route around the bad chip. Third, the operator would be notified of the change so maintenance could be scheduled. Finally, the computer would resume operating as though nothing had happened. You see, NECEN's design is redundant. Every component has a duplicate or backup. If a circuit goes bad, another circuit takes over until the problem is fixed. To disable the machine, you'd have to sever wires on two or three different chips, and since we can't fly, that's impossible."

"I'm not sure I agree with you, Ned," said Corbin. "I heard the same thing about NECEN's security system, and the Harlequin managed to find a weak spot. We have to do the same thing. I'm convinced we can make NECEN fail. We just have to find its Achilles' heel."

"It's a waste of time, Professor."

"Humor me, Ned. I'm an old man. Let's examine exactly how NECEN reacts to a component's failure. You said the system pauses and then figures out an alternate path. Computers can't figure out anything without a program."

"You're thinking of the hardware failure routine," said Ned.

"Can we modify it?"

"It's stored in ROM."

"Read-only memory," mused Corbin.

"That's right, Professor. We can't change read-only memory."

"Of course not," agreed Corbin, sounding just a bit disappointed. He'd have to find a different angle. "How exactly does the hardware failure routine get control?" he asked.

"Through an interrupt," said Ned, without elaborating.

"Explain what you mean," prompted Corbin.

"Surely you know what interrupts are," responded Ned, his tone almost insulting. Not even Corbin was immune to his impudence.

"Yes, I do," replied Corbin, ignoring Ned's manner, "but I want to know exactly how NECEN handles them."

"Okay," agreed Ned, reluctantly. "We're talking about hardware failure interrupts. When a component fails, an interrupt is sent to the main processor. As soon as the interrupt arrives, the main processor stops what it's doing and gives control to the hardware failure routine. It's part of the operating system. Once the routine works out a path around the bad component, control goes back to the application program. You know this. Why am I explaining it to you?"

"We're looking for a weak spot, Ned," Corbin reminded him. "Sometimes weak spots are so obvious that you overlook them. You say that the main processor stops what it's doing and gives control to the hardware failure routine. How does it know where that routine is?"

"What are you driving at, Professor?"

"Computers are stupid, Ned. You can't just tell them to give a particular module control. You have to tell them where the routine is. You have to say something like: Give control to the module starting at memory location 1000."

"You're right," Ned agreed. "NECEN uses an interrupt table. One entry on the table holds the address of the hardware failure routine. When an interrupt occurs, the processor's hardware takes the address from the table and branches to it."

"Let's clarify that," said Corbin. "An interrupt occurs. The processor looks to the interrupt table, finds the address of the hardware failure routine, and branches to that address. An operating system routine now has control. It finds a way around the bad component, notifies the operator, and then gives control to an application program."

"Right," agreed Ned.

"That takes time," continued Corbin. "The hardware failure routine needs at least a few microseconds to find an alternate path through the system. During that time, the bad component is still broken. Won't it keep generating interrupts?"

"Sure," said Pete. "When a component fails, it sends interrupt after interrupt after interrupt, until the problem is fixed or bypassed."

"Why doesn't the processor react to those subsequent interrupts?"

"They're masked," answered Ned. "After the processor accepts the first one, it ignores the others."

"How are they masked?"

"There's a switch in the interrupt table," replied Ned.

"What if we reset that switch?" suggested Corbin.

"I see what you're driving at, Professor," said Ada. "We could throw the system into an endless loop!"

"Exactly," agreed Corbin. "All we have to change is one bit." A slight smile betrayed his pride in his solution. Intellectually, at least, he had beaten NECEN.

"But if *Gossamer* can't fly, how do we change the switch?" asked Ned.

"We're in the middle of a sort routine," answered Corbin. "What if we modify the program instructions to tell NECEN to change the switch for us?"

"That's beautiful!" said Ada, grinning broadly. "We give NECEN an order to self-destruct." She clapped her hands and laughed. "I like it!"

"You're forgetting one more thing," cautioned Ned. "There's a backup computer. If NECEN fails, it takes over."

"I know all about the backup," responded Corbin. "In fact, I suggested it. It's located somewhere in New Jersey, far enough away from Manhattan that a single incident won't damage both computers. At the moment, it's completely independent. Until the backup machine gains control, it can't be accessed via telephone line, so our friend, the Harlequin, could not have modified its operating system. If NECEN fails, a hardware switch activates it, and he can't change the hardware. We want the backup to gain control, because we control it. It represents NECEN B.H."

"B.H.?" Ada wondered aloud.

"Before Harlequin." Corbin grinned. He glanced outside. "The others are returning," he said, still grinning. "Why don't you two work out the details while I explain the plan to them?"

"I think I have an idea," said Ada. "Let's go back to my bubble, Ned." Strangely subdued, Ned nodded his assent.

"Keep it simple, Ada," called Corbin as they hurried off. "The best plans are the simple ones."

There was still hope.

18 *Achilles' Heel*

"Hi Gramps," said Susie, as she dropped through the hatchway.

"Hi, Susie," Corbin replied, affectionately. Ignoring the dull pain that had reappeared in his side, he hugged her. He'd been so wrapped up in *Gossamer*'s problems, he'd almost forgotten about his granddaughter. His mood darkened. He should have insisted they turn back as soon as they found her. If anything happened to Susie, he'd never forgive himself.

"Okay if I go up front with Ada?" Susie asked.

"Sure, honey," replied Corbin. "She and Ned are busy, though, so don't disturb them."

"I won't," Susie promised. She waved and hurried away. Corbin watched her leave. Ada, he realized, had become a role model, and that pleased him. At least something positive had come from this trip.

"Good news," said Sylvia, as she slid through and dropped to the floor. "I think we'll be able to fly again. Not one hundred percent, of course, but some."

"Excellent," said Corbin, trying to regain his optimism.

"Have you come up with anything, Professor?" asked Pete. He squeezed through the hatch, pulling it closed behind him.

"I have an idea. Ada and Ned are working on the details right now."

"Let's hear it," said Pete.

"In a nutshell, we're going to trick NECEN into shutting itself down."

"I like it already," said Sylvia, smiling. She seemed delighted with the idea of having the machine defeat itself.

Corbin chuckled. "It does have a certain appeal, doesn't it?" he said. "We're going to take advantage of the way NECEN works. Either of you know exactly what a machine cycle is?"

"Only vaguely," admitted Pete. Sylvia nodded. After several trips inside computers, she probably understood machine cycles as well as anyone.

"How about interrupts?"

"Strike two," said Pete. Sylvia nodded again. Her firsthand experience had given her a unique perspective.

"The functions of an operating system?"

"I have a rough idea," said Sylvia, "but I've never been inside a system as large as NECEN. Better start from scratch."

"Agreed," said Pete. "Take your time, Professor."

"Ada and Ned are going to need some time anyway, so we may as well," said Corbin. "Let's start with the basics. Like most computers, NECEN's main processing unit contains an instruction control unit, an arithmetic and logic unit, and several registers." (Fig. 18.1)

"What are registers?" asked Pete. When the mission began, he might not have asked that question, but the possible consequences of ignorance had become too great to let a little thing like embarrassment stand in the way of his understanding.

"Registers are small units of high-speed storage, usually a word

FIGURE 18.1 The processor consists of three primary components: an instruction control unit, an arithmetic and logic unit, and several registers. The instruction control unit decides which instruction the computer will execute next. The arithmetic and logic unit executes it. The registers hold control information and intermediate computational results.

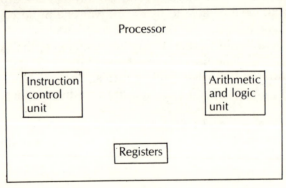

FIGURE 18.2 A machine cycle. During instruction time, or I-time, the instruction control unit fetches the next instruction from main memory. During execution time, or E-time, the arithmetic and logic unit executes it.

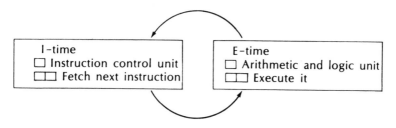

or less, located in the processor," replied Corbin. "They hold control information and computational results. Let me get back to the machine cycle, though.

"A machine cycle consists of two distinct steps." He sketched a diagram to illustrate the concept (Fig. 18.2). "During instruction time, or I-time, the processor's instruction control unit fetches a single instruction from main memory. Now the second phase begins: during execution time, or E-time, the arithmetic and logic unit executes the instruction. That completes one machine cycle. Next, control returns to the control unit, which starts a new cycle by fetching the next instruction. That basic cycle—fetch/execute, fetch/execute—is repeated over and over again, until the computer is turned off."

"Slow down, Professor," said Pete. "You say the instruction control unit fetches the next instruction. How does it know which one is next?"

"Excellent question, Pete. It leads me right into my next point. I could have used you in some of my classes. I'll start with an outline." He paused, and wrote:

1. Instruction time (instruction control unit)
   a. Get address from instruction counter.
   b. Fetch instruction at this address.
   c. Increment instruction counter to point to next instruction.
2. Execution time (arithmetic and logic unit)
   a. Execute instruction in instruction register.

"Picture a program stored in main memory," Corbin continued. He started a new diagram (Fig. 18.3a). "Assume the first instruction is

FIGURE 18.3

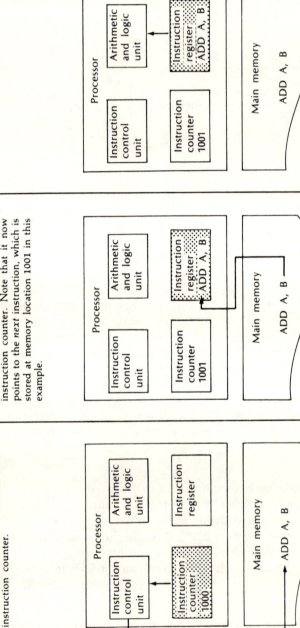

a. As a machine cycle begins, the instruction control unit fetches the instruction whose address is found in the instruction counter.

b. As the instruction flows over the bus and into the instruction register, the control unit has time to increment the instruction counter. Note that it now points to the *next* instruction, which is stored at memory location 1001 in this example.

c. Finally, the arithmetic and logic unit executes the instruction.

at byte 1000, the second at byte 1001, the third at 1002, and so on. The operating system gets the program started by loading the first instruction's address into a register called the instruction counter." He added the register to his diagram.

"The first machine cycle begins. The control unit looks at the instruction counter, finds an address—1000 in my example—and fetches the instruction stored at that address. As the instruction flows over a bus and into the instruction register, the control unit has plenty of time to bump up the instruction counter (Fig. 18.3b). Finally, the arithmetic and logic unit executes the instruction (Fig. 18.3c). When the next machine cycle starts, the instruction counter already contains the next instruction's address. The cycle is repeated over and over again."

"Interesting," said Pete. "And the computer never varies from that basic cycle?"

"That's right," answered Corbin. "We're going to take advantage of that predictability. Computers are stupid. If the address in the instruction counter points to an instruction that tells the computer to destroy itself, it will, because it can't do anything else."

"But," argued Sylvia, "modern computers just don't fail anymore."

"You have a point," admitted Corbin, "but I think we've found a weak spot. Let me lay a bit more groundwork, and then I'll tell you what it is."

"Fair enough," said Pete.

"Earlier, I compared an operating system to a traffic officer. There's a bit more to it. An operating system's basic purpose is to make the computer easier to use. It's a collection of software routines that sits between the computer's hardware and the application programs. Communicating directly with the hardware is tedious, so the operating system assumes responsibility, acting as an interface. That simplifies the programmer's job.

"On big machines like NECEN the operating system has additional responsibilities too. At any given time the computer might be working on dozens of different programs. Whenever you have several programs competing for the same resources, conflicts are inevitable. Two or more programs are going to want the processor at the same time. Two or more programs are going to want the same main memory space or the same external device. The operating system resolves these conflicts."

"Does that mean the operating system gets involved whenever an application program needs more space or some input data?" asked Pete.

"That's right. Each application program is assigned a certain amount of main memory space. As long as the program is executing its own instructions to process data stored in its own space, it doesn't need the operating system. However, if the program needs more data, or more space, or access to any other system resource, it must ask the operating system for help. The operating system communicates with the channels too, telling them when to start an I/O operation and sensing when one has finished its work. The operating system is a collection of programs that manages the computer system's resources."

"So the operating system really coordinates everything that happens on the computer," suggested Sylvia.

"That's right," agreed Corbin. "It's an absolutely crucial component. In fact the operating system is so crucial that access to it is highly restricted. The only way to communicate with the operating system is through an interrupt."

"What's an interrupt?" asked Pete.

Suddenly, Susie entered the room. "Ada says she and Ned won't be too much longer," she announced. She took a seat on the floor. "Maybe five minutes."

"Great!" exclaimed Pete. "Thanks, Susie. Go on, Professor."

"Okay," said Corbin. He smiled. "Susie has just given me a perfect lead-in. She entered the bubble and said something. We stopped what we were doing and shifted our attention to her. We noted her message and then resumed our conversation. That pattern resembles what happens when a computer is interrupted. When an application program or an external device needs the operating system's attention, it generates an electronic signal called an interrupt. The signal is sensed by hardware. In response, the computer stops what it was doing and gives control to the operating system. The operating system performs a support function. Then the computer goes back to what it was doing when the interrupt occurred."

Corbin began to draw a series of sketches. "Here, look at this (Fig. 18.4a). Imagine our application program is in control. The instruction counter contains the address of an instruction in that program. The instruction is fetched and executed. Then the next instruction is fetched and executed. The cycle goes on and on. The program reaches a point where it needs input data. It isn't allowed to get the data itself. Because it needs the operating system's help, it generates an interrupt.

"An interrupt is an electronic signal. When the signal is sensed by hardware, the address in the instruction counter is copied to a save register (Fig. 18.4b). The instruction counter, remember, holds the address of the next instruction in our application program. Saving it will allow the computer to resume processing our program's instructions later.

"Now, the computer's hardware has to transfer control to the operating system. To do that, it needs the address of the operating system's first instruction. That address is stored in a fixed location in main memory. Because the operating system's address is always stored in the same place, hardware always knows where to find it. The address is copied from memory into the instruction counter (Fig. 18.4c)."

"So the operating system gets control next," suggested Sylvia.

"That's right," said Corbin. "Because the instruction counter holds the address of the operating system's first instruction, that first instruction will be fetched and executed. Thus the operating system can start the input operation (Fig. 18.4d). Eventually, the operating system will copy the address of our program's next instruction back into the instruction counter (Fig. 18.4e), returning control to our program. See how it works?"

"I think so," said Pete. "How is this going to . . ."

"We're ready, Professor," interrupted Ada, as she and Ned walked into the meeting room.

"Excuse me for a second," said Corbin. He turned to Ada and Ned and nodded. "I assume you have a plan."

"Yes we do," said Ada. "I think it will work, Professor." She seemed excited. "First, we turn off the interrupt mask . . ."

FIGURE 18.4 a. As Professor Corbin's example begins, an application program is in control.

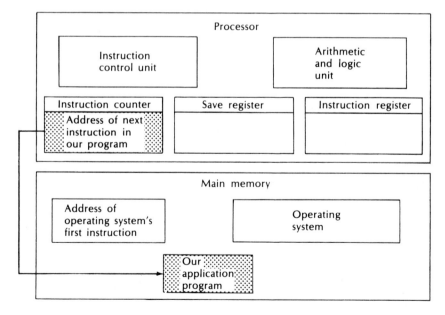

b. The application program needs input data, so it issues an interrupt. In response, hardware copies the contents of the instruction counter into a save register,

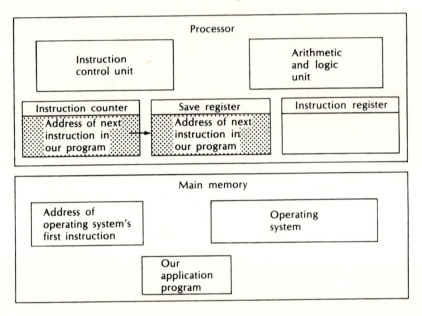

c. and copies the address of the first instruction in the operating system into the instruction counter.

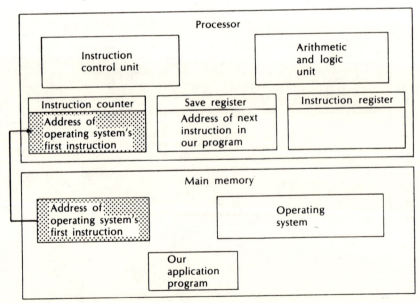

d. Because the instruction counter contains the address of an operating system instruction, the operating system is in control. It can start the input operation.

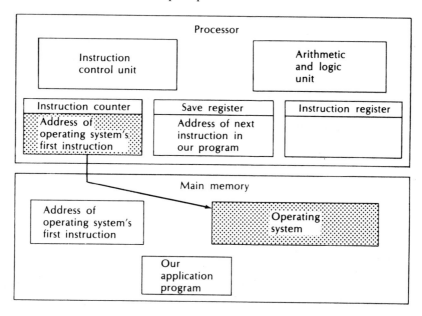

e. Finally, the operating system copies the address of our program's next instruction back into the instruction counter, returning control to our program.

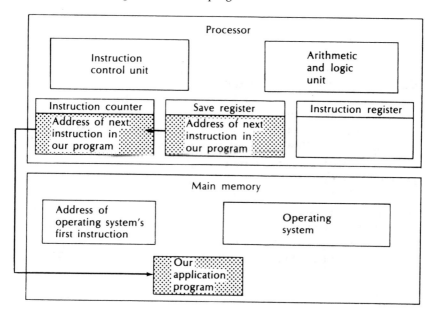

"Interrupt mask?" asked Pete.

"It's a control switch, Pete," said Corbin. "One bit. If it's on, subsequent interrupts are ignored. I'll explain it to you later. Continue, Ada."

"Well," she went on, almost bubbling with enthusiasm, "once we turn the interrupt bit off, we'll tell the system to start an I/O operation to our communication port. Then we'll land in the instruction counter. When the interrupt happens, the system will move us to a save register. The save register is near the channel linkage register, right Ned?"

"That's right," he agreed.

"A short flight transfers us to the channel linkage register," Ada continued. "We can fly, can't we, Sylvia?"

"A bit," Sylvia replied. She looked confused; she wasn't following this conversation.

"Once there, we flow to the channel. On our way through, we use the laser to break a wire. That causes a hardware failure. Meanwhile, we're on our way back home."

"The only problem," said Ned, "is that we have to change bit values here on disk. Will the laser work, Sylvia?"

"I'm not sure what you mean," said Sylvia.

"We have been talking in computerese, haven't we?" apologized Corbin. "The basic plan is to modify some instructions here in this sector. Then, when we're read into NECEN, the new instructions will change a few key control bits and send us back to SMF."

"Oh, I see," said Sylvia. "That's why you want to know if the laser can change bit values on disk."

"That's right," said Ada.

"I don't know," Sylvia admitted. "We've never tested it on disk."

"We know that bits are recorded on disk by aligning a few surface molecules. We're small enough to see the molecules; maybe we can line them up ourselves," suggested Corbin.

"It's worth a try," agreed Ada. "What are we waiting for?" She seemed eager to begin.

Once again Pete helped Ada through the hatchway. Ned followed, carrying the laser. They descended and started toward the sector's low-order bits. Anxiously, the others watched as the two experts stopped several bytes away. Ada pointed to a spot on the surface. Ned fired. A brilliant flash illuminated the ship. Ada shook her head; it hadn't worked. Ned changed positions and fired from a different angle. Ada stooped to inspect the results. Triumphantly, she threw a fist into the air! It worked! They could change bit values.

"Let's get back to the plan, Professor," suggested Pete. There was nothing to do but wait anyway. "I'm beginning to get a sense of where you're headed. We're going to plant a bomb of sorts and let NECEN bump into it."

"Good analogy, Pete," said Corbin. "Actually, it's more like a Trojan Horse. If it works, NECEN will shut itself down, and our people should be able to regain control."

"And interrupts are the key, right?" suggested Sylvia.

"That's right," said Corbin. "There are two types of interrupts I didn't mention before: one for program failures, and one for hardware failures. It's that latter one we'll key on.

"You see, in some ways a computer resembles a living organism. Like a brain, the processor coordinates all the other components. When a component fails, special circuits, acting like nerves, sense the failure and send the processor an interrupt. Now, sensing an error is a lot like sensing pain. When we hurt, we continue to hurt until something relieves the pain. When a hardware failure is sensed, the circuitry sends the processor an interrupt, and it continues to send interrupt after interrupt until the problem is fixed. That's NECEN's Achilles' heel."

"Go on," prompted Pete. Both he and Sylvia focused their full attention on Corbin now. This plan made sense! Only Susie ignored him. Glancing at his granddaughter, Corbin smiled. She stared through *Gossamer's* side, watching Ada. He sensed her concern for Ada's welfare. His former student and his granddaughter had become fast friends.

He turned back to Pete and Sylvia. "When the first interrupt arrives," he continued, "hardware grabs the address of the operating system and copies it into the instruction counter. As far as the processor is concerned, though, nothing has changed. It still works by following its basic machine cycle."

Pete anticipated the next step. "Because the address in the instruction counter points to the operating system, the operating system's first instruction is fetched next, right?"

"Exactly, Pete," said Corbin.

"But how does that help us, Professor? That's just standard procedure."

"You're right, Pete," agreed Corbin. "I'm coming to the real heart of the plan right now. Remember what I said about the error-checking circuitry sending interrupt after interrupt until the bad component is fixed? Well, what would happen if the system actually *accepted* all those interrupts? Imagine it. The first interrupt arrives, and the address of the operating system is placed in the instruction counter. The operating system's first instruction is executed. But then, a second interrupt arrives. Hardware, in its simple-minded way, copies the address of the operating system into the instruction counter. During the next machine cycle, the first instruction in the operating system is fetched and executed all over again. Then a third interrupt arrives. Do you see what's happening?"

"Sure!" said Sylvia. "An endless loop." She chuckled. "I like it. Work through the logic, Pete. An interrupt occurs, so the operating system's first instruction is executed. A second interrupt occurs, so, once again, the operating system's first instruction is executed. As long as the interrupts keep coming, that first instruction is executed over and over again. The only way to stop the interrupts is to fix the error. The system can't fix the error until it gets beyond the first instruction. But it can't get beyond the first instruction until the interrupts stop. Catch-22!"

"Exactly," said Corbin.

"But it doesn't work like that," argued Pete. "Computers do not drop into endless loops following a minor hardware failure."

"No, of course not," agreed Corbin. "Do you know why?"

"No," admitted Pete.

"One bit," said Corbin, answering his own question. "One stupid bit. It happens to be the first one in the instruction counter. As long as it's off, the computer accepts all interrupts. And, it's always off. Except, of course, when an interrupt is being processed. Remember how the operating system's address is stored in main memory?"

"Sure," said Pete.

"The first bit in that address is *on*. When an interrupt happens, that address is copied into the instruction counter. Now, the instruction counter's first bit, the mask bit, is on, so subsequent interrupts are ignored. The operating system can go about its business undisturbed."

Pete smiled. "And we're going to turn it off," he said.

Corbin nodded, grinning broadly. Sylvia laughed. They were about to tell a computer to destroy itself, and it felt good.

19
Sabotage

"What's so funny?" asked Ned, as he dropped through the hatch and reached up to take the laser from Ada.

"I just told them about our plan," chuckled Corbin.

"I fail to see the humor in an interrupt."

"I didn't think you would, Ned," said Sylvia. She shook her head and laughed again. "But the idea of telling a computer to destroy itself has a ring of poetic justice."

"I never looked at it that way," said Ada, swinging into the bubble. She grinned. "You're right, though. It does have a certain appeal."

"Did you change the program?" asked Pete. He reached up to close the hatch.

"No problem," replied Ada.

"Give us an overview of the changes," suggested Corbin.

"Certainly, Professor." Ada grabbed a pad of paper and sketched the new version of the sort program (Fig. 19.1). "We changed three instructions. *Gossamer* rides the first one—a no-op."

"A no-op?"

"That's right, Pete," continued Ada. "A no-op is an instruction that doesn't do anything. Essentially, it tells the computer to waste some time. Its purpose is simply to carry *Gossamer* to the processor via the instruction register.

"The second instruction," she went on, "is the key one. It tells the computer to change the mask bit in the operating system's entry point address." She paused and looked at Pete.

"I told him about the mask bit," said Corbin.

FIGURE 19.1 As part of their plan, Ada and Ned modified a portion of the sort program. When they returned to *Gossamer*, Ada outlined the new instructions.

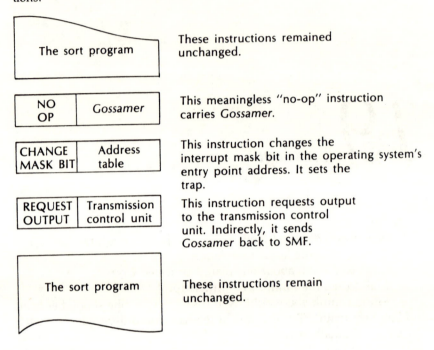

| The sort program | | These instructions remained unchanged. |

| NO OP | Gossamer | This meaningless "no-op" instruction carries *Gossamer*. |

| CHANGE MASK BIT | Address table | This instruction changes the interrupt mask bit in the operating system's entry point address. It sets the trap. |

| REQUEST OUTPUT | Transmission control unit | This instruction requests output to the transmission control unit. Indirectly, it sends *Gossamer* back to SMF. |

| The sort program | | These instructions remain unchanged. |

Ada smiled. "The third instruction," she continued, "starts an output operation to the transmission control unit. I/O requires the operating system's help. That means an interrupt. Following any interrupt, the instruction counter's contents are copied to a save register. We want to get to that save register. The no-op will carry us to the instruction register. We'll have to fly from there to the instruction counter. If we make it in time, we'll flow to the save register when the interrupt happens.

"The channel linkage register is right next to the save register. We'll have to fly to it, too. After the interrupt, NECEN's operating system will get control and start the output operation. The first thing the channel will do is read the contents of the channel linkage register. If Gossamer is in there, we'll flow to the channel. Once we hit the channel, we'll fly to the data bus and head for home."

"Can we do all that flying, Sylvia?" asked Pete.

"As long as we're talking about short hops, I think so," Sylvia replied.

"We considered that," said Ned. "The flights are all between adjacent registers. There is something we may have overlooked, though."

"Oh," said Corbin. "What's that?"

"Memory protection," replied Ned. "When we enter memory, we won't be allowed to change the interrupt bit."

"What is memory protection?" asked Pete, suddenly serious. Their plan depended on changing that bit. Wouldn't anything go right on this mission?

"It's a technique for protecting programs from each other," explained Corbin. "Imagine my program and your program are both in main memory. For some reason, I decide to store data in space assigned to you. If I were allowed to do that, I could destroy part of your program. The operating system won't let me—that's memory protection. Basically, memory protection restricts each program to its own space."

"That's where the plan breaks down," interjected Ned. "When we enter main memory, we'll be stored in an application program region. The operating system's address will lie outside our region, so memory protection won't let us change the interrupt mask bit. The plan won't work."

"Correct me if I'm wrong, Ned," said Ada, "but memory protection only applies to application programs, doesn't it? If we can get into the operating system, we can do anything we want."

"Good point, Ada," said Corbin. "We want the processor to execute an instruction that changes one bit in the address table. If we can make NECEN think the instruction comes from the operating system, the processor will execute it. That's right, isn't it Ned?"

"Yes," he agreed.

"Obviously," continued Corbin, before Ned could qualify his answer, "the processor must be able to distinguish an operating system instruction from an application program instruction. How does it do that?"

"Just before the instruction is executed, the processor checks the program state bit in the instruction counter," replied Ned.

"Show us," said Corbin, pushing a pad and a pencil at him.

Quickly, Ned drew a sketch (Fig. 19.2). "The instruction counter," he said, "sits in a special register. The register holds one word which, on NECEN, is 64 bits long. The low-order 32 bits hold the address of the next instruction. The other 32 hold control information. The high-order bit is the interrupt mask bit; we've already discussed it. The next

FIGURE 19.2 NECEN's instruction counter occupies a 64-bit register. The low-order 32 bits hold the address of the next instruction. The high-order 32 bits hold control information. The very first bit is the interrupt mask bit. It is followed by the program state bit.

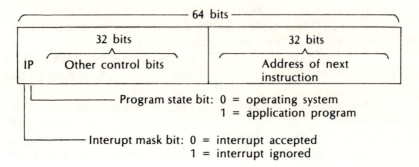

bit defines the program state. If it's on, the system is executing an application program. If it's off, the operating system has control.

"Just before the arithmetic and logic unit executes an instruction," he continued, "hardware checks to be sure that all the memory affected by the instruction is within the program's assigned memory space. If it is, fine, the instruction is executed. If it isn't, hardware checks the program state bit. If the bit is on, the instruction must have come from an application program, so the program is terminated. If the bit is off, the operating system must have been in control. Since the operating system can do whatever it wants, the instruction is executed."

"Why don't we just change the program state bit?" asked Pete. To him, the solution seemed obvious.

"You don't understand," said Ned, contemptuously. "Memory protection limits a program to its own region. Both the interrupt mask bit and the program state bit will lie *outside* our region, so we won't be allowed to change them. Professor Corbin's plan won't work."

"Where is the instruction counter, Ned?" asked Corbin.

"It's a register. It's in the processor."

"I know that. Where is the instruction counter in relation to the instruction register? Are they close to each other?"

"Certainly. Side-by-side."

"The solution is obvious. Ada just explained our plan. *Gossamer* rides the first instruction, so we'll be fetched first. As soon as we reach the instruction register, we fly to the instruction counter. On our way, we'll use the laser to change the program state bit to zero. The instruction that changes the mask bit will be fetched next. By the time it reaches the processor and is executed, the program state bit will be 0, so the processor will think it came from the operating system."

"Can you think of any reason why that won't work, Ned?" asked Pete.

Ned thought for a moment. "No," he said, finally.

"Then it's settled. Any other . . ."

"What's that!" interrupted Susie. She pointed overhead toward a massive, shadowy figure that had suddenly moved between *Gossamer* and the dim light. As their sector continued its steady rotation, a shape gradually took form: the access mechanism had stopped over their track.

"Unless I miss my guess," said Corbin, "we're about to be read into main memory. Better get back to our bubbles and strap ourselves in. The first step might be bumpy."

"Let's go," ordered Pete. Quickly the meeting broke up. One revolution of the disk, and *Gossamer* would move into main memory. One revolution. It seemed to take forever. Finally, the outline of the access mechanism reappeared in the distance. Soon it dominated Corbin's field of vision.

Now the read/write head hung directly overhead. *Gossamer* leaped from the disk surface. As the craft ascended, Corbin looked back at the string of bits following them upward. The 1-bits seemed to glow; the 0-bits seemed empty and dull. Zeros and ones, one and zeros. Even today, after a lifetime of working with computers, he found it difficult to believe that so much could be accomplished by manipulating those two simple symbols. Zeros and ones . . . Wait a minute! Those two bits read 1 1. They were *supposed* to read 0 1. Ada must have made a mistake. A 1-bit in the first position would leave the interrupt mask bit on, not turn if off. With the mask bit on, the plan would not work. *Gossamer* would escape, but the Harlequin would still control NECEN. That bit *had* to be corrected.

For the moment, however, as *Gossamer* flowed through the access mechanism and into the disk controller, Corbin sat powerless. Had he misread those bits? He hoped so. Time would tell. He forced himself to relax, settling back to enjoy the miniature universe.

After the near darkness of the disk drive, the electronic components inside the control unit seemed even more beautiful than before. The ship traveled just under the board's surface, the protective coating filtering the light to an eerie green. The bubbles plunged briefly beneath the surface, then quickly rose through tiny pins to join a set of fine, hairlike wires that led to a chip. Again Corbin experienced the sensation of passing through an electronic field. Bit values read and parity checked, the bubbles joined another set of fine wires, left the chip, and, once again, flowed across the board's surface.

The familiar silver ponds and golden lakes came next. Then *Gossamer* joined a bus and, an instant later, entered a channel. Just beyond the channel, Corbin knew, lay NECEN. A brief wait inside a buffer seemed to last forever. Finally, *Gossamer* moved again.

The ship entered a huge cylinder. NECEN! Components lined the inner surface. The bus line flowed through the cylinder's center. Gold-plated connectors and tiny coolant tubes glinted in the diffused light that filtered through various cracks and openings. There would be no wind inside NECEN; circulating freon cooled this massive mainframe.

Gossamer streamed past bank after bank of memory boards. Finally, the system selected one and shunted the ship off the main bus. Crossing a board, it flowed smoothly to a chip. Tiny pins led to fine wires. The wires, in turn, carried *Gossamer* to the chip's surface. Selecting eight contiguous bits, it came to rest.

"How long until the sort program is executed, Ada?" called Pete.

"Not long," she answered. "A fraction of a second, real time; we might sense a few minutes."

"Everybody stay put," ordered Pete.

"We can't," said Corbin, quietly. "We have a problem."

"You're kidding!" exclaimed Pete.

"I wish I were," replied Corbin. "One bit is wrong. It's a key bit in the instruction that resets the interrupt mask bit to 0. It has to be changed."

"No it doesn't!" shouted Ned. Momentarily shocked, no one moved. That was all the time Ned needed. Vaulting from his seat, he hit the floor running. With a start, Pete realized his objective—the laser! Reacting with the speed and grace of a trained athlete, he tore off his seat belt and raced toward the meeting room, but Ned arrived first. Grabbing the laser, he pointed it down the aisle toward Pete. "Stop or I'll shoot!" he warned.

Pete's momentum carried him a few steps into the meeting room. Frightened, Ned backed up toward Ada's bubble. "I *mean* it!" he shouted, waving the laser menacingly. Pete stopped, his hands raised above his head.

"Put that laser down, Ned," Pete ordered.

"No way, sir," snapped Ned, sarcastically. "You go back to your bubble and sit down." Pete hesitated. Again Ned waved the laser. Then he spun toward Ada and Sylvia. "You stay put, too," he warned. Taking advantage of Ned's momentary inattention, Pete reached up and unlocked the hatchway. Ned spun back toward him. Without a word, Pete slowly backed up toward his bubble and sat down.

"That 1-bit was no mistake," bragged Ned. "Why don't you tell them what I've done, Professor?"

Corbin sighed. "With a 1-bit in that position, the instruction is meaningless," he said. "It won't change the interrupt mask bit. We'll get out, but we won't disable NECEN."

"Exactly," sneered Ned.

"But why?" asked Ada.

"Did you ever hear the name Ned Lud before?"

"No," she admitted. "You're the first Ned Lud I've ever known."

Frantically, Corbin searched his memory. Ned Lud. He knew that name. Of course! "The Luddites," he said, quietly.

"Very good," said Ned. "Tell them about the Luddites, Professor."

Corbin glanced past Ned toward the control module. Slowly, stealthily, Sylvia moved toward the front hatchway. Preoccupied, Ned couldn't see her. Corbin realized that he would have to keep Ned's attention. "Back in the early 1800s," he began, "the Luddites ran around England smashing labor-saving machinery. They feared mechanization would put them out of work. Their martyr or patron saint was a guy named Ned Lud—thus the Luddites. Old Ned was a revolutionary of sorts, I guess."

"Your grasp of history is almost as impressive as your grasp of technology, Professor. Ned was my ancestor; I'm named after him."

"Shall I tell them the rest, Ned?" Nervously, Corbin glanced toward the control module again. Sylvia had slipped outside and climbed to the top of her bubble. He couldn't give her away! He forced himself to look at Ned.

"What do you mean, Professor?"

"History, I think, compassionately views the Luddites as crackpots," Corbin answered. "For a time, anyone who tried to block progress was branded a Luddite; it's not a term of respect. Old Ned's image is even less flattering. He was feebleminded. Today we'd call him crazy or mentally unbalanced."

"That's not true!" exploded Ned. "He was a great man, a brilliant man. Way back in 1779 he foresaw what technology would do to us. He foresaw the unemployment, the exploitation, the pollution, the dehumanization. He foresaw all that! And he was *right!*" Ned's voice had risen to a shrill pitch. "Feebleminded! *Ha!* He wasn't crazy. He was a genius, centuries ahead of his time."

"How can you say that, Ned?" argued Ada. "You are without a doubt the most technological person I've ever met."

Ned turned to face her. Corbin held his breath. Would he notice Sylvia's empty bubble? He waved the laser at Ada, his attention focused on her. "That's right," he replied, his voice back under control. "I'm an expert; I have credibility. If I say technology is bad, who's going to disagree with me? Another technologist? I'll pick him apart?" Ned's voice cracked again. Clearly, he found it difficult to control his emotions. That could prove dangerous. "People will listen to me," he went on. "Especially after we show them how easily we gained control of their precious NECEN."

"What makes you think you're even going to have the opportunity to present your position?" challenged Pete. "As soon as we get back, you'll be arrested. You know that."

"After this mission fails, I'll surrender to you, Pete. My good friend, Georgie Hacker, better known as the Harlequin, will simply add a new demand to his growing list: my release."

"Georgie Hacker!" gasped Ada.

"That's right, Ada," sneered Ned. "Georgie Hacker. He told me all about you."

"You realize, of course," interjected Corbin, "that he's using you."

"And how might he be doing that, Professor?"

"You're an idealist, Ned. You're misguided, but I'll recognize your idealism. The Harlequin is in this for the money and the power. You're just a pawn to help him get what he wants."

"Nonsense! Georgie and I are friends. He's doing this to embarrass the government and to demonstrate the stupidity of this national data bank concept. I'm surprised you're not with us, Professor."

"I did oppose NECEN," admitted Corbin. "I still do. I'd like to see the plan discredited. But, my friend, the end does not justify the means." A quick glance revealed Sylvia approaching the hatchway, almost directly over Ned's head.

"In this case, it does, Professor. Besides, I'm holding the laser, so my opinion counts more than yours."

"If Georgie Hacker has suddenly become an idealist," said Ada, "why is he asking for a billion dollars?"

"That's the only way to get this government's attention," answered Ned. "Besides, we plan to use the money to publicize our position."

"Ha," sneered Ada. "If you believe that, I have a bridge I'd like to sell you. I know him better than you possibly could, Ned. He's in this for himself, not for some crazy cause. You are unbelievably naive. I think you inherited your ancestor's stupidity."

"Don't antagonize me, Ada," warned Ned, waving the laser toward her.

Taking advantage of Ned's outburst, Corbin glanced overhead again. Sylvia had reached the hatchway. Silently, he signaled Ada: keep it up!

"Did he ever tell you his plans for taking over the government, Ned?" Ada continued, challenging him. She swung into the aisle and took a step toward the meeting room. Ned stepped back. "Did he ever talk about his intellectual elite?"

"Yeah," said Ned. "He's right, you know. We would do a better job than the clowns who run things now."

"I've heard that before," interjected Corbin. "The guy's name was Hitler. He defined elite differently, but the concept is the same." Corbin and Ada were playing a game now, forcing Ned to switch his attention back and forth, between them.

"Watch it, Professor," warned Ned, waving the laser again. Corbin noted Ned's position. He stood near the opening to Ada's bubble, too far from the hatchway for Sylvia to mount an attack. If only he'd move toward the bubble's center.

Suddenly, a young voice rang out. "You really are a jerk, Ned!"

Susie! What was she doing? Concerned, Corbin stepped from his chair and started toward the meeting room.

Shocked, Ned stared at the little girl in disbelief. She was just a kid! Confused, he swung the laser toward her.

"Leave her alone, Ned!" warned Ada, jumping to Susie's defense. She stepped toward him again. "I can't believe your arrogance," she chided. She was close enough now to poke a finger into his ribs. "You and Georgie are going to take over the government. Ha! That's really idealism." Confused, Ned retreated before her steady advance. "You don't believe in technology, but you technologists are going to run things. The elite. Don't make me laugh. You guys couldn't organize a one-man band."

Had it been Pete attacking, Ned might have fired, but this was Ada. Shaking his head, he stepped back again. He swung the laser, brushing her hand away. "That's enough!" he shouted. "I'll fire, Ada. I really will."

Suddenly, like a cat, Sylvia dropped on him, knocking him to the floor. Leaping to her feet, she lashed out with her right foot and knocked the weapon from his grasp. It flew into the passageway toward Ada's bubble. Ada grabbed it.

Now, Pete entered the fray, brushing past Corbin, positioning himself between Ned and Ada, cutting off Ned's access to the weapon. "Got the laser, Ada?" he called over his shoulder.

"Got it!" Ada replied.

Advancing slowly, arms outstretched like a linebacker moving in for the kill, Pete approached the fallen hardware expert. Ned scrambled to his feet, terrified, and backed away. Suddenly, Sylvia groaned and dropped to her knees, clutching her head. Pete shifted his attention to her. "Sylvia," he whispered.

In desperation, Ned leaped, grabbed the edge of the opening, and pulled himself through the hatchway. Triumphantly, he slammed it closed. His muffled voice could barely be heard inside *Gossamer*. "You can't get out," he shouted. "You won't be able to change that bit. The mission is a failure."

For the moment, Pete ignored him. He hurried to Sylvia's side. She sat on the floor, leaning against the wall. He placed an arm around her shoulder and held her. "Are you okay?" he asked, quietly.

Sylvia smiled. "The exertion got to me, Pete. That's all. I'll be fine in a few minutes." She looked at him and smiled again. "Honest," she said. She relaxed and leaned against him.

Suddenly, *Gossamer* moved. "Oh my god!" cried Ada, "it's the instruction fetch." Taken by surprise, Ned lost his balance. Inside, the others, huddled together on the meeting room floor, watched in horror as he slid slowly across the bubble. Desperately he struggled for a hand-hold, but there were none. He continued to slide, almost in slow motion. Then, he broke free, falling toward the chip just below.

"No!" screamed Ada. She dropped to her knees and stared through *Gossamer*'s side. There, receding farther and farther into the distance, lay Ned, his arms outstretched, pleading. "What's going to happen to him?" she asked, sadly. Her voice trembled with the strain of the past few minutes.

"He's gone," said Corbin. "We'll never see him again."

"But what will *happen* to him?" Ada insisted.

"I don't know," admitted Corbin. "Maybe, if he's lucky, the fall killed him. If he survives, he'll be stuck inside the computer for the rest of his life. He won't last long, though. He'll probably die in less than an hour, real time."

"That's terrible." Ada cried. Susie moved to her side, comforting her.

"Yes. Yes it is," agreed Corbin. He turned his attention to Sylvia. "How is she, Pete?" he asked.

"I think she's okay," Pete replied.

As *Gossamer* left the chip and flowed across the memory board the crew sat quietly, thinking of Ned. They had beaten him, but that fact brought no joy. He may have been sullen, self-centered, and impossible to work with, but they respected him as a talented colleague. No one really wished him ill. And now he was gone.

Gossamer joined the bus that would take it straight to the instruction register. A melancholy silence hung over the crew. "Looks like Ned won after all," Pete said, sadly. "We won't have time to fix the error. We failed."

20 *The Processor*

"There's still a chance," said Corbin, taking command. "Listen carefully, because we won't have time to go over this twice. Return to your stations the instant *Gossamer* stops. Susie, you move back in with Ada. That will get us down to four active bubbles for the parity check."

"Okay, Gramps," Susie answered, meekly. She seemed frightened. Perhaps she realized the danger they faced. Maybe losing Ned had affected her.

"Won't that change our instruction, Professor?" asked Pete.

"It doesn't matter," Corbin replied. "We're riding a no-op, so our bit pattern is irrelevant, but we do need an even number of 1-bits to pass the parity check." He swung toward Sylvia. There was no time for lectures now. "Our instruction is being fetched," he continued. "The bus will drop us in the instruction register. As soon as possible, take off and fly to the instruction counter. You'll have to guide her, Ada."

"Roger," replied Sylvia.

"Okay, Professor," agreed Ada.

"Pete, stay in bubble 3. Ada, give him the laser." Without comment, Ada handed over the weapon. "We're going to change a few bits on the fly. I'll identify them."

"Got you, Professor," said Pete.

Their plan, Corbin knew, could be reduced to two steps: set a trap, and escape. Because Ned had changed a 0-bit to a 1-bit, the trap had been rendered harmless.

Reluctantly, Corbin admired Ned's ingenuity. He had sabotaged only the first part of the plan. The subsequent output operation would still be carried out. *Gossamer* would escape. The Harlequin would retain control. From Ned's perspective, that must have seemed the best of both worlds. Only chance had revealed that 1-bit to Corbin. Had he missed it, no one would have known why the mission failed. Had he missed it, he and SMF, not Ned, would become scapegoats for the Harlequin's victory. But he had seen it, and now Ned lay dead or dying inside a computer.

Corbin faced a difficult decision. If he did nothing, *Gossamer* would escape. Susie would be safe. The Harlequin would still control NECEN, but Ned would bear the blame. Trying to change that bit could prove dangerous. If they failed, they might all share Ned's fate. No one would blame him if he quit now.

But Pete would know. And Sylvia. Ada, too. He had their respect; he didn't want to lose it. Then there was Susie. She'd come this far. Step-by-step, she'd grown into the mission. She'd never forgive him if he quit now.

Finally, Corbin thought about Ned. If the crew had given up, if they hadn't fought for one more chance, Ned would still be alive. If they quit now, Ned's death would have been in vain. As long as the slightest chance of success remained, they had to keep fighting!

The bus ended in the instruction register. *Gossamer* jerked to a stop. Immediately, the crew members sprinted to their stations. Sylvia started the engine. Slowly, ponderously, *Gossamer* rose.

Looking down from his flight chair, Corbin studied NECEN's processor (Fig. 20.1). The clock lay to his right. He pictured it working like a metronome, its precisely timed electronic pulses driving the system. Tick! I-time. An instruction is fetched. Tick! E-time. The instruction is executed. Tick! I-time. The next instruction is fetched.

Gossamer, he knew, rode a meaningless instruction, a no-op. The instruction had already been fetched; that was how the ship had reached the processor. He knew the arithmetic and logic unit had already started to execute it. The fact that it did nothing meant nothing to NECEN. E-time would still consume one full clock cycle.

The next time that clock ticked, NECEN would fetch the instruction Ned had changed. Another pulse, and the arithmetic and logic unit would execute it. *Gossamer* had but two ticks of the clock to accomplish its mission.

Again Corbin looked down at the processor. *Gossamer* glided slowly over the instruction register. The clock lay near the processor board's far edge. Closer at hand were the instruction control unit and the arithmetic and logic unit. An array of work registers used to hold computational results lay behind him. Their objective, the instruction counter, lay just ahead. Beyond it were still more control registers.

FIGURE 20.1 Looking down, Corbin saw the processor laid out before him. *Gossamer* was directly over the instruction register, flying toward the instruction counter. Later, an interrupt would transfer them to the save register. From there, the ship would fly to the channel linkage register.

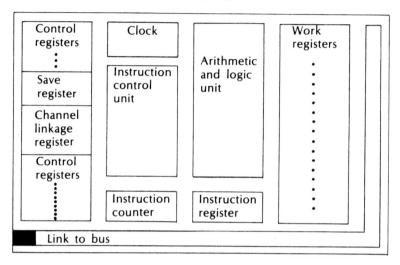

Mentally, he reviewed the plan, searching for some small detail he may have overlooked. The immediate objective was to fix the instruction Ned had changed. One more tick of the clock and that instruction would be fetched. However, even if they were able to fix it, NECEN would not execute it because the program state bit in the instruction counter was on. With that bit on, NECEN would know the instruction had come from an application program. An application program is not allowed to modify main memory outside its own region. The bit *had* to be turned off.

Thus, *Gossamer* moved toward the instruction counter. Once there, Pete would use the laser to turn off the program state bit. That mission accomplished, the ship would hurry back to the instruction register to await the arrival of Ned's instruction. Again, one bit would be changed. The corrected instruction would tell NECEN to turn off the interrupt mask bit in main memory. With the program state bit set to zero, NECEN would execute that instruction. The trap would be set.

The next objective was to escape. The path home led through the channel. The nearest door to the channel, the channel linkage register, lay too far away; *Gossamer*, in its present state, could never fly to it in time. However, right next to the channel linkage register lay the save register. Following an interrupt, the contents of the instruction counter would flow to that save register. The instruction immediately following Ned's would ask the operating system to start an output operation, thus generating an interrupt. If *Gossamer* could manage to return to the instruction counter before the interrupt occured, it could flow to the save register along with the instruction counter's contents. Once there, a short flight would carry it to the channel linkage register.

The operating system, he knew, would signal the channel to start the output operation. The channel, in response, would read the contents of the channel linkage register. If *Gossamer* reached that register in time, the ship would flow to the channel along with the register's contents. Once they reached the channel, they were home free.

Only one task would remain: springing the trap. As the ship flowed through the channel, Corbin would select a target of opportunity, probably a fine wire, and instruct Pete to sever it with the laser. If all went well, the result would be a never-ending series of interrupts causing an endless loop. Computers are completely predictable, and they would take advantage of that predictability.

The plan made sense; it just might work! But success, Corbin knew, depended on perfect timing, perfect execution, and a great deal of luck. One mistake, one bad break, one miscalculation, and they might never leave NECEN alive!

"We're over the instruction counter," called Ada.

"Good," replied Corbin. "Pete, do you know how to read the bits in a register?"

"Not really, Professor," he admitted.

"Look directly below you. The register is a long, narrow, black rectangle."

"Okay, I see it."

"Look inside the register. You should see a string of little black squares."

"I see them."

"Good. Each square is a flip-flop circuit. Each flip-flop holds one bit. Stare at one, you should see a pattern inside it."

Pete selected one of the tiny squares and stared intently. Finally, against the black background of the chip's surface, a faint pattern emerged. "I think I see it," he said.

"Describe it," insisted Corbin.

"Looks like two little gray squares linked by a fine wire."

"That's it. Now look even more carefully. One of those little squares should glow slightly. The other one should be flat and dull."

"They both look dull," said Pete. "No, wait a minute. I see what you mean. The right one glows very faintly."

"Which bit are you looking at?"

"The second one."

Corbin paused and looked for himself. "You got it, Pete. That's a 1-bit. If the right side glows, it's a 1-bit; if the left side glows, it's a 0-bit."

"How do I change the value?" asked Pete.

"Aim at the glow," replied Corbin. "The extra energy from the laser should overload the circuit and force it to flip."

Without another word, Pete climbed onto the work table, pushed open the hatch, and slid partway through. Wrapping the laser's shoulder strap around his arm, he rested his elbows on the edge of the hatchway and prepared to fire. A hand signal indicated that he was ready.

"Can you hear me?" called Corbin. Pete nodded. "It's the second bit, Pete. It's on. Do you see it?" Again Pete nodded. That's the program state bit. Turn it off! Fire!"

Staring intently down the barrel, Pete pulled the trigger. Nothing happened! He shook his head, gripped the laser more tightly, and pulled the trigger again. Still nothing happened.

"Fire, damn you!" he bellowed. Swinging the laser away from his shoulder, he shook it, violently. Perhaps something had jammed when Ned dropped it. Perhaps he could clear it.

Again he positioned the laser against his shoulder, took aim, and pulled the trigger. This time, a brilliant flash of intense light shot toward the instruction counter. The beam struck the center of one grey square. For an instant, the square glowed brightly. Then, suddenly, the glow cascaded across the narrow wire to the other side. The program state bit now read zero. Pete breathed a sigh of relief.

"Bingo!" shouted Corbin. A twinge in his side tempered his excitement. Ignoring the pain, he turned toward Sylvia. "To the instruction register," he called. "Quickly."

Pete slipped back inside as *Gossamer* lumbered through the still air. "I just changed the program state bit, right?" he asked.

"That's right," said Corbin.

"Next we have to change the interrupt mask bit. Isn't it right next to the program state bit?"

"Yes, it is."

"Why don't we change it now?"

"It wouldn't do any good, Pete. We have to make the change down in the address table, not here."

"Why?"

"Changing the mask bit now, up here in the instruction counter, would be like yanking the hook out of the water before the fish bites.

The problem is timing; we're setting a trap for NECEN, and we have to spring it at just the right time. We want the interrupt mask bit to be zero *after* we break a wire in the channel. We're concerned about the mask bit's *future* value, not its present value. The instruction counter holds the present value. The mask bit's future value is stored in main memory.

"Suddenly, I have more respect for programmers," said Pete. "I thought my profession demanded attention to detail."

"Thank you, Pete," called Ada. "I'll remember that."

Pete grinned, and relaxed just a bit.

"Anything we can do to help, Professor?" asked Ada. Anything beat sitting and waiting.

"Except for guiding Sylvia, not really," answered Corbin.

Ada reached across the aisle and touched Susie's arm. "Guess this is one of those operations that involves more brawn than brains." she said. Susie flashed a tense smile.

"We're nearing the end of the instruction counter, Pete," said Corbin. "When we reach the instruction register, the bad instruction should be in there. We have to change bit number 8. We start counting at zero, so that's the ninth bit."

"Got you," said Pete. Again he climbed onto the table, pushed through the hatchway, and prepared to fire.

Corbin turned toward *Gossamer*'s control module. "Sylvia," he called. "Hover on my command!"

"Roger!" she replied.

Bit by bit, Corbin noted the ship's progress. *Gossamer* seemed to crawl over the surface. Why were they moving so slowly? If the arithmetic and logic unit started executing the instruction before Pete could change it, the plan would fail!

Finally, the ship cleared the first byte. Now, the target bit lay directly below. Corbin stared at the flip-flop circuit. The bit read 1; it had to be reset to zero. "Hover!" he shouted. His side ached, but he couldn't worry about it now.

Gossamer stopped in midair, hovering, almost perfectly still. "Hit the right side, Pete," called Corbin. "Turn it off."

Carefully, Pete took aim. Suddenly, the ship dropped. Then it steadied. "Hold it still, Sylvia!" shouted Corbin.

"Tell Pete to make it quick, Professor," she called back. "The engine is overheating."

Again, Pete took aim. Just as he fired, *Gossamer* dropped again; the shot missed its mark. Corbin held his breath. Once more, Pete took aim. A bright flash shot from the laser and exploded in the target bit's center.

The right square glowed brightly; the charge cascaded to the left. He'd done it! Now they had but two ticks of the clock to hurry back to the instruction counter.

An ominous rumble shook the ship. The engines labored. Steadily, *Gossamer* dropped toward the chip's surface. "Return to the instruction counter, Sylvia," called Corbin. "Land on the first eight bits you come to." She started toward their objective. Still the fragile craft dropped, its engines sputtering, its rotor blades grinding. The instruction counter was so near, but it seemed so far away. If *Gossamer* could reach it in time, its bubbles would become bits again and flow effortlessly through the processor's circuits. They couldn't fail now! Not after all they'd done!

Pete pulled the hatchway closed behind him and jumped to the floor. Corbin swung the work table against the wall. *Gossamer* would soon rejoin the electronic circuits, and they didn't want to be caught between bubbles. Together they hurried through the passageway. Quickly Corbin pulled himself into his seat and fastened his belt. Glancing down, he saw the contents of the instruction register changing. The output instruction had been fetched. Soon NECEN would execute it. *Gossamer* had to reach the instruction counter before that happened. If they were late, if the output instruction were executed before they reached the instruction counter, they might never escape NECEN. One tick of the clock was all that separated them from sharing Ned's fate.

One bubble cleared the edge of the instruction counter. One by one, the others followed. Still the ship dropped, riding barely above the chip's surface. Valiantly, Sylvia fought the controls, struggling to extract the last possible measure of performance from the dying ship. With a thud, *Gossamer* landed. Each bubble touched one of the instruction counter's bits. They had made it!

Just in time! With a jerk, *Gossamer* left the instruction counter and, crossing a network of fine wires, flowed to the save register. The output operation had begun. Eventually, Corbin knew, the contents of this save register would be reloaded into the instruction counter. Their presence had changed several bits, but that didn't matter. If all went as planned, NECEN would shut itself down long before this save register was reloaded.

Soon, the processor, acting under control of the start I/O routine's instructions, would notify the channel that output data were to be sent to the transmission control unit. The channel, in turn, would get the channel linkage register's contents. That register was their next objective. Once more, *Gossamer* had to fly.

"Next register, Sylvia!" shouted Corbin. "Think we can make it?"

"I'll try," she replied. "Is it in front of us, or behind us?"

"You'll have to move toward bubble 7," said Ada.

"Roger." Once again, the rotors turned. The sound seemed even louder than before. Reluctantly, *Gossamer* rose, but just barely. Slowly, bit by bit, its bottom scraping the surface, the ship crossed the save register.

The channel linkage register lay just ahead. Afraid to look, Corbin closed his eyes and tried to ignore the laboring engine and the grinding rotor blades. Suddenly, *Gossamer* landed. Cautiously, he opened his eyes. Sylvia had done it!

And not a moment too soon. In an instant, *Gossamer* moved toward the channel. Once again, the bubbles flowed over parallel wires. Once again, the ship joined a bus line. But this time was different. This time, they were heading home!

21 *Escape*

The bus ended. *Gossamer* rested in a channel. Corbin pictured the channel's structure (Fig. 21.1): two boards, a processor board and a memory board, side-by-side, plugged into two separate bus lines running across the channel's base. One, a control bus, linked the channel's processor and NECEN's main processor. The other tied NECEN's main memory to the channel's memory, and then continued on to the transmission control unit.

An instant before, the ship had barely managed to reach the channel linkage register in NECEN's main processor. The channel had read that register, copying its contents across the control bus and storing them in a channel register. Thus, *Gossamer* clung to the channel's processor board. Soon, a message would move from NECEN's memory, through the channel's memory board, and out to the transmission control unit. That message would carry them home, but only if they could reach the other board. *Gossamer* would have to fly once more.

"Sylvia," called Corbin. "We have to transfer to that other board." He pointed toward their target. "The message will come through there. The two boards are plugged, side-by-side, into the channel's base. Near the bottom is a set of tabs that link the memory board to the data bus. That's our objective." Far below, the golden tabs glinted in the dim light. *Gossamer* could almost fall to them.

"When do we leave?" asked Sylvia.

"As soon as possible. When you reach the tabs, hover until a message arrives."

"That may be a problem," warned Sylvia.

FIGURE 21.1 Corbin formed a mental image of the channel. It consisted of two boards: a processor board and a memory board. One bus linked the processor board to NECEN's main processor. Another linked the memory board to both NECEN's main memory and the communication interface. *Gossamer* clung to the processor board; thus the ship would have to fly once more.

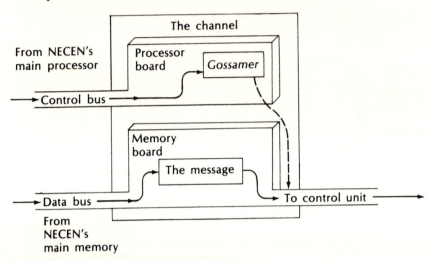

"I know," he admitted. "We don't have much choice, though. The message could come at any time, and if we wait up here, we might miss it. If that happens, we'll never get home."

"We're on our way," said Sylvia. Once again, she started the engine. Reluctantly, the rotors turned. *Gossamer* pulled away from the processor, wobbling slightly. Suddenly, Sylvia cut the engine. The ship began to drop quickly toward the bottom of the channel, its rotors spinning noisily as the air rushed through them.

"Something wrong?" called Pete.

"No," replied Sylvia. "I'm saving the engine. We need the power to hover."

Corbin sat quietly, watching. To his left, the processor board raced past. To his right, the memory board drew closer and closer. *Gossamer* continued dropping. Sylvia restarted the engine. Again the rotors caught the air; the ship's descent slowed. Carefully, she searched for the tabs, spotted them, and maneuvered toward them. Like a gigantic skyscraper, the memory board towered overhead. *Gossamer* hovered near its base, waiting for a message. The engine sputtered and coughed; the rotors screamed in protest.

"We're overheating again," warned Sylvia. "I can't hold it much longer."

"Can we land?" suggested Pete.

"It's risky," warned Corbin. "When that message comes, we won't have much time."

"The front rotor shaft is about to snap," countered Sylvia. "If we don't relieve the pressure, time won't matter anyway."

"Sounds like we don't have any choice," concluded Pete. "Get as close to the tabs as you can and take us down."

"Roger," agreed Sylvia. With a bump, *Gossamer* landed. The engines stopped.

"Watch the bus, Sylvia," instructed Corbin. "At the first sign of a glow, move."

"Got you, Professor," she replied.

Corbin turned his attention to the last stage of his plan. In some way, they had to damage the channel just as *Gossamer* left it. He searched for a target. Then he spotted a nearby chip. He identified it as a switching circuit, but its function didn't matter. Much more important was the fine wire that protruded, barely visible, from one edge. That wire would be the target.

He swung from his chair and stepped quickly into bubble 3, where Pete, laser in hand, already stood waiting. "Do you see the chip directly in front of us?" he asked, pointing to it.

"Sure do," replied Pete. He, too, pointed. "That one, right?"

"That's the one. Look near the top left edge. There's a fine wire sticking out."

Pete stared, then he chuckled. "I see it, Professor. Now I know how William Tell felt when he had to shoot an apple off his kid's head."

"It's our best bet. There aren't too many components we can destroy with that little laser."

"Do I have to *destroy* it?"

"Sever it, Pete. If you just hit it, you'll overload the circuit, and the heat will generate an interrupt, but, as soon as the wire cools, the interrupts stop. If they stop, our Trojan Horse won't work. Hot wires cool; broken wires don't regenerate. Break it."

Pete pushed open the hatch and took his position. Almost immediately, a telltale glow brightened the bus: a message approached. Sylvia spotted the glow and started the engine. It sputtered, then died.

"Let's go, Sylvia!" shouted Corbin. "The message is coming." They *had* to reach that line. If they missed the message, they might never escape!

"I see it," replied Sylvia, in a calm, controlled voice. She understood the danger, but like Pete, she seemed to improve in a crisis. Again she worked her controls, smoothly and precisely, repeating the starting sequence. Again, the engine sputtered and coughed. Finally, it caught. Slowly, reluctantly, *Gossamer* rose, its engine protesting as it drove the ship forward.

"Fire the instant we touch, Pete!" shouted Corbin. His last two words echoed in his ears. It seemed quiet. Then, he realized what had happened. The engine had stopped!

Slowly, *Gossamer*'s momentum carried it toward the tabs. At the same time, gravity dragged the ship down. If they reached the tabs, they were home safely. If not, they were doomed. The glow marking the message moved steadily toward the bus. Soon it would flow past. The outcome no longer rested in their hands. They were so close. They couldn't fail now! With a jolt, the ship hit something, but what? Anxiously, Corbin looked down. Gold! They were safe! "Fire, Pete!" he shouted. "Fire!"

A flash of light shot from the laser and streaked toward its target. The threadlike wire began to glow. Another flash, then another and another, found the mark! The wire glowed red, but still it wouldn't break. *Gossamer* moved now, leaving the golden tabs and entering the data bus. One last shot struck the wire. A wisp of smoke curled upward, then the target disappeared from view. Reluctantly, Pete pulled the hatch closed behind him. Maybe that last shot had severed the wire. Maybe it hadn't. There was nothing more he could do.

Gossamer crossed the data bus and entered the transmission control unit. A chip shifted the bubbles from parallel back to serial. The next chip, Corbin knew, would check parity. For some reason, that bothered him.

He remembered their first trip through the transmission control unit. NECEN, they thought, would expect odd parity, so five bubbles, including Ned's, had been occupied. But the Harlequin had surprised them, resetting the machine to even parity. Consequently, *Gossamer* had been shunted toward an unknown chip. Had they passed through it, the chip would have tried to give them a sixth 1-bit by sending a jolt of current through bubble 7. The resulting shock might have killed them all. Instead, they had flown over it.

Now *Gossamer* headed back out through the transmission control unit. Susie shared a bubble with Ada. He shared the meeting room with Pete. Three bubbles, including Sylvia's, were occupied. That meant odd parity. Their line *expected* odd parity. The parity changer, Corbin decided, would not be a problem this time. Unless, of course, he was wrong. In its present state, *Gossamer* could not fly. If the ship headed toward the parity changer, they could do nothing to stop it.

Gossamer dropped below the board's surface. When the ship emerged, it would enter either the parity changer or a buffer. Corbin held his breath. Suddenly, the light returned. A fine wire led to a chip—a memory chip. The buffer! Nothing could stop them now! Once a message reached the transmission control unit's buffer, the computer forgot it. They were home free!

Corbin walked confidently into Ada's bubble. He stopped in front of his granddaughter and took her hand. She stared back at him, fear in her eyes. "We're safe now, Susie," he whispered. "Everything is going to be okay."

She smiled. "I knew we could do it." There was only a hint of a tremor in her voice. Grabbing his neck, she hugged him, tightly. His side ached, but he didn't care. They were safe.

"I want you to move back to bubble 3 where you were before," he continued. "You'll be right between Ada and me. We'll be home before you know it, honey."

"I'm sorry, Gramps. I know I shouldn't have come."

He hugged her again. "Don't be sorry, Susie. You were very brave. You did fine."

"I should have stayed back in Washington. I caused all kinds of trouble."

Gently, he lifted her chin and stared into her eyes. He smiled. "That was wrong," he agreed, "but I'm glad you came. I'm proud of you."

"And now we need you again, Susie," said Ada. She stood directly behind them. "With Ned gone, if it wasn't for you we'd have only four people. We need five to get through the network. That's why you have to move to bubble 3. It's important."

"That's right, Susie," agreed Corbin. "You shouldn't have come, but you did. And now we need you—we really do."

Susie smiled. "I was scared, Gramps," she admitted.

"Me, too, Susie. Me, too." He hugged her again and kissed her cheek. "I have to go now." He turned and walked toward his own bubble. As he entered the meeting room, he stopped and glanced back over his shoulder. Susie walked toward him, toward her assigned station. She seemed so confident, so mature. He felt proud of his granddaughter. He turned to Pete. "We're on our way home, my friend," he said quietly.

Pete swung the folding table against the wall and put the laser away. Finished, he checked the hatchway latch, and then laid a hand on Corbin's shoulder. "Hope I got it Professor," he said. "That wire was smoking, but I didn't see it break."

"We'll know soon enough," said Corbin. "We did our best. That's all anyone can ask."

"Guess you're right," agreed Pete. "Still, I wish we knew."

"So do I, Pete, so do I." The two old friends started toward their stations.

"Tell me, Professor, that last flight . . ."

"You mean the one between the two channel boards?"

"Yes, that's the one. We were already in the channel. Why did we have to change boards? We didn't do that on input."

"There are two paths, two separate bus lines, linking a channel to a computer, Pete," replied Corbin. "A control bus allows the main processor and the channel's processor to communicate with each other. We were in a register in NECEN's main processor, so we followed the control bus to the channel's processor. The message was in main memory, so it took the data bus to the channel's memory. We had to switch boards to join the message."

"Why are there two bus lines?"

"It has to do with the computer's architecture. Why don't you come in here and I'll show you."

Pete had already started toward him. The big man slid into bubble 4's work chair. "Go to it," he said.

"Okay," agreed Corbin, with a smile. "Let's start with microcomputer architecture." He picked up his pad of paper and sketched another diagram (Fig. 21.2). "Most micros," he continued, "are designed around

FIGURE 21.2 Microcomputers are typically constructed around a single bus line. All data movement and all control signals must pass over the same bus, making it difficult to do more than one thing at a time.

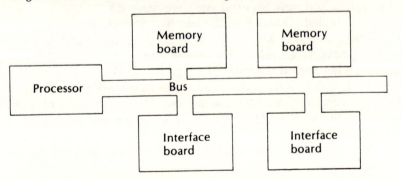

a single bus line. Control signals move from the processor to memory over the bus. Other control signals move between the processor and the various interface boards over the same bus. Data move between the processor's registers and memory, or between main memory and an interface board over the same bus. The single bus is the only path linking the internal components.

"There are some real advantages to single-bus architecture. For one thing, it's simple. It's also relatively inexpensive. There are some disadvantages, too, though. With only one line, only one operation can take place at a time. When data are flowing from memory to an interface board, for example, the processor can't fetch instructions from memory. If the processor is transferring data from a register to main memory, the bus is not available to copy other data from memory to a printer interface. For all practical purposes, a single bus line is limited to one activity at a time. That's no problem on a single user micro. Mainframes, however, support multiple users. Remember our discussion of channels?"

"Sure," said Pete. "The channel is a small computer with its own, independent processor. It takes care of controlling input and output, so the main processor is free to work on something else."

"That's right," said Corbin. "Freeing the processor to work on another program is essential if several users are to be supported, but the independent processor, by itself, isn't enough. Two processors and one bus line is a bit like two plugs and one socket. If we're to take advantage of multiple processors, we need multiple bus lines. That's why most mainframes use a multiple-bus architecture." He sketched another diagram (Fig. 21.3), tore the sheet from his pad, and handed it to Pete.

Suddenly, *Gossamer* moved again. "Better get back to your bubble," said Corbin.

"I'm on my way." Pete slid from the seat and dropped to the floor. Crawling on all fours to avoid any possibility of falling, he returned to his chair and fastened his seat belt. "Continue, Professor," he called, staring at the new diagram.

"In a minute, Pete," replied Corbin. "We're about to enter the message-switching computer, and I want to watch the show."

The laser optics seemed even more beautiful than before. All around him, brilliant pulses flashed by, again and again. He leaned back, relaxed, his face bathed first in red, then blue, then yellow, then green. He glanced behind him. A stream of laser pulses moved with them. The fiber optics cable reminded him of a freeway on a rainy night, with traffic marked by streaks of light moving in opposite directions. But no freeway ever looked like this! It took his breath away.

FIGURE 21.3 Mainframes, on the other hand, typically use a multiple-bus architecture. In this sketch, two separate data buses link main memory to the main processor and to the channel, respectively. With two bus lines, the main processor and the channel can access main memory simultaneously.

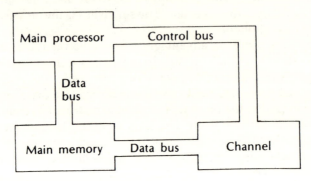

Abruptly, *Gossamer* left the fiber optics cable and entered the message-switching computer. Soon they would return to the satellite and begin the final stage of their journey. Corbin was ready. As he sat looking through *Gossamer* at the message-switching computer's internal components, he knew he would never see a computer in quite the same way again. Still, the time had come to go home.

"Professor," called Pete.

"Yes." Reluctantly, he turned back to his friend.

Pete waved the diagram at him. "You were talking about multiple-bus architecture," he said.

"So I was," agreed Corbin. "Where were we?"

"You'd just compared a single-bus architecture to two plugs and one socket," replied Pete.

"I remember. The problem boils down to efficiency. That's why mainframes support multiple users. That's why they use channels. The idea is to have several things going on at the same time. That way, we can take maximum advantage of the computer's power. We can't do several things at the same time with a single bus."

"The diagram I gave you shows a multiple-bus architecture. Note that one bus links the processor with main memory. The processor uses that bus to fetch instructions. Over that bus, data move from memory to a register or from a register to memory. But note that it's only used to link the processor and main memory; input and output operations use different bus lines.

"Concentrate on how the channel is attached to the computer. Two bus lines are involved. A control bus links the main processor and the channel's processor. The main processor uses it to tell the channel to start an I/O operation. The channel uses it to send interrupts to the main processor when an I/O operation is finished.

"A separate data bus links main memory and the channel's memory. On input, data flow over that bus into main memory. On output, data flow from main memory over that bus. Note that, because they have different paths to main memory, the main processor and the channel can access memory simultaneously."

"You said NECEN has at least five channels," recalled Pete. "I assume each one has its own set of bus lines."

"That's right," said Corbin. "With five channels plus the main processor, six different regions of main memory can be active at the same time."

"That's amazing."

"And now," said Corbin, "if you don't mind, Pete, I want to sit back and enjoy the rest of the trip. I may never see this again."

"I understand, Professor. See you in Washington."

Corbin leaned back and relaxed. Any second now, *Gossamer* would leave the message-switching computer for the satellite. He remembered how he had panicked earlier, and smiled. This time he would enjoy the trip.

Susie's soft voice broke through his concentration. "Gramps."

"Yes, Susie," replied Corbin. He looked at her, sitting there in bubble 3, and once again felt proud. She had done well.

"I feel bad about Ned."

"We all do, honey," he replied, gently.

"Maybe, if I hadn't yelled at him, he'd still be alive."

"No, Susie," said Ada. "You did the right thing. If you hadn't spoken up when you did, I would have, or Pete would have. Ned might have shot us. What happened to him was his own fault, not yours."

"And if Ada or Pete hadn't acted, I would have," added Corbin. "He would have shot me, too. Ada's right, Susie."

"That was a very brave thing you did," said Pete, joining the conversation. "Don't blame yourself for what happened to Ned. He almost killed all of us."

"Thanks," said Susie. Corbin watched a shy smile form at the corners of her mouth. "Still, I wish it hadn't happened."

"We all do," agreed Ada.

The crew fell silent, each person lost in his or her own thoughts. Finally, *Gossamer* started toward the satellite. Corbin watched the world fall away. He'd done his best. Perhaps the Harlequin had been defeated, perhaps not, but he'd done his best, and no one could ask more than that. He felt satisfied.

22 *Success*

NECEN's clock ticked. The instruction control unit looked to the instruction counter, found an address, and sent it over a bus to main memory. The control unit incremented the instruction counter. The processor waited.

The memory controller accepted the address. Quickly it computed the physical location of the desired word. Sixty-four electronic switches opened; sixty-four bits flowed to the bus. Back to the instruction register they raced. To memory, they were just sixty-four bits. To the processor, however, they held an instruction. Carefully, the instruction control unit checked the bit pattern, verifying the instruction's validity.

Then, something strange happened. Eight of those bits seemed to rise above the instruction register and fly toward the instruction counter. A human being faced with such an unusual circumstance would have wondered. A human being might have spotted *Gossamer* and, perhaps, reacted. But no one told NECEN to wonder. So it didn't.

Again the clock ticked. The arithmetic and logic unit took control. The instruction told the processor to do nothing, so it did nothing. It didn't object. It didn't complain about this waste of its valuable time. Computers don't think. They don't reason. They follow instructions. An instruction is an instruction; the computer doesn't care. This instruction told NECEN to do nothing, so it did nothing.

Again the clock ticked. Again, the instruction control unit looked to its instruction counter. An address flowed to main memory; the counter was incremented. The processor waited. The next instruction entered the instruction register.

Again the clocked ticked. The arithmetic and logic unit scanned the instruction. It told the processor to change one bit in main memory. That bit lay outside the program's address space. The arithmetic and logic unit checked the instruction counter's second bit: the program state bit. A 1-bit would have made the instruction illegal; an application program cannot change the contents of memory outside its own region. The bit read zero. A tiny fraction of a second before, that bit had read 1, but *Gossamer* had changed it. Clearly, the instruction had come from an application program. Clearly, the program state bit's setting was wrong. But the computer didn't care. Right now, that bit read zero; the instruction was legal. A pulse of current crossed the bus toward main memory; a single bit changed from 1 to 0. The interrupt mask bit had been reset. The trap was baited.

Again the clocked ticked. Mindlessly, the instruction control unit looked to the instruction counter. An address flowed to main memory. The instruction control unit incremented the instruction counter, and waited.

The next instruction entered the instruction register. Again the clock ticked; the arithmetic and logic unit had control. The instruction told it to start an output operation. Key control information moved from main memory to the channel linkage register. An electronic signal flashed over the command bus to channel 1. Now the arithmetic and logic unit waited for the channel to respond. As it waited, it did not notice that the channel linkage register's contents had changed. It had no reason to notice; no one told it to. But *Gossamer* had entered the channel linkage register.

A signal returned over the command bus; the channel would assume responsibility for the output operation. Satisfied, the arithmetic and logic unit released the processor. The clock ticked. Mindlessly, the instruction control unit fetched the next instruction.

Meanwhile, the channel read the main processor's channel linkage register. Sixty-four bits flowed from NECEN's main processor, across a bus, and into the channel's instruction register. *Gossamer* had escaped NECEN. The channel knew only that its next instruction had arrived.

The channel's clock ticked, and its arithmetic and logic unit took control. The instruction told it to send a stream of output data to a telecommunication line. Obediently, it asked main memory for the data. Obediently, main memory placed them on the data bus. As the data flowed through the channel's memory, *Gossamer* joined the message stream. The channel neither noticed nor cared. No one had told it to.

Surely NECEN's main processor must have suspected something. First came an instruction telling it to do nothing. Somehow, during the execution of that instruction, the program state bit had magically changed to 0. Then came an instruction that modified a key bit in the address table. An output operation followed. The pattern made no sense; no programmer would write such an absurd sequence. It required very little imagination to realize that something was wrong.

But computers have no imagination. Already the prior instructions were forgotten. The clock ticked. The instruction control unit did the only thing it could. It looked to the instruction counter and fetched the next instruction.

Byte by byte, the channel copied the message from NECEN's main memory into its own memory. Meanwhile, NECEN's main processor executed several more instructions. Suddenly, a tiny wire near the channel's data bus overloaded, and then snapped. The channel's error-checking circuitry sensed the hardware failure, and sent an interrupt to the main processor. NECEN's hardware sensed the interrupt and copied the instruction counter into a save register. A single word moved from main memory to the instruction counter. The interrupt ended.

The clock ticked. NECEN's instruction control unit looked to the instruction counter, found an address, and fetched the instruction stored at that address. Thus, the operating system's first instruction flowed to the instruction register. The clock ticked. The arithmetic and logic unit gained control. Obediently, it executed the instruction.

Back on the channel, the tiny wire was still broken. The channel's error-checking circuitry had one and only one job to do—report such failures to the main processor. Thus, it sent another interrupt. A human being would have hesitated. A human being would have remembered the interrupt sent just a few nanoseconds before, and given the main processor time to respond. But hardware cannot reason.

The second interrupt arrived as the main processor executed the first instruction in the operating system. Had the first bit in the instruction counter been 1, hardware would have ignored this second interrupt. But the first bit had been reset to zero by *Gossamer's* crew. NECEN accepted the new interrupt. The instruction counter's contents flowed to the save register. A word from memory moved to the instruction counter.

The clock ticked. The instruction control unit looked to the instruction counter and fetched the next instruction. It flowed from memory, over the bus, and into the instruction register. Again the clock ticked. Obediently, the arithmetic and logic unit executed the new instruction.

A human being would have noticed something wrong. A human being would have balked at executing the very same instruction once again. A human being would have wondered. But computers can't wonder. Computers do what they are told. Repeating the same instruction was absurd, but computers have no sense of the absurd. Thus, once again, NECEN executed the very first instruction in the operating system.

Meanwhile, the channel's error-checking circuitry, mindlessly, mechanically, sent yet another interrupt to the main processor. As the arithmetic and logic unit finished executing the operating system's first instruction, the third interrupt arrived. Hardware checked the instruction counter's first bit and accepted the interrupt. The instruction counter's contents flowed to the save register; a word flowed from memory to the instruction counter.

The clock ticked. The instruction control unit looked to the instruction counter and fetched the next instruction. Again the operating system's first instruction flowed to the instruction register. The instruction control unit neither noted nor cared that it had fetched the same instruction for the third consecutive time. It was designed to do one and only one thing: fetch the instruction whose address it found in the instruction counter. It could do nothing else. Computers don't think. They respond.

Over and over again the cycle continued. The channel, sensing a machine failure, sent an interrupt to the main processor. The processor, seeing no reason to ignore the interrupt, accepted it, copied the instruction counter into the save register, and moved the address of the operating system's first instruction into the instruction counter. The instruction control unit fetched the first instruction in the operating system; then the arithmetic and logic unit executed it. A new interrupt arrived. Again the operating system's first instruction was fetched and executed. Another interrupt arrived. Over and over and over again, the same instruction was fetched and executed.

Computers are predictable. They are precise. If you tell a computer to add 2 + 2, it will get 4. If you didn't *mean* to tell it to add 2 + 2, it will *still* get 4. A computer is a machine—nothing more. NECEN was being told to execute the same instruction over and over again, so it did. Like a dog chasing its tail, the machine was completely unaware of the absurdity of its actions.

Did NECEN repeat this single instruction ten times? A hundred? A thousand? No. In the first second after the first interrupt, a million more arrived. In that first second, that single instruction executed a million times! During the next second, it executed a million more!

Four seconds passed. Four million times this single instruction was executed, again and again and again. Still the interrupts came. Still the computer's hardware copied the same address to the instruction counter.

Again and again the instruction control unit fetched the same instruction. Again and again the arithmetic and logic unit executed it.

Sitting at his control console, the Harlequin typed a command. A second passed; NECEN did not respond. That seemed unusual. He had reprogrammed the operating system to respond immediately to his commands—he had top priority. Another second passed. Still NECEN refused to respond. Far more intelligent than any computer, he knew something had gone wrong. He reacted. But his mind functioned chemically, not electronically. He responded in milliseconds, not nanoseconds. Frantically, he typed command after command through his control console, but NECEN ignored him.

The Harlequin controlled the operating system, but the problem lay in the hardware. A hardware failure means a malfunctioning machine. It is senseless to execute instructions on a malfunctioning machine; thus, a hardware failure has the very *highest* priority. He controlled the hardware through the operating system's instructions, but those instructions could not be executed until after the hardware failure was repaired. He could do nothing.

On NECEN, every component had its duplicate; when one failed, an alternate path was quickly established. Redundancy did not stop at the component level, however. Miles away, somewhere in central New Jersey, lay a complete backup system, with its own main processor, main memory, channels, control units, and peripherals. The Harlequin had no access to the duplicate system. Its telephone lines had not yet been activated. Its operating system did not reflect the Harlequin's changes. The government still controlled it.

In between the two systems sat a ten second timer. With each machine cycle, a tiny fraction of a second ticked off the clock. If it ever reached zero, hardware would automatically switch to the backup machine. Whenever it got control, the operating system reset the timer to ten seconds. Normally, the operating system executed several times each second. Under extreme conditions three or four seconds might pass before it reset the clock. Barring machine failure, the timer would never reach zero.

But something had gone wrong. Seconds passed. Because the processor executed the same instruction over and over again, the operating system never reached the instruction that reset the clock. Microsecond by microsecond, it moved toward zero. Like an alarm clock, it could not reason; when the timer reached zero, it would react.

Finally, inevitably, the magic moment arrived. One more microsecond passed; the timer read zero. Without a thought, new hardware sprang into action. Key data and program disks were switched to new control units. Communication lines were rerouted to new transmission control units. A new processor turned to the first instruction in its operating system. Logically, NECEN still existed. Physically, it occupied new hardware, hardware not controlled by the Harlequin. The government was back in control.

The new hardware had one more task to perform. With preordained timing, another switch fell into place. Its power cut, the hardware that had been NECEN died. Interrupts and machine cycles ceased. Main memory lost its contents. Disk drives spun slowly to a stop. Its power gone, the machine lost its hold over the physical site. The massive door swung open. Seizing their opportunity, NECEN's operating personnel rushed into the room. The crisis had ended. The Harlequin had lost.

23 *The Hero Returns*

Again the world seemed to rush toward them, but this time Corbin felt no fear. The mission had ended. Perhaps they had defeated the Harlequin. Perhaps not. But he'd done his best, and no one could ask for more. He felt satisfied, contented.

Again the Chesapeake came into view. Now the Potomac River lay clearly outlined, far below. Washington appeared, its buildings growing larger and larger. He picked out their target, an antenna. An instant later, the antenna caught *Gossamer*. For a moment, the ship rested in the message-switching computer's memory.

Now the journey's final leg began. *Gossamer* passed through a modem and entered a local analog line. This time, Corbin remained in his seat, fascinated by the experience. The microcomputer's communication interface board passed the ship into main memory where, once again, it rested for a time. Finally, *Gossamer* flowed to the output unit. They were home!

Had it really been only seconds since SMF officially started the mission by flashing the "all systems go" signal? When *Gossamer* left, eight lights had glowed. Now, those same eight lights still glowed. The time had come to signal their return.

"Pete, bubble 7," said Sylvia.

"Roger."

"Professor, bubble 6." One by one, she read their assignments. One by one, they took their positions and verified them. She pushed the output button. Now only five lights glowed. They formed the code for the letter M: Mission accomplished! Quickly she ordered them into new positions; again she pushed the output button. The light pattern displayed the code for the letter K: all systems A-OK!

Once again, red laser light coursed around the ship. The walls of the output unit seemed to shrink, slowly at first, then more rapidly. The laser stopped. A red-tiled hemisphere swung away to reveal the SMF control center. Gigantic human figures moved in slow motion through the room. Corbin blinked back tears of joy. They were home.

A technician approached and looked inside; Sylvia flashed him the all clear signal. Smiling, he held up a hand-lettered sign. "Congratulations!" it said. "You did it!" The sign, Corbin knew, had been printed on a sheet of typing paper, but the letters looked ten feet tall. The crew cheered. Sounds of congratulation filled the passageway.

A robot moved into view. "Strap yourselves in," ordered Sylvia. "Let's not have any accidents now."

As he watched the robot approaching, Corbin thought about Ned. An arid desert, NECEN's memory board provided neither food nor water. Ned would live out his life, what was left of it, alone, hungry, and thirsty. What a terrible way to die. Soon technicians would descend on NECEN. Perhaps they would find his remains, but Corbin doubted it. He would never see Ned again.

He remembered the early miniaturization experiments. In those days, after a few hours, people automatically returned to normal size. He pictured Ned's body expanding, destroying NECEN's internal components. He pictured those components crushing and deforming Ned's body. But it would not happen. The problem had been solved. Only the laser beam could bring him back.

Poor Ned. Like the Luddites, he was misguided. They had tried to stop the industrial revolution by breaking machines. He had tried to stop the information revolution by breaking computers. Like his ancestor, he failed to realize that progress occurs in human minds, not merely in the products of those minds. Progress cannot be stopped. It can, however, be controlled and channeled. Had that been Ned's goal, he might have succeeded.

Ned's message was simple, and Corbin accepted much of it. Humanity was moving much too fast. Humanity had adopted yet another new technology without adequately considering its implications. Corbin had been saying the same thing for years. He understood Ned's frustration. Perhaps a grand gesture might have had an impact; perhaps Ned's plan would have worked. As Corbin reflected on his own feelings, he realized that he shared at least some of Ned's objectives. He would carry on the fight, but not in the same way. He could never accept Ned's means.

"Pete," he called. By now, the robot had finished its work. *Gossamer* rested on a red tile, bathed in laser light.

"Yes, Professor."

"What do we tell them about Ned, Pete?"

"What do you think, Professor?"

"I think we should say Ned died in the line of duty."

"I can't do that. We have to catch the Harlequin. Something in Ned's background might provide a clue. We have to treat him as the Harlequin's ally."

"Do what you must in private, Pete. In public, let him be a hero."

For a moment, Pete said nothing. Quietly, he walked into Corbin's bubble. He looked directly at his old friend. "I don't know, Professor," he said, softly, shaking his head. "I just don't know."

Suddenly, the red glow disappeared. "We're back!" shouted Sylvia. Ada hugged Susie. Smiling, Pete and the professor shook hands. They had made it! "Exit through my bubble," continued Sylvia. "Same way we got in." Corbin walked slowly toward the front of the craft. He took his granddaughter's hand. He dropped to one knee and hugged her. They were safe! At just the right speed, two perfectly normal technicians rolled a set of stairs into place. *Gossamer* was home. They were really back home.

Pete exited first. As he stepped from the ship, uniformed men and women surrounded him, applauding and cheering. Ada stepped out; the cheers continued. Professor Corbin and his granddaughter came next; the applause grew. Finally, Sylvia, their captain, left the ship. They were home.

The mass of uniformed technicians parted to make way for General Custer and his staff. The general walked directly to Pete, saluted, and shook his hand. "Congratulations, Major," he said with a smile. He turned to Susie. "And I am especially happy to see you, young lady. I was afraid we lost you."

"Thank you, General," replied Pete. "We were as surprised as you when we found her on board. She did fine, though."

The general nodded. "I'm sure she did." He looked over the rest of the crew. "Where is Ned Lud?" he asked.

Pete glanced at Corbin. The professor ignored him; he was on his own. Carefully, he considered his answer. Finally, he began. "We lost Ned, General. He deserves a medal, sir."

"You all deserve medals," said the general. He turned to Corbin.

"Professor," he went on, "the President has convened his cabinet. He's waiting for you."

"General," interrupted Pete. "Professor Corbin needs medical attention."

"I can wait," said Corbin. "I have a broken rib or two, General. Pete wrapped it, and I feel about as good as I'm going to feel for the next month or so. Let's go see the President."

"Don't worry about Susie this time," offered Ada. "She and I have plans for the next few hours."

"Is that so," said Corbin, smiling.

"Ada's going to show me the computer center, Gramps," said Susie. "It's all right, isn't it?"

"Sure, Susie."

"Shall we go, Professor?" said the general.

Corbin kissed his granddaughter one more time. "I'm ready," he said.

The conference room looked the same. The Cabinet, the chairman of the Joint Chiefs of Staff and the directors of the FBI and the CIA were all present, along with the leaders of the Senate and the House. One thing had changed, though. Today, Corbin was a hero.

As he entered the room, everyone stood and applauded. Hypocrites. Had the mission failed, he would have been their scapegoat. "Corbin blew it again," they would have said. "It's Corbin's fault." But he had succeeded. Now they honored him. Suddenly, he wanted nothing more than to be back home, away from this madness.

Gradually, the applause died. The President rose. "Today," he began, "a team of brave men and women risked their lives to recapture the NECEN computer center from perhaps the most dangerous hacker our nation has ever faced. We owe that crew a debt of gratitude. Unfortunately, because of the mission's sensitive nature, the nation will never know what happened today. They do, however, know the name of Professor William Corbin."

Again the applause began; the President signaled for quiet. "This nation owes you a great deal, Professor," he continued. He gestured toward the Senate majority leader. "At the request of Senator Tompson, we have arranged for you to address a joint session of Congress tomorrow morning." He faced Corbin and smiled. "Perhaps we can learn something from this incident, Professor." Again, everyone applauded. The President took his seat. Corbin had the floor now.

He waited for the applause to die down. "Mr. President, assembled guests," he began. "The success of this mission can be attributed to the entire team and not to any individual. There is no better pilot than Captain Potter. I've know Major Pete Smith for years, and he is simply the best at what he does. Ada Byron is a true software expert. Ned Lud was an outstanding hardware man; we'll miss him. Without any one of these people, we would not have succeeded. Even my granddaughter did her part. It is they and not I who deserve the credit.

"As for me, my only wish is to return home. I have no desire to address a joint session of Congress, and will *not* do so. I will not allow you to present me as NECEN's savior." An angry murmur filled the room. Addressing Congress was an honor afforded few men; how *dare* he reject it! "I'll say what I have to say here," continued Corbin. "Perhaps you'll listen this time. Perhaps not. So be it."

The mood in the room turned suddenly tense. As he glanced from face to face, Corbin sensed that some understood his decision and respected his stand. Others were insulted. Others, he imagined, resented the loss of an opportunity to be seen in public with the latest hero. A few, of course, opposed him for the old reasons.

The President broke the awkward silence. "Professor Corbin," he said. "I respect your decision not to address Congress. As for today, you will have the undivided attention of this group for as long as you want it." His determined look flashed around the table. He meant it. Corbin would have their attention.

"Thank you, Mr. President," said Corbin. "As most of you know, I opposed the concept of a national data bank from its very inception. Many of you misunderstood my position; a few of you misrepresented it. Some of you accused me of fearing a computer takeover. Today, for the last time, I'll restate by concerns. I hope you listen." He stared directly at Senator Tompson. The Senator looked away.

"The problem with a national data bank, even a partial one, is simple. It has nothing to do with hardware, or software, or data. The problem is people. People rob banks because that's where the money is. People attack data banks because that's where the information is.

"Knowledge is power. If there is any place on earth where that old adage doesn't require proof, it's here in Washington. Knowledge *is* power. You all know that. Information is the raw material of knowledge, so information is power. Computers are information-processing machines. That makes them very powerful machines indeed. If you don't think people will try to take over a national data bank, you are incredibly naive.

"The proposed national data bank represents the greatest concentration of governmental information imaginable. Whoever controls it controls the country. NECEN is a small piece of that national data bank.

By controlling it, the Harlequin, one human being, controlled much of the East Coast's transportation and much of its economic activity. A few hours ago, you were desperately trying to pull together the funds to meet his demands. Who was in control? You? Or him?" Corbin paused, his gaze moving from face to face, around the table. One by one, he seemed to challenge each person in the room. No one took up his challenge.

"The more information we store on a computer," he continued, finally, "the more tasks we control through it, the more inviting a target it becomes. That's the problem. When you focus information, you focus the raw material of power. Read a history book. The pages are filled with people who craved power. The governor of my home state is paid seventy thousand dollars a year. Two years ago, the *losing* candidate spent over five million dollars trying to win that office. She didn't do it for the money. Because a centralized data bank represents power, it's a tempting target. People will try to control it. It's just a matter of time before they succeed.

"The military would never consider concentrating all its forces in one place; a single, well-directed blow could wipe them out. Concentrating all our information in one place is equally stupid. Losing our resources is an obvious risk, but with information, we face an even greater danger. Information, you see, can be used against us. The Harlequin demonstrated that. If we aren't careful, our own resources can defeat us.

"Note that I am talking about information, not computers. A computer is just a tool, a machine. Machines are amoral. You don't blame the automobile when a bank robber uses it to escape from the scene of the crime. You don't blame the gun when a human being aims it and shoots it. You don't blame the computer when someone misuses the information stored on it. Worry about people, not computers.

"You say you have outstanding security on NECEN. You think security will protect the system from intrusion. Don't kid yourselves. NECEN is the state of the art, the most reliable, most secure computer ever built. But one man, the Harlequin, apparently acting alone, penetrated that computer and took control away from you. One person.

"I know what you're thinking. The Harlequin is a genius. No one else could have done what he did. Baloney! Georgie Hacker is a very bright young man, but there are thousands of others just as bright out there. All they need is the money, the motivation, and the time, and they can break into NECEN, too.

"Vault doors, the traditional symbols of security, are rated on a time scale. Faced with a two-hour door, a skilled thief, equipped with the proper tools, will need about two hours to break through. Faced with an expensive eight-hour door, that same thief, equipped with even better, more expensive tools, will need eight hours of steady work to gain entry. Nobody makes an unbreakable safe; there is no such thing. Security is a function of time, skill, and money. Give a skilled thief the right tools and enough time, and there is no such thing as security.

"On a computer, sophisticated security features are effective against accidental or casual intrusion, but give me enough time, enough money, and the right tools, and I'll break your security. The outcome is inevitable. If I want to access your computer, I will. An expert who is willing to spend the time and the money can break any security system that exists.

"There's another problem with a national data bank, too. It will fail. A computer is a very fragile thing. Do you have any idea how we managed to regain control of NECEN? We changed one bit. I know the government spent almost twenty million dollars on that machine. It is, as I said before, the state of the art, the most reliable, most secure computer ever developed. It's an engineering masterpiece. But we crippled it by changing *one bit*." Again Corbin paused and glanced around the table. His revelation had achieved the desired effect. A few people didn't believe him. Others didn't want to. Most appeared shocked. But he had undermined their faith in technology. None, he was sure, would ever again accept a claim of absolute security without challenge.

He resumed his lecture. "Imagine if a terrorist could shut down our entire military establishment by flipping a single light switch in the Pentagon. Imagine if The White House could be destroyed by extracting a single nail. That's how fragile a computer system is. And that's why large, centralized systems are certain to fail. It's just a matter of time.

"I know you find that hard to believe. Most people don't understand computers. To them, what happens inside the machine is about as clear as what happens inside an atom. To them, computer output is gospel. To them, a computer's contents are simply inaccessible. However, to an expert, breaking into a computer is child's play, and sabotaging a computer is easy.

"What are the implications of a national data bank? Clearly government will have a great deal of information that it does not now possess. I don't deny that. Government will be more efficient, with less duplication of effort. That fact can't be denied either. Thoroughness and efficiency are powerful arguments. But there are risks.

"At best, you, the representatives of this government, will find yourselves communicating with your new tool through a new priesthood of computer experts. Who really controlled ancient Egypt, the

Pharaohs or the temple priests? You're going to share your power with a new, technological elite. The data bank will be a major source of your power. But you won't control it. They will. And they'll speak a language you won't be able to understand.

"That's the *best* possible outcome. What happens if someone inside that new priesthood suddenly realizes his or her true power and decides to exercise it? What if some government official manipulates the data to support a political position? What if another Harlequin breaks in and gains control? Or organized crime? Or a foreign enemy? What happens when the computer fails? Don't pretend it can't happen; the Harlequin just proved it can. You may not realize it, but he did you a favor. He showed you what could happen. We regained control. We were lucky. Next time, we might not be.

"My point is simple: when you concentrate information, you create an irresistible target. NECEN represents perhaps one fourth of a true national data bank. Even today, it is one of the most tempting targets ever created. That is an unacceptable risk. Drop it. Centralize only what is absolutely necessary. Don't concentrate your forces unless you are prepared to lose them all.

"With that final bit of wisdom, I take my leave. I intend to go home and enjoy my retirement. I don't want awards and I don't want honors. I want peace. I sincerely hope you've listened this time. If you haven't, then so be it. Thank you, Mr. President, and good-bye." Without another word, without waiting for a reaction, he turned and walked out the door.

24 *Until Next Time*

The cab left the mountain road and followed the narrow, gravel pathway into the heart of the forest. Professor Corbin and his granddaughter relaxed in the back seat, breathing the fresh, mountain air through the open windows. Beyond a rise, a chain link fence blocked the way. The cab rolled to a stop near a gate. Corbin watched the squat, dwarflike robot emerge from its guardhouse and amble toward them. "This is private property," said Duke, politely. "I cannot allow you to continue."

Smiling, Corbin poked his head out the window. "It's me, Duke," he said, softly. "Open the gate, please."

"Good afternoon, Professor," replied Duke. "Welcome home."

"It's good to be home, Duke. Any news?"

"Nothing to report, sir," said the robot. The gate slid open. "You've been gone for quite some time. We missed you."

"Thank you, Duke. I've missed being home. The cab will drive us to the house. When it returns, let it out, please."

"Certainly, Professor," replied Duke.

Corbin pulled his head back inside and leaned forward to talk to the driver. "The house is a few hundred yards up this road," he said. "There's a spot where you can turn around." The driver nodded, and drove through the gate. A few minutes later, he stopped in front of the cabin. Corbin paid the fare. He and Susie stepped out and he watched the cab drive away. He felt content. This was where he belonged.

Calmly, he walked to the door, pushed a button, and repeated the code words: "Strawberry. Mississippi. Inconsistent."

The door buzzed; he pushed it open and stepped inside. Familiar sights and smells greeted him like old friends. Without a word, he started toward his favorite spot, the observation room. Silently, Susie followed him. She understood her grandfather's moods.

Side by side, they crossed the living room, descended the spiral staircase, and walked through the library. Now and then Corbin paused to touch some familiar object. They passed through a door and entered the observation room. The water falling into the rocky glen far below looked even more beautiful than he remembered. With obvious relish, he dropped into his favorite chair. He reached for his granddaughter and took her hand. "Some adventure, wasn't it, Susie?" he said.

She smiled. "Yes it was, Gramps." She seemed mature and confident. She'd grown during the mission.

Once again they fell silent. Susie broke the spell this time. "I've decided what I want to be when I grow up, Gramps," she announced.

"What's that, Susie?" he asked.

"A programmer, just like Ada."

"You like Ada, don't you?"

"She's nice. Can she come to visit sometime?"

"Anytime, Susie. I like Ada, too."

"Will you teach me how to program, Gramps?"

"Sure, honey. We'll start tomorrow morning."

"Great!" She leaned over his chair and kissed his cheek. "Okay if I go out and explore the forest for a while?"

"Sure, Susie." She'd missed the mountains, too, he realized. "Take Cedric with you, though."

"Okay, Gramps." Again she kissed him. Then she ran off.

Corbin leaned back in his chair, totally at ease. He loved this place; it would be a while before he left again. Contented, he fell asleep. He awoke sometime later, refreshed. The television played. He hadn't remembered turning it on. Perhaps he was growing old. He recalled how the miniaturization experiments had aged Sylvia. He'd been gone two days; it felt like a month. He felt older.

The news anchor smiled from the screen. The Harlequin had been defeated; the government, once again, controlled NECEN. In a prepared statement, the President thanked Professor Corbin for his invaluable assistance. He did not, of course, mention SMF. Secrets are secrets.

Then came the bombshell. By presidential order, NECEN would be shut down. The Harlequin had demonstrated a fundamental weakness in the system, pointing out a need for further study. For now, the old-fashioned, decentralized ways would have to do. Corbin smiled. The President had listened; perhaps there was hope. But the announcement seemed understated. The President had not rejected the national data bank concept. Instead, he'd ordered further study. Corbin's years in Washington had taught him to read between the lines. NECEN still had powerful supporters. A battle had been won; the war still raged.

He turned back to the news. The President had sent Congress a new computer security bill. It would require, among other things, detailed security audits of sensitive computer systems, and fail safe human access to any hardware controlling or utilizing public communication networks. The White House press secretary described the bill as long overdue. In response to a question, he admitted provisions of the bill would have made the Harlequin's takeover impossible, but he denied any relationship between the bill's timing and the recent problems with NECEN. Corbin chuckled. Perhaps before he died, a Washington official would give the nation's citizens credit for some intelligence, but he doubted it.

Some opposed the bill, of course. Senator Jacobs called it unnecessary. After all, he argued, hadn't we just regained control of NECEN from an extremely bright hacker? We had learned a great deal from that incident. The loophole that had allowed the Harlequin to penetrate NECEN's security would be fixed. The system would be even better than before. Security problems were a thing of the past. Corbin shook his head. Why do they keep making the same mistakes over and over again?

Now Senator Tompson appeared. He opposed shutting down NECEN. The system, he argued, was already returning benefits. The East Coast depended on NECEN. To shut it down now would destroy all that American science and technology had accomplished. Given a weak case, Tompson always appealed to patriotism. To govern efficiently, he went on, the government absolutely required a centralized computer system. The same old arguments. He repeated the same old arguments. It would, Corbin realized, happen again.

The interview with Senator Tompson continued. The President's computer security bill, he suggested, combined with improved security procedures on NECEN, would ensure against a future Harlequin. To Senator Tompson, the computer security bill represented NECEN's salvation. To Senator Jacobs, it seemed unnecessary. Why, wondered Corbin, didn't they listen to each other? Couldn't they sense the inconsistency of their positions? Why did they insist on ignoring the real problem—NECEN itself? They jockeyed for political advantage. They fought for position without understanding what they fought over. Ignorance is *not* bliss. It is ignorance.

He'd heard enough. He flipped open the arm of his chair and pushed a button. The news disappeared. Now the screen displayed his

electronic mail. He scanned through the bills, receipts, and advertise-
ments, pausing to dictate replies to an occasional personal note. Then,
one brief message caught his attention. Pete and Sylvia had decided to
marry! The wedding would take place within the month, and he and
Susie were invited. Smiling, he dictated a reply. "About time, my friend.
Congratulations. Of course, we'll be there." A command transferred the
message to Pete's computer.

Perhaps Ada would be there, too. Maybe he and Susie would have
a chance to visit her. He looked forward to that. Ada had a special
quality about her, a strength of character. He admired her as a friend
and as a professional.

He wondered if she'd seen the day's news. He wondered how she
would react to the continued infighting over NECEN. Somehow, he
knew she shared his concern.

He began to tire. Age had stolen his stamina. His publisher expected new editions of two books in the coming year. He'd need help,
a coauthor. Perhaps Ada would be interested. He'd ask her. He needed
help fighting NECEN, too. Again Ada might be the one. He was aging.
He needed a successor, someone to carry on the fight. He looked forward
to talking with her.

He turned back to the screen and requested the next message. A
very special note appeared. He read it. Then he reread it.

Dear Professor Corbin:

Congratulations on your victory. [It had to be you.] Until next
time.

                                        Respectfully,
                                        The Harlequin

Until next time. Yes, Georgie, he thought. Maybe next time, I'll be
on your side.

Glossary

At times, computer people seem to speak a foreign language. To help you understand it, we've compiled this glossary. It contains brief definitions intended to convey general meanings of key words. For those who are interested, more precise definitions can be found in the publications of the American National Standards Institute (ANSI) and the International Standards Organization (ISO).

Access mechanism   On disk, the part that holds the read/write head. Like the tone arm on a stereo turntable, the access mechanism moves, positioning the read/write head over the track containing the desired data.

Access method   A software routine that translates a programmer's request for input or output into the physical commands required by the external device.

Address   A location in memory. Often, the bytes or words that comprise memory are numbered sequentially; the byte's (or word's) number is its address.

Analog   Data represented in a continuous physical form. The height of a column of mercury is an analog representation of a temperature. Computer data are transmitted over local telephone lines by converting them to continuous wave form. Contrast with DIGITAL.

Application program   A program written to perform an end user task. A payroll program or a computer game are application programs. An operating system is not.

Architecture   See COMPUTER ARCHITECTURE.

Arithmetic and logic unit The part of a computer's processor that executes instructions.

Backup Extra hardware, software, or data intended to keep a computer system running in the event that one or more components fail.

Base In a number system, the number used to define positional values. For example, decimal uses base 10, while binary uses 2 as its base.

Batch processing A type of computer application in which data are collected over time and then processed together. For example, payroll data might be collected throughout the week and then processed on Friday.

Binary A base 2 number system that uses the values 0 and 1.

Bit A binary digit.

Bit bucket Computer slang. The depository for truncated or overflow bits.

Board See CIRCUIT BOARD.

Boot A small routine that is read into main memory when the computer is turned on, and which reads the rest of the operating system into memory.

Buffer Temporary storage used to compensate for the different speeds of adjacent devices.

Bug An error in a program.

Bus A set of parallel wires used to transmit data, commands, or power.

Byte Eight bits. On many computer systems, the smallest addressable unit of main memory.

Cable An electrical connector; often, a shielded, serial wire.

Calculator A device for performing arithmetic that requires human intervention at each step.

Central processing unit See PROCESSOR.

Channel A device used to attach input, output, and secondary storage devices to a large computer system.

Channel linkage register A register used to pass control information from the main processor to the channel or from the channel to the main processor.

Character A single letter, digit, or other symbol. On many computers, each byte of memory can hold a single character in coded form.

Chip A tiny square of silicon that holds thousands of integrated electronic circuits.

Circuit board A flat board on which chips are linked by electronic paths embedded in the surface. Examples include processor boards, memory boards, and interface boards.

Clock A device that generates the regular electronic pulses that drive a computer.

CMDF   Combined Miniature Deterrent Force, the original name of SMF.

Code   (1) A set of rules for representing characters as bit patterns. (2) To write a program.

Command   (1) A control signal that tells a hardware component to perform a specific function. For example, a fetch command tells the memory controller to transfer the contents of a single memory location to a bus, while a seek command tells a disk controller to position the access mechanism. (2) A request from a programmer, an operator, or a user to an operating system asking that a specific function be performed. For example, a request to load a program.

Communication interface   A device that links a communication line to a computer system.

Computer   A machine that processes data under control of a stored program.

Computer architecture   The physical structure of a computer: in particular, the way in which a computer's components are linked together.

Computer crime   Any criminal activity in which the computer is the victim or an accomplice.

Computer jock   Computer slang. An individual whose life seems to revolve around computers. This term is often used to describe a skilled, knowledgeable, productive individual who, unfortunately, suffers from a narrow "computers only" viewpoint.

Computer junkie   Computer slang. An individual who seems addicted to computers. Similar to COMPUTER JOCK, but more negative. Computer jocks are productive. Computer junkies are game players.

Computer program   A series of instructions that guides a computer through some process.

Console   A device, often a keyboard/display unit, used by an operator to communicate with a computer.

Contiguous   Next to, adjoining.

Continuous   Unbroken, connected.

Control bus   A bus used to transmit control signals.

Control unit, instruction   See INSTRUCTION CONTROL UNIT.

Control unit, I/O   An electronic device that links an I/O device to a channel.

Controller   A device or electronic circuit that controls a computer component.

CPU   Acronym for central processing unit.

Data   Raw, unstructured, unprocessed facts.

Data bank or **Data base**   A collection of related data.

Data bus   A bus used to transmit data.

Data fetch   See FETCH. The act of copying the contents of a memory location into a register in the processor.

Data processing   Converting data into information.

Data stream   A set of data moving as a continuous stream through a cable or a bus line.

Debug   To remove errors (BUGS) from a program.

Demodulation   The reverse of modulation. Converting data from analog to digital form.

Digital   Data represented as individual, discrete digits. Contrast with ANALOG.

Discrete   Opposite of continuous. Separate, independent.

Disk, magnetic   A flat, platelike surface on which data can be stored magnetically.

Disk controller   An I/O control unit dedicated to one or more disk drives.

Diskette   A thin, flexible magnetic disk often used on small computer systems.

Display   A TV-like screen that displays data.

Endless loop   A loop without an exit. Repetitive logic that executes over and over again, without end.

Even parity   See PARITY BIT. A parity rule specifying that the sum of all the bits, including the parity bit, be even. Contrast with ODD PARITY.

Execution   The act of carrying out an instruction or performing a routine.

Execution time   The time during which an instruction is executed by the arithmetic and logic unit.

Fetch   To locate a unit of data or an instruction in main memory and send it, over a bus, to the processor.

Fiber optics   A data communication medium on which laser light pulses are transmitted over a glass fiber cable.

File   A collection of related records.

Flag   See SWITCH. A marker used to indicate that an event has occurred.

Flip-flop   A common memory circuit that stores one bit.

Floppy disk   See DISKETTE.

Garbage   Computer slang. Meaningless data.

Gossamer   The miniaturization craft featured in the story. The word means light, thin, and filmy.

Hacker   Computer slang. Similar to a computer jock or a computer junkie, but usually applied to an individual who gains illegal access to a computer system via a communication line.

Hard disk A rigid disk. Contrast with FLOPPY DISK or DISKETTE.

Hardware Physical equipment. Contrast with SOFTWARE.

Hexadecimal number system A base 16 number system, often used as a shorthand for representing binary values.

High order In number system notation, the position associated with the largest integer power recorded. Generally, the leftmost digit in a field. Contrast with LOW ORDER.

Index A list of the contents of a disk pack or other storage medium showing the locations of each file or program.

Information The meaning a human being assigns to data. Processed data.

Information processing See DATA PROCESSING.

Initial program load or IPL The process of loading the operating system when the computer is first turned on. Big systems are IPLed; small systems are booted.

Input Transferring data from an external device into a computer's main memory.

Instruction One step in a program. Each instruction tells the computer to perform one of its basic functions.

Instruction control unit The part of a computer's processor that decides which instruction will be executed next.

Instruction counter A special register that holds the address of the next instruction to be executed.

Instruction register A special register that holds the instruction being executed by the processor.

Instruction time or **I-time** The time during which the next instruction is fetched from main memory and interpreted by the processor's instruction control unit.

Interface On a small computer, an electronic component, often a board, that links an external device to a computer. More generally, an electronic component that links two different devices.

Interrupt An electronic signal that causes a computer to stop what it is doing and transfer control to the operating system in such a way that the task being performed at the time of the interrupt can later be resumed.

Interrupt bit On NECEN, a bit whose setting determined if hardware would accept or ignore an interrupt. A similar control bit is found on many real computers.

Interrupt masking The process of selectively ignoring interrupts based on switch or control bit settings.

I/O Input/output.

I/O control unit   See CONTROL UNIT, I/O.
IPL   See INITIAL PROGRAM LOAD.

K   When referring to memory, 1024 bytes or words.

Line   A communication medium connecting two or more points.
Local   Connected to a computer by regular electric wires. In close proximity to the computer. Contrast with REMOTE.
Logical I/O   Input or output operations performed without regard for the physical structure of the data.
Long-distance   Remote. Contrast with LOCAL.
Low order   In number system notation, the position associated with the smallest integer power recorded. Generally, the rightmost digit in a field. Contrast with HIGH ORDER.

Machine cycle   The basic operating cycle of a processor during which a single instruction is fetched, interpreted, and executed.
Magnetic disk   See DISK, MAGNETIC.
Mainframe   The processing unit of a large computer system, or the processing unit plus other components contained in the same physical cabinet as the processing unit of a large computer system.
Main memory or **Main storage**   Memory that can be directly accessed by the processor.
Mask bit   A control bit whose setting determines if hardware will accept or ignore an interrupt. See INTERRUPT MASKING.
Masking, interrupt   See INTERRUPT MASKING.
Memory   The computer component in which instructions and data are stored.
Memory board   A circuit board that holds memory chips.
Memory controller   A device that controls access to memory or storage, accepting an address, computing the physical location of the desired storage unit, and writing data to or reading data from that storage unit.
Memory protection   See STORAGE PROTECTION.
Message   A group of related characters or symbols transmitted between two points.
Message character   A character that precedes or follows a message transmitted over a communication line.
Message-switching   Routing messages by receiving, storing, and forwarding them.
Microcomputer   A small computer system. A typical microcomputer is composed of a microprocessor, main memory, and one or more input/output devices.

Microprocessor   A processor on a single integrated circuit chip. The processor in a microcomputer system.

Microsecond   One millionth of one second.

Microwave   A electromagnetic wave that is used to transmit data.

Millisecond   One thousandth of one second.

Minicomputer   A small, digital computer, smaller than a mainframe but bigger than a microcomputer.

Modem   An acronym for MOdulator/DEModulator. A device that converts data from the computer's internal digital form to analog wave form, and back again. Used to link computer equipment to a telephone line.

Modulation   Converting data from digital form to analog wave form.

Motherboard   A metal or plastic framework that holds a computer's circuit boards. Often, circuit boards slide into slots on the framework, and are electronically linked by bus lines.

Multiple-bus architecture   A computer architecture in which more than one bus line is used to link components. Often, separate bus lines are provided for commands, addresses, and data. Often, independent bus lines link the main processor and main memory, the channel processors and the main processor, and the channel memories and main memory.

Multiprogramming   One computer concurrently executing several programs.

Nanosecond   One billionth of one second.

National data bank   In the story, a proposed, centralized collection of governmental data. Such a system was actually proposed in the 1970s.

NECEN   The NorthEast CENtral computer system; a fictional, centralized computer system featured in the story.

Nerd   Computer slang. A computer junkie utterly lacking in certain basic social skills and completely unconcerned about his physical appearance. (Note: this term is rarely applied to a young woman.) The term can also refer to a non-computer person who exhibits the same negative social skills and physical appearance.

NETEN   The NorthEast TElecommunication Network; a fictional telecommunication network featured in the story.

Network   A group of computers linked by communication lines.

Nonvolatile memory   Memory that maintains its contents even when power is lost. Secondary storage is nonvolatile; random access memory (RAM) is, typically, volatile. Contrast with VOLATILE MEMORY.

No-op   A valid computer instruction that does nothing.

Odd parity   See PARITY BIT. A parity rule specifying that the sum of all
the bits, including the parity bit, be odd. Contrast with EVEN PARITY.

Open   To prepare a file for processing. For example, opening a file on
disk involves checking the index to find the track and sectors where
the file's data are stored.

Operating system   A collection of program modules that control the
operation of the computer. A typical operating system allocates
resources, schedules programs, controls access to input and output
devices, and manages data.

Operator   The person who operates a computer system.

Output   The act of transferring data or information from the computer's
main memory to an external device.

Packet switching   A data transmission technique in which a message
is broken into discrete, digital packets. The packets are then transmitted independently over a high-speed line, and the message is
reassembled at the other end.

Parallel   Side-by-side. Parallel processing involves performing two or
more tasks at the same time. Parallel data transmission involves
sending bits, side by side, over parallel wires. Contrast with SERIAL.

Parity bit   In memory, an extra bit appended to the data bits, that allows
a computer to check the bit pattern for accuracy. See EVEN PARITY
and ODD PARITY.

Peripheral hardware   Input, output, and secondary storage devices attached to a computer system.

Personal computer   A small, inexpensive microcomputer system mar-
keted for use by individuals.

Physical I/O   The act of transferring a physical block of data to or from
a peripheral device. For example, on diskette, each physical I/O
operation might transfer one sector; on a printer, each physical
I/O operation might transfer one line.

Picosecond   One millionth of one millionth of a second.

Polling   Asking a series of terminals or buffers, one by one, if they have
data to transmit. A technique for determining who gets to transmit
data next.

Port   The point at which a communication line enters a computer
system.

Power surge   An unpredictable or unanticipated burst of electrical power
that can destroy computer circuits and media. Power surges can be
caused by turning electrical motors on or off, by utility company
load-switching, by lightning, and by other phenomena.

Primitive command   A machine-level hardware command: for example,
a fetch command whereby a processor requests data from main

memory, or a seek command whereby a disk controller is told to position the access mechanism.

Processing (1) Executing instructions. (2) Converting data into information.

Processor The component of a computer that selects and executes instructions. The processor contains a clock, an instruction control unit, an arithmetic and logic unit, and registers.

Program See COMPUTER PROGRAM.

Program state The status of an executing program: for example, waiting or ready, supervisor or application.

Programmer A person who writes computer programs.

Programmer, application A person who writes or maintains application programs.

Programmer, system A person who writes or maintains system programs such as operating systems or data base managers.

Programmer/operator A person who both programs and operates a computer.

PROM Acronym for programmable read-only memory.

Protocol A set of rules for establishing communication between two devices.

Prototype A model or pattern.

RAM (random access memory) Memory that can be directly addressed, read, and written by the programmer. The main memory of a computer is generally RAM. Contrast with ROM.

Read/write head The component that transfers data to or from the surface of disk or magnetic tape.

Record A collection of related data. For example, all the data related to an employee's pay would constitute that employee's payroll record; all the data related to a student's academic performance would constitute that student's academic history record.

Redundancy The repetition of data in two or more places.

Register Temporary storage used to hold data or instructions in the processor. Often, the current instruction, the data being manipulated by that instruction, and key control information are stored in registers. Registers are part of the processor.

Relative address An address relative to a reference point: for example, the tenth byte away from the beginning of a program, or the third record in a file.

Relative record number The location of a record relative to the beginning of a file: for example, the fourth record in a file. Given the actual track and sector of the first record in the file, it is possible to compute the address of any other record, given its relative record number.

Remote Distant. Linked to a computer via communication lines.

ROM (read-only memory) A type of memory that cannot be modified by the programmer.

Routine A program module.

Salami game Computer slang. A computer or electronic crime in which data or electronic funds are manipulated, modified, copied, or stolen in such small increments that the victim does not realize a crime has been committed.

Save register A register used to hold data or control information temporarily: for example, the register used to hold the contents of the instruction counter following an interrupt on NECEN, the computer described in the story.

Schematic A diagram.

Secondary storage Nonvolatile memory such as disk or magnetic tape used for the long-term storage of program instructions and data. Generally, the data and instructions currently being processed by a computer are stored in main memory; all other data and instructions are stored in secondary storage.

Sector A fixed-length element of disk or other magnetic storage that holds a single physical record. A common sector length on microcomputer systems is 256 characters.

Security Software, hardware, and procedural elements that are intended to protect or safeguard computer equipment, data, or programs.

Seek time The time needed to position a disk's access mechanism over a specific track.

Serial One by one. Serial data transmission involves sending a stream of bits, one after another, over the same wire. Contrast with PARALLEL.

Single-bus architecture A computer architecture in which all internal components are linked by a single bus line.

Slot On a motherboard, one of several openings into which a circuit board can be plugged.

SMF The Special Miniature Force, sometimes called the Small Missions Force. A fictional secret government agency featured in the story.

Software Programs.

Special-purpose computer A computer designed to perform a single task.

Spooling On input, transferring data to secondary storage and holding them for eventual processing. On output, transferring data to secondary storage for eventual output to an output device. A technique used to make batch processing applications more efficient.

Storage Memory.

Storage protection A facility that prevents one program from destroying, changing, or (in some cases) accessing regions of memory belonging to another program.

Stored program A series of instructions placed in a computer's main memory to control that computer. Distinguishes a computer from a calculator.

Switch See FLAG. A marker used to indicate that an event has occurred.

System pack The disk pack that contains the operating system.

System programmer See PROGRAMMER, SYSTEM.

Tapeworm Computer slang. A program or routine that moves itself from computer to computer, often over a communication line. Usually several computers are involved. Often, like an organic tapeworm, the electronic tapeworm acts as a parasite, doing damage or stealing data as it moves.

Telecommunication Transmitting signals over long distances by means of telephone lines, radio signals, or other media.

Telephone network A network of telephone lines.

Terminal Hardware placed at the entry or exit point of a communication network for the purpose of entering or obtaining data.

Timer See CLOCK.

Token An electronic signal, often part of a protocol. See TOKEN-PASSING NETWORK.

Token-passing network A communication network in which the right to transmit is determined by an electronic signal called a token that is passed from terminal to terminal. Only the terminal holding the token can transmit data over the line.

Track One of a series of concentric circles on a disk surface on which data can be stored. Tracks are often subdivided into sectors.

Transaction An exchange between a user and a computer that accomplishes a single logical function. For example, all the steps involved in requesting cash from an automatic teller machine constitute a single transaction.

Transaction processing Processing transactions as they occur, rather than in a batch. Contrast with BATCH PROCESSING.

Transient error An error that occurs occasionally, or at unpredictable intervals.

Transmission Sending data from one location to another over a communication line.

Transmission control unit or **TCU**   A control unit that links a transmission line or lines to a computer system.

Trojan Horse   Computer slang. A seemingly innocuous or insignificant routine, stored in a computer's main memory, that, when activated, allows a hacker access to the system or destroys programs or data.

VACCINE   Computer slang. A program reputed to cure VIRUS. See VIRUS.

VIRUS   Computer slang. A mythical program that moves from computer to computer, stealing machine cycles. Legend suggests that a VIRUS epidemic was cured by VACCINE. See VACCINE.

Voice print   A technique for verifying an individual's identity by the pattern produced by his or her voice.

Volatile memory   Memory that loses its content when the power is turned off. Contrast with NONVOLATILE MEMORY.

Wait state   A condition whereby a given task or process must await the completion of an event before it can resume.

Word   The basic storage unit around which a computer system is designed. On all but the smallest microcomputers, a word consists of two or more bytes.